D0597119

The Fiery Spiral Trilogy

— BOOK TWO —

The Rising Tide

BY HELEN BRAIN

CATALYST PRESS
Vinton, Texas

Catalyst Press

Vinton, Texas

The Rising Tide, Book 2, The Fiery Spiral trilogy

For further information,
email info@catalystpress.org.

Originally published in 2017 in South Africa
by Human & Rousseau, an imprint of NB Publishing.

FIRST EDITION 10 9 8 7 6 5 4 3 2 1
Library of Congress Cataloging-In-Publication
Number: 2020947985

Cover design and illustrations by
Karen Vermeulen, Cape Town, South Africa

For Ted

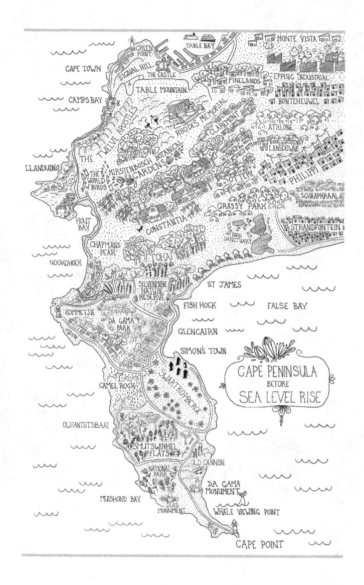

CAPE PENINSULA
BEFORE
SEA LEVEL RISE

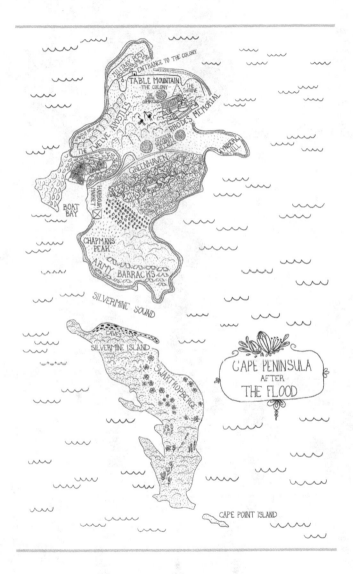

MILITARY POST

ENTRANCE TO THE COLONY

TABLE MOUNTAIN
THE COLONY

THE SHRINE

THE TWELVE APOSTLES

RHODES MEMORIAL

IMPERIAL HILL

GREENHAVEN

HARBOUR MARKET

BOAT BAY

CHAPMANS PEAK

ARMY BARRACKS

SILVERMINE SOUND

CAVES
SILVERMINE ISLAND

SWARTKOPBERG

CAPE PENINSULA
AFTER
THE FLOOD

CAPE POINT ISLAND

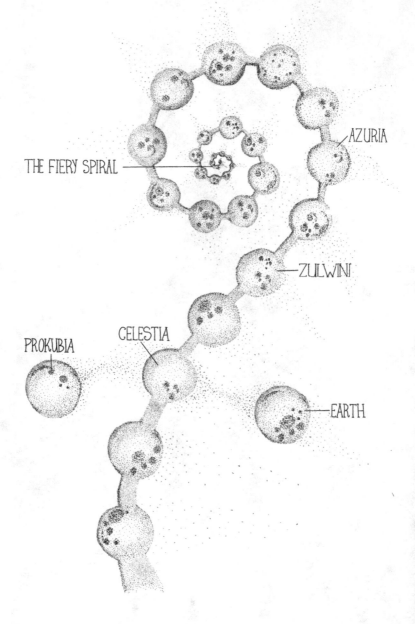

THE FIERY SPIRAL

AZURIA

ZULWINI

PROKUBIA

CELESTIA

EARTH

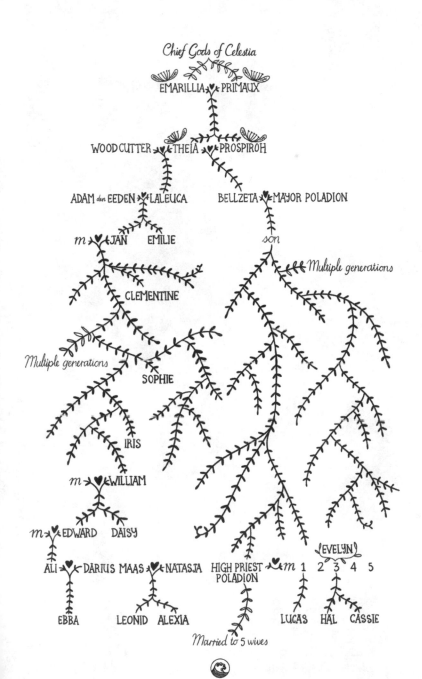

Chief Gods of Celestia

EMARILLIA ♥ PRIMAUX

WOODCUTTER ♥ THEIA ♥ PROSPIROH

ADAM *den* EEDEN ♥ LALEUCA   BELLZETA ♥ MAYOR POLADION

m ♥ JAN   EMILIE   *son*   *Multiple generations*

CLEMENTINE

Multiple generations

SOPHIE

IRIS

m ♥ WILLIAM

m ♥ EDWARD   DAISY

ALI ♥ DARIUS MAAS ♥ NATASJA   HIGH PRIEST ♥ *m* 1   *EVELYN* 2 3 4 5
                                  POLADION

EBBA   LEONID ALEXIA   LUCAS HAL CASSIE

Married to 5 wives

Prologue

Long ago, before Earth was created, all living creatures journeyed through numerous worlds during numerous lifetimes. God or mortal, they faced trials that proved them worthy to move onwards, closer to the Fiery Spiral that burns with love and is the heart of all that is.

But not every living being wanted to face their trials. Those who lacked the courage to look in the eye the thing that frightened them most stayed in their world, coming up against the same weakness again and again, until they had confronted and conquered it. Then, strengthened and purified, they were ready to move on.

It was such a weakness that caused a conflict between the gods of Celestia. A conflict that lasted millenia and resonated far beyond their own world. The cause of the conflict was a powerful necklace. Their battleground was Earth.

Myths of Celestia:
The birth of Theia and Prospiroh.

Under the branches of a spreading Ficus tree, the great Goddess Emarillia and her husband Primaux awaited visitors. The queen, belly swollen, was embroidering a pattern of fern fronds on a tiny vest. For many years they had longed for a baby, and soon their child would be born.

"The elemental gods," a herald announced.

Four shimmering figures emerged from the forest. The first was a woman dressed in fiery red that vibrated against her ebony skin.

The second woman was so pale she was almost translucent. Her robe was gray-white and a spray of mist surrounded her.

Behind her the two men were as striking as the women. One had hair the color of soft earth and a beard as thick as lichen. His robe was a rich loamy brown. The last man was tall, with long hair that rippled like water. His robe was aquamarine with a border that curled like the crest of a wave.

"Your majesties, we are here to pay homage to your child," the Earth god said with a bow. "In time, you will leave this world and move upwards to the next. This necklace gives your child the power to rule over each of our elements, earth, fire, wind and sea."

"Used well, it will bring balance and harmony to Celestia, and all the worlds below us." The Water God's voice rippled like a mountain stream.

The queen's robes fluttered as the Wind Goddess's words blew across the clearing. "But used badly, it will cause untold pain and destruction."

The four gods stepped forward and knelt at Emarillia's feet. The Fire Goddess presented the necklace to the queen. But instead of moving back like the other gods, she rested her hands on the queen's swollen belly. "You carry two children, your majesty."

The queen laughed. "There's only one baby, of that I am certain."

"There are two, my queen." The Fire Goddess flared up, making the amulets sparkle in the sudden light. "I feel them in your womb."

"We have consulted the oracles." Primaux's rich voice echoed through the trees. "There is one child. We thank you for your gifts."

It was time for them to leave, but the four gods had gathered together, whispering.

"My queen," the Water God said at last. "We request that the amulets be divided between the two children. The boy, Prospiroh, must have dominion over fire and air. The girl, Theia, will govern earth and water."

"There is only one child," the queen insisted. "Such a beautiful necklace will never be split."

That night the queen went into labor. She delivered a baby girl, a healthy child with hair like flame.

"She's a bonny, strong baby," the midwife said. "You rest now, your majesty."

Suddenly the queen arched her back and screamed. There was a flurry among the women. The midwife felt her belly. "There's another baby."

For hours the queen battled. The first baby was lying backwards, and she was tired. Finally, the baby emerged, bottom first, screaming, streaked with blood. The queen collapsed, exhausted.

The women whispered to each other as they washed the baby in the stone basin. He was healthy and strong, but a birthmark covered the left half of his face like black velvet. They wrapped him in a blanket and put him on her breast. The queen was too tired to open her eyes.

He seized her nipple in his mouth and fed hungrily. They brought the little girl and lay her in the crook of the queen's other arm.

When the queen finally opened her eyes, she took one look at her son's face and shrieked. "He's damaged. The king will never accept a child so ugly." She pushed the child off her breast. "Get rid of him," she cried. "Take him into the forest and leave him for the wolves. The king must never know he was born."

She sobbed bitterly, rocking her red-haired daughter as the nurse wrapped the screaming baby boy in a sheep-skin and called the queen's most trusted guard. "This baby is deformed," the nurse whispered. "Take it into the forest and leave it there. Never tell anybody or I will have you killed."

A horse was already waiting, and the guard rode away. But instead of going into the forest, he turned toward the distant mountains. Beyond them lay a small town where his wife waited; his sad-eyed wife with the barren womb.

Chapter One

It's been two weeks. Two weeks without Micah, and I have no idea if he's dead or alive. I miss him. His lithe body, his hair so black that it glints blue when the sun shines on it. His eyes like quicksilver, always moving, searching, analyzing, planning. Greenhaven doesn't feel right without him. Especially now that we're trying to repair the damage caused by the earthquake.

Shorty rounds the corner, bringing another wheelbarrow of mud. He is as different to Micah as anyone could be. As round as Micah is slim, as grubby and disheveled as Micah is neat. As transparent as Micah is guarded.

"Here you go," he says, tipping the mud onto the old tarpaulin piled with straw and animal dung.

Jasmine is up to her knees in the mixture, treading and churning it with her feet. It squelches between her toes and she laughs. She looks fiercer with her long hair gone—more determined. She's always been feisty, but since she came out of the bunker and met Leonid she's showing a toughness and focus I never expected. Just like Micah, all she thinks about is the Resistance, about overthrowing the government. Leonid, perched on the thatch roof, is slathering the mixture onto the gable that stands above the front door.

He empties the bucket onto the wall, crawls crab-like across the thatch, and ties it to the rope that Fez has rigged up. He lowers the bucket, his forehead in its customary frown, his sturdy body keeping balance effortlessly as the bucket spins around and then clanks onto the stoep. Isi, my Africanus dog, opens one eye, checks that I'm alright, stretches so the sun can warm her belly, and goes back to sleep. I wish I could relax like her but the question torments me:

Why hasn't Micah come home?

Did the soldiers shoot him when he led them away from us? Did he fall down the mountain? Maybe he's lying there still, wounded, with no one to help him.

Or he's been caught—and he's back in prison, being beaten by General de Groot, tortured, for leading the Resistance. For being everything the High Priest and General hates.

"He'll come back, Miss Ebba," Shorty says, hearing me sigh. "Didn't you say he survived being thrown out of the Colony? He's a tough one, that one; wily as a jackal. You don't have to worry about him. He always makes a plan. Always ends up crowing like a rooster on top of the dung heap."

I hope he's right. I thought I'd lost him back then when he disappeared from the Colony. I grieved for years. And then he turned up at Greenhaven, and we were no longer children. We weren't locked in a bunker deep in Table Mountain being supervised by guards 24/7. Our love could grow and blossom. Oh, please, please, Micah, please come home.

Then Isi's head shoots up. She runs to the edge of the stoep, barking—the sharp bark that means danger.

"What is it?" I call to Leonid. "Can you see anything?"

Shielding his eyes from the sun, Leonid peers out over the roofs of Greenhaven. He can see across the orchard and the vineyards to the gates of the farm. "It's an army carriage," he yells.

"Quick, Letti," Shorty shouts through the front door.

"This way. Fez, come on."

The twins hurtle out of the house. They've rehearsed this for days. After Victor told the High Priest they were hidden in the house, Shorty set up a hiding place in the forest, deep in a thicket where the soldiers will never find them. They dash across the meadow and disappear between the trees before the carriage turns the corner.

Cold sweat pools on my forehead. This is it. I've waited for the army to come since the day of the earthquake. Since the most important man in Table Island, in the whole world, was stung to death by my bees, on my farm. I throw off the blanket and stand up. My knees shake.

Jasmine is by my side. She reaches up and adjusts the sling holding my broken collar bone in place. "Don't let them see you're scared," she says. "Put your chin up. Act invincible."

My eyes dart from the carriage thundering down the drive to the outbuildings. It's not too late to hide. In the barn, in the poultry coop—there are a hundred places where I can conceal myself until he's gone. But they'll find me eventually. The general has a whole army he can send to tear the place apart. They mustn't find Fez and Letti. I have to protect them. I have to face whatever punishment they have planned for me.

Isi snarls as the carriage approaches, teeth bared, the ruff of white fur standing up on her back.

"Isi, come here." She runs up the stairs and positions herself between me and the carriage that has come to a halt.

Jasmine presses her arm against mine. "It's Atherton," she mutters as the carriage door opens and we glimpse the tall pale man seated inside. "Better than Zungu."

I have no doubt that he has come to fetch me on Major Zungu's orders. I'm going to have to pay for the death of the High Priest. And the person who will decide

my punishment is the most feared man in Table Island
City: General Magnus de Groot.

Chapter Two

"Stand up to him," Jasmine whispers as the captain jumps down from the carriage. I glance at her. She's pulled on a sun hat with a wide brim. Will he see that her hair is cut short underneath it? Will he realize she's the same "boy" who tried to rescue Letti and Fez?

"Go inside," I mutter. "Don't let him get a close look at you." I push myself in front of her, take a deep breath, and look him straight in the eye. He's only slightly taller than me, but he's fit and strong, and I'm still getting over the flu and the accident. I can't let him see how wobbly I am.

"Yes, Captain. What can I do for you?"

"Miss den Eeden," he says, saluting. "You are to come with me."

I swallow. *Don't act scared.* "Are you arresting me?"

"Simply following General de Groot's orders."

Aunty Figgy comes out then with my shoes. "Be strong," she whispers as she cups my face with her warm hands. "I will ask the Goddess to help you."

I feel for the necklace around my neck—the family heirloom that should hold four precious amulets but now is nothing but an empty necklace. I had one amulet, but the High Priest took it, and now I have none. How can the Goddess protect me if I don't have the amulets that once belonged to her? If I have lost the only one I ever had and have failed to find the others, despite Aunty Figgy urging me to make it my first priority?

Atherton paces alongside the carriage, his eyes

narrowed as he scans the forest. He knows they're in there somewhere. I have to get him away from Greenhaven. Away from Letti and Fez.

"I'll be back soon," I call to Leonid, still perched up the ladder. "Please finish this repair, then check the fence around the paddock."

He raises his eyebrows, then gives a brief nod. He knows what I'm saying. I'm telling Captain Atherton that I'm not finished here. I'm coming back, and that nobody, not even the general, will stop me.

If only I believed it.

I step inside the carriage, and Captain Atherton sits opposite me, just as he did two weeks ago, when he and Major Zungu forced me to go with them. That day Zungu stole the amulet from me and the dark forces were released. Already those forces have done so much damage—the carriage crashed, the High Priest was killed, they've caused an earthquake and kept Micah from coming home. What will they do next?

Isi runs alongside the carriage, barking until we reach the gate and turn toward the city. Will I ever see her again? Will I ever see this land again, the land my Khoi ancestors freely wandered for thousands of years before my European ancestors colonized the land and built Greenhaven?

I am the last remaining den Eeden. What will happen to the farm if I don't return? I should have written a will, leaving it to...I have no idea who. I want it to go to the people I have known my whole life—Micah, Jasmine, Letti, and Fez. But only Citizens are allowed to own land in Table Island, and the only Citizens I care about enough are Hal and Cassie. I can't leave it to them.

Where is Hal? I've been expecting an angry visit

from him but neither he nor Mr. Frye have been near Greenhaven. When Leonid went to market last week, soldiers turned him back at the top of the LongKloof. He's heard rumors of a military coup, overthrowing the Prosperites. If it's true, I wonder what will happen to the Poladion family.

We climb Wynberg Hill and turn toward the sharp point of Devil's Peak. Just beyond it lies Table Mountain, where the Colony lies deep in the gray rock.

I should have used my wealth to get everyone out. I should have tried harder. But it seemed everyone wanted something different from me. Aunty Figgy insisted I had to find the amulets so the Goddess could return. Mr. Frye wanted me to make money from the farm. Micah wanted me to help the Resistance overthrow the government. Then there were my Sabenzis, and the 2,200 people trapped in the mountain. I really wanted to help them start new lives in the open, to feel the sun on their faces, and to see how beautiful our world still is, in spite of the Calamity that nearly wiped it out. And it seems I didn't manage to please a single person.

We pass Claremont Security Village, the group of tall cone-shaped houses, clustered together like seeds in a sunflower head. From there, it's a short ride along the base of the mountain and we reach the road that zigzags uphill to the shrine and offices.

The horses take a corner too fast. I groan as my broken shoulder hits the window. Atherton jumps up and I grip the edge of the seat. He's going to open the door and throw me into the road. But the coachman regains control, the carriage steadies, and he sits down. Not long now. Just a short drive along the potholed road, past the slopes where the High Priest's ostriches run, kicking up clouds of dust in the bare ground and scratching for food in the ruins of the old university.

We reach the shrine. Soldiers have ripped the gold wheat sheaves—the emblem of the Prosperites—off the doors. They are busy on the roof, pulling off the copper sheets that made the building glint like a jewel.

I look up the mountainside, tracing the path we took when we escaped from the prison. Micah was with me as we climbed through the night. I find the shadow in the rockface that conceals the cave. The place where we sat together watching the sunrise while the others slept, and he said the words I longed to hear. "No matter what happens," he said, "remember I'll always love you."

He's gone, and I will never see him again.

The carriage stops at the entrance to the Shrine offices. A group of soldiers are gathered around the statue of the High Priest, trying to pull it down with ropes.

I can't read Captain Atherton's stony face as he opens the carriage door and gestures to me to get out. "Follow me."

The flight of stairs flanked by stone lions looms over me. At the top is the colonnade that leads to the High Priest's offices. The last time I was here, the Council warned me there would be no more chances.

The door opens behind the colonnade, and a man appears. A stocky, uniformed man with a sneering expression, the one person I don't ever want to see again. Major Zungu.

I try to read his body language as he begins to descend the stairs. He's marching with his usual gait—shoulders back to balance the weight of his heavy paunch, arms stiff by his sides. He is as hard and impenetrable as the marble steps.

Reaching me, he salutes Captain Atherton and snaps, "This way."

My breath snags in my throat as he leads me along a narrow passage to one side of the stairs. Is this the way we came when we escaped? He unlocks a door in the wall, and now I'm certain. He's taking me straight to the dungeon.

My mind whirls. I can't go in there. I stop, look back, wondering if I can run for it. But I know the violence he's capable of. I rub my sore shoulder, recalling how he grabbed the amulet, punched me in the stomach, and threw me so hard against the carriage window that my head was cut. There's no way of escaping him. I have to go where he's pointing—down the gloomy passage opening up before me.

We turn a corner and descend a steep flight of stairs lit with burning torches. My heart constricts with each step.

"This way," Zungu says again as a guard unlocks the heavy padlock and opens the gate.

"Where are you taking me?"

He gestures with his thumb to the right, down a gloomy, damp corridor.

The air down here is cold and so stale, my lungs feel like they'll never fill up. Someone nearby is whimpering. Who is it? It can't be Micah. He always used to tell me never to let the bullies see that I was scared. It was a tactic that worked for him again and again in the bunker when the Year Ones came looking for trouble. If the general has arrested him, he won't be crying in his cell. Who is it then?

I clench my fists and force myself forward.

Evelyn, Hal and Cassie's mother, sits on the stone floor in the first cell, head bowed. She glances up, sees me. She scrambles to her feet and runs to the bars, grips them with tight fists, her thumb a bloody mess where the nail used to be. She's always been so groomed and pretty. Now she is haggard, her robe dirty and torn as though someone has tried to rip it off. The stab wound in her arm is festering.

My gut twists. Is Major Zungu going to pull out my nails too? He's standing back, face blank, as Evelyn screams, "Get us out of here. Get us out." She bangs on the bars until blood drips from her thumb.

I bite my lip, not knowing what to say. I'm in as much trouble as she is.

Her face darkens. "You always were a self-absorbed little bitch," she snarls.

Her screeches follow us down the corridor. "We're the chosen ones of Prospiroh. He will punish you for this. You'll lose everything—your house, your farm, your friends. You'll be poorer than the dirty boat people. Don't say I didn't warn you."

I keep my eyes on the ground as Zungu leads me past three more cramped cells, each holding another of the High Priest's wives. I feel their gazes bore into my back. "Murderer," the blond wife hisses, and they all pick it up, chanting, "Murderer, murderer," as I pass.

We turn down a passage to the left. Zungu does not slow down. The stench of sewage hits me, and I cover my nose with my sleeve. The cells are bigger here. Zungu stops at one, crowded with fourteen of the High Priest's children. They stare at each other like they've given up. The youngest one, a toddler, slumps against the wall, eyes fixed on the floor. He's wearing nothing but a shirt. He's filthy. They all are. Filthy and half-starved. I can't believe this is the happy family I shared meals with after Shrine.

They recognize me and jump up, running to the bars. "Ebba, Ebba," they call. "Let us out. Please, Major, we want to go home."

Their cries slice through my core but Major Zungu gestures to hurry up, so I follow him around another corner. The youngest wife, Nomkhululi, is waiting for us. She cradles a tiny baby, her face wracked as she reaches one thin arm to me through the bars. "Please, take my baby. They're going to kill us. She hasn't done anything to hurt anyone." Tears run down her face and the baby gives a feeble wail. "Please, ask the general if you can fetch her."

I stare, seeing not her but my own mother holding me when I was just a few hours old, and she faced down the army. "Major Zungu?" I turn to him. "Please?"

He reaches in and shoves Nomkhululi in the face. She falls, protecting the baby with her skinny arms.

"Move along," he snaps to me. "Hurry up."

My legs shake so badly, I fear I might fall too. I hold the wall with one hand, and creep after him. He's going to throw me into a cell and torture me, I know it. I just know it.

Is Micah here? Have they tortured him too?

We turn down another passage, going deeper into the mountain. The air is staler, the smell of mold and damp squeezing the air from my chest. I don't know how much longer I can carry on.

Then we reach the next cell, and there, lying on the floor, is Hal. Seeing me, he limps forward, his eyes hopeful in his misshapen face. "Ebba, I knew you'd come and save us."

I can barely look at him—the missing teeth, the open sore on his cheek. "Save you?" I whisper. "How?"

"Please." He presses his face against the bars, just inches from mine.

"There's nothing I can do, Hal."

"You've got powers from the Goddess. You know you have."

I swallow. "Not anymore. Your father stole my amulet. Where is it? I have to get it back."

"They're raping Cassie," he says, his voice cracking. "Every night—I hear them taking turns. You've got to get us out of here."

"I'm so sorry Hal," I reach for his hand. "I think they're arresting me too."

He looks taken aback, and then the light in his eyes seems to go out. He lifts his lip and spits in my face.

"If we'd got married, this would never have happened. First you kill my father and now you won't even save me. You took me in, you really did, with your dewy-eyed innocent act. You're nothing but a two-faced murdering slut..."

Is that a smirk on Major Zungu's face? He's loving showing me how I'm going to suffer once I'm in my cell. Enjoying seeing the Poladions yelling abuse at me. Cold sweat pools on my forehead. In the next corridor someone bashes their fists against the bars. Is it Micah?

We turn a corner and I'm face to face with Cassie. One eye swollen shut, her hair matted with dried blood. She squints at us with her remaining good eye, expression wild, desperate.

"Please help me," she gasps. "Help me, please Ebba. They're...they're...hurting me."

I flinch as she reaches out—there's a huge bruise on her arm. "Please, I'm your friend. I gave you my favorite robe—the turquoise one, remember? Remember, Ebba? I gave you shoes too. Don't leave me here."

I swallow. What can I possibly say?

"They're going to shoot us all," she sobs. "Stop them, Ebba, please stop them."

I fall against the wall as the room spins. "I can't do anything." My voice bounces off the narrow walls, sounding louder than it is. "I'm sorry."

She lifts her chin and her one good eye half closes. For a moment she looks like her father, the High Priest. She turns her back, repulsion plain in the lift of her shoulders. Like Hal, she thinks I'm choosing not to help her.

They're all going to die. And it's my fault. If I'd just

married Hal, none of this would have happened. But
Micah....What about Micah? Where is he, my love? There
are still two cells ahead of us.

I stagger forward, hoping beyond hope that he isn't
trapped behind those iron bars. I'd rather imagine him on
the mountain, in the open air with the sky above him and
the sun on his cheek, even if he's dead.

Three more steps and I'm next to the bars.

A figure huddles in the corner, arms wrapped around
thin legs, head resting on his knees. He doesn't look up.

"Lucas," I call. "Lucas."

At last he half lifts his head and looks at me.

"What have they done to you?" I gasp.

His face is smeared with blood. His nose has been broken. But it's his eyes. They're dead. Totally dead.

I can't bear it. He's the one who found me last time I
was locked in these cells, who gave me the key and the
map, who helped me find Micah, Jasmine, and the twins
so we could all escape.

All these people are going to die. If only I hadn't gone
to the shrine that day. I should have stayed at home...
but then they would have killed my Sabenzis.

Major Zungu unlocks the cell door, marches over, and
kicks Lucas in the face. Lucas makes no sound. Just a small
grunt as he falls sideways.

I'm going to vomit. I grip my clammy hands together.
There's only one more empty cell, and we're at the end of
the corridor. Ahead lie the locked gates where the guards
sit. The same place that Lucas bribed the guards with
drugged wine so we could escape.

Zungu kicks open the door to the empty cell. "Hurry
up," he snarls.

This time there will be no Clementine and her little
boy to help me, no Lucas to bring me the key. I'll never see
Isi or Greenhaven again, never laugh with my Sabenzis,

or work with Aunty Figgy in the kitchen. If Micah comes back, I'll be gone. General de Groot will take Greenhaven for himself. He'll kill everyone—the twins, Jasmine and Leonid, Aunty Figgy...

I can't go inside. I can't. My feet slow. I have to save them. I have to do whatever it takes.

Footsteps sound on the stairs and the hem of a bright green robe comes into view. It's Mr. Frye. The guards open the gate for him.

I run to him and collapse into his arms.

"Please, Mr. Frye, I'm begging you. Tell the general I'll do everything he says. I'll tell him everything I know. Just don't let him kill me."

I freeze. What have I said? Did Major Zungu hear? He's glaring as though I'm a cornered rat that he's going to pulverize with a kierie. What if the general asks about the Resistance? About Micah? Did I just promise to betray them?

The voices of the Poladion family echo down the corridors. Cassie sobbing, Evelyn screeching, Hal calling me, ordering me to get him out. The baby starts to cry, a thin wail that shatters me like glass.

Only Lucas is silent. Head drooping, he sits and waits, as if dead already and waiting to be buried.

"The general is waiting," Major Zungu snarls, pointing to the stairs. "You do not want to keep him waiting."

"Just remember, you are extremely wealthy," Mr. Frye says quietly as we reach the top of the stairs, go through another set of locked doors, and turn down a carpeted passage leading further into the mountainside. "Wealth is power. Use it."

Me? Power? I'm a sixteen-year-old girl up against a general and his whole army. I've enraged every Citizen in Table Island. The people from Boat Bay don't like me any better. I've got no family except a half-brother who hates me and a half-sister I've never met. I'd hardly call that power. I'm more like a hen waiting to have its neck wrung.

Major Zungu stops in front of the white door marked Council Chamber. He opens the door and gestures with his huge hand. "After you."

I glance around, heart scudding. There must be another way out.

"Come on, Ebba," Mr. Frye says firmly. "No dillydallying." He puts his arm in the small of my back and guides me into the Council room.

I've seen the middle-aged man sitting at the table before. Is he Oliver's father, Mr. Adams? Cassie and Hal's friend Oliver who came to lunch at Greenhaven? Mr. Frye sits next to him.

"There in the center," Major Zungu orders.

I go to the spot he points out, stand there, trying to control my shaking knees.

A door opens and Captain Atherton says, "All rise."

Two guards enter, followed by the general. He takes his seat between Zungu and Atherton and the guards stand behind him with faces of stone.

Zungu leans over and whispers in his ear. They glance up at me then carry on muttering to each other.

Then silence. The general glares at me and taps his pen against the table top. Every tap counts down the seconds I have left to live. He's going to demand I betray my friends. And when I've done it, he'll kill me. But I know I'll do it. I will. I can't, I just can't, go back into those cells. I can't die. I need to go home to Greenhaven, no matter what it takes. Even though every cell in my body screams at me, *What kind of person are you, offering to betray the Resistance that your parents fought and died for? The movement that Micah has dedicated his life to?* I stare at the floor, too ashamed to lift my head.

The general clears his throat. This is it.

"Miss den Eeden, are you ready to take the oath?"

My head shoots up. What is he talking about?

"The oath of allegiance," the general says. "You acted bravely and loyally by assassinating a corrupt leader. Without thinking of your own safety, you brought about the downfall of the previous regime. As a reward, you are to be given a place on the Table Island Council."

Has Major Zungu told him what I said in the dungeon? Does he think I'm one of them now? "I...I didn't kill the High Priest," I stutter. "It was an accident."

"Repeat after me," the general says, my words sliding off him like oil on water. "I do solemnly swear to serve General Magnus de Groot, President and Supreme Ruler of the Republic of Table Island City, and to..."

If I become a Council member, if I swear allegiance to General de Groot, it really and truly makes me one of them—one of the enemy. My Sabenzis will never forgive me.

"Do I have to?" I mutter.

He stops talking and stares at me with those cold blue eyes. They look weirdly bright against his coppery skin, drilling into me like he can see inside my skull. I twist my robe, weighing up the alternatives. I'm going to have to say yes. Mr. Frye catches my eye and gives a tiny nod. His words echo in my head: "Remember you're wealthy, and wealth is power. Use it."

Maybe they want me on the Council not because they think I'm a traitor but because of my wealth. And having a position of power could help the people I love. Maybe they have Micah somewhere else? What if the general decides to send guards to arrest Letti and Fez? And there's the two thousand people in the bunker. It'll be much easier to get them out if I'm helping make the decisions. Surely Jasmine and Leonid and Micah will understand that.

"Sorry," I say, lifting my right hand and trying to look calm. "I'm ready."

"Repeat after me: I do solemnly swear to obey General Magnus de Groot, President and Supreme Ruler of the Republic of Table Island City, and to serve the Council to the best of my ability. I will be loyal, diligent, and untiring in executing my duty."

I mutter the words after him and take the chair Major Zungu pulls out for me at the white marble table. General de Groot, Major Zungu, and Captain Atherton are on one side. Mr. Adams, Mr. Frye, and I sit on the other.

"Item one on the agenda," Captain Atherton says, opening and turning the pages of a large leather bound book.

"Gentlemen...and lady...we are in a crisis situation," General de Groot says. He pauses.

"We are in a crisis situation," he repeats. "We are running out of food. The reserves in the Colony are reducing daily. Without their produce, there is nothing to trade, no way to feed the army or the Citizens or to prevent rebellion. We have to find a new way to produce enough food to keep our Islanders fed. Mr. Adams, your syndicate produces grain on the Mainland. Can you increase your yield? Can we import more into the island?"

"Unfortunately not," Mr. Adams says. "We don't have the water resources for much of the year."

"Hmmm," the general says, steepling his fingers. "What is your opinion, Miss den Eeden?" He fixes his stare on me.

His muscles bulge through the sleeves of his uniform, reminding me that he's in charge. He's looking at me now with those strange eyes that shine like metal. "Can Greenhaven produce more food?"

I stare with my mouth open, like a stupid person. Is this why he wanted me on the Council? For Greenhaven's produce? I have to produce more food to feed the Citizens and the army, while in the bunker, the people I grew up with are starting to go hungry?

"Let me answer that," Mr. Frye says with a smile. "Greenhaven has plenty of empty land to expand. However, labor remains a problem. Without sufficient laborers, no more expansion is possible. Isn't that right, Ebba?"

Suddenly I get what he means. Here is the most important person in the island, in the whole of the world, and he's asking me to help him. Now's my chance to get what I want.

"Well, General," I begin. My voice sounds squeaky in the big marble-lined chamber. "We could produce more food, but as Mr. Frye says, we don't have staff." I take a deep breath and brace myself for his reaction. "There are two thousand teenagers in the Colony. If you released them, you'd have a powerful workforce. I could have some at Greenhaven and you would release them from the slavery that the High Priest kept them in."

He snorts. "Ebba, Ebba, such an idealist. Where would we put them all? How would we feed and clothe and house them? It would be cruel to release them with no preparation. Life in the Colony is all they've ever known, being fed three times a day, provided with everything they need. You seriously want them released into this dangerous world where there's not enough to go around? It would be dog eats dog." He chortles. "And once they start breeding..."

He and Zungu are mocking me. A blush burns my face.

But I may never get this chance again.

"You can't keep them in there indefinitely. You've told us already they're running out of food and growing medium, thanks to the High Priest and his corruption."

The general's eyes narrow and harden as he watches me. Have I gone too far?

But he sits back and nods slowly. "You may have a point

here, Miss den Eeden. You may have a point. They need to be prepared for life up here. What do you suggest?"

I exhale slowly. "They should learn to read and write," I say. "They need to know to keep out of the sun, how to build shelters, where to find water...they need to know some basic medicine, how to..."

"One thing at a time. We should start with reading and writing. I'll instruct the tutors to begin daily lessons. Does that make you happy, my dear?"

"Yes. Thank you."

Mr. Frye beams at the three men. "Well done, General. You're already proving to be a wise and generous leader. Now, how many of the young people in the Colony could you spare? Greenhaven really does need a greater workforce."

The general gestures with his head to Major Zungu and Zungu leans over. Captain Atherton passes the leather book over. They bend over it, muttering. The general jabs the page with his stubby finger. At last he looks up.

"I can give you fifty girls," he says.

"Fifty?" I swallow as the logistics hit me. "Where will they sleep? I haven't got room for fifty."

Major Zungu nods. "They will be in the care of the army. They will sleep in a temporary barracks located outside Greenhaven Farm. They will be transported to Greenhaven at 0800 hours, six days a week, and return to the barracks at 1700 hours. Guards will supervise them for the duration. You will feed them three meals per day."

"How am I supposed to find food for an extra fifty people a day?" I begin to waver. I can't take responsibility for an extra fifty people, plus the army guards. But if I don't, they'll be stuck in the Colony, and probably starve to death.

"In time the food they produce will be more than enough to feed them and you'll have plenty over to sell to the City. It's your duty, Miss den Eeden, to help solve this crisis."

Under the table, Mr. Frye's knee nudges mine. I remember his words. "Bargain with him."

"General," I begin, "this is an interesting opportunity, but it's also a major adjustment for Greenhaven. I'm not certain that we want to expand so quickly. Perhaps in a year or two, when we're a little more established."

He narrows his eyes. I'm hitting home. I push forward. "However..." I pause. "However, I could perhaps be per-suaded if you were to do something for me. Something to make up for the inconvenience."

He leans forward. "What? What is it you want, Miss den Eeden?"

I swallow the boulder in my throat. If I don't ask now, I'll never get it. "If I could have full citizenship for my friends...please."

He thinks a bit, then picks up his pen. "Names?"

"Jasmine Constable, Letti Sinxo, Fezile Sinxo, um, Micah Maystree." I look to see if they're responding to his name, but their faces are blank. Major Zungu is tapping his fingers on the table. I bite my lip. Is that everyone? No, there's Shorty. We were so mean to him when we suspected him of being the High Priest's spy. And then we discovered it was Victor who was the traitor and that Shorty had been loyal all along. This is a way to make up for it. "And Shorty...I mean Troy Julius." Is there someone else? Think, Ebba. You're forgetting something.

Zungu's fingers tap faster.

I'd better move on. "And then..."

The general narrows his eyes. "There's more?"

"I want to select the fifty workers from the Colony myself."

He nods. "Granted. Moving on to the next item..."

I don't really listen to the discussion that follows.

Something about new laws regarding importation of wheat from the Mainland, and means of transport. Instead my mind goes to the Colony, to the workers I will be choosing to work with me on Greenhaven. I wish I could get Ma Goodson out as well. Maybe I can ask about her next time we have a meeting, or Mr. Frye might have a better idea.

I'm still thinking about the new labor and how best to use them on the farm when the general says, "That concludes the business of the day. Next item—the execution. All Council members are required to attend."

Chapter Three

"Come along, Ebba," Mr. Frye says. The others have left the Council chamber..

"Who...who are they executing?"

He can't meet my eye. "You don't know? The Poladion family. Now come along."

"But..."

"Look, I'm as upset as you are. The Poladions are—they *were* my friends. But times have changed, and we must adapt if we are to survive. And it's extremely important we don't do anything to annoy the general or we might be next. We must play it the general's way."

He tucks his hand into my arm and leads me down the passages and out onto the colonnade. The general and the other Council members are gathered halfway down the flight of stairs. Below them, like a broken tooth, stands the empty plinth. The soldiers are dragging away the statue of the High Priest, jeering and scoffing. I recall how he died for real, the swarm of angry bees, his screams, his gasps for breath.

He was a brutal killer, thinking nothing of ordering me to be sacrificed. But this is his family they're about to execute. *They* haven't done anything wrong. They were kind to me when I came out of the Colony. They welcomed me into their home, and gave me a taste of what family life could be.

A door opens in the wall, and the wives and younger children enter. Evelyn is carrying the toddler, who gazes with huge eyes at the soldiers. Nomkhululi is sobbing, bent over the baby she clasps to her breast. Cassie comes out next. She is the only one to lift her eyes. Seeing me half hidden behind the pillar, her face convulses. I turn away.

Surely, he can't be doing this. I've seen the general at the Shrine with his family. He's a father. He can't be about to kill these innocent children. But he's impervious to the sobs and wails echoing around the courtyard. Back straight, hands locked behind his back, his cold eyes trained over every inch of the courtyard, checking that all is orderly, that the guards are ready with their rifles.

Hal and Lucas aren't here. It's a game. It must be. This is just an elaborate method of intimidation. Psychological torture. He just wants to scare them all shitless, and then let them go at the last minute.

My mouth goes dry as the door opens again and Hal limps out, followed by a guard with a rifle.

"Please, de Groot," he yells, his voice booming up the stairs. "I'll work with you..." The guard hits him with the butt of his rifle and he staggers. The general hasn't even glanced at him. Hal's face twists as he catches sight of me and Mr. Frye. "Ebba," he yells. "*Do* something."

Mr. Frye squeezes my upper arm. "Ignore him," he mutters. "It's every man for himself now."

A moment later, Lucas emerges. His thin shoulders are twisted, his steps jerky as he staggers across to the far wall. He already looks half dead.

The soldiers line the family up next to Lucas. Another line of soldiers stands facing them, rifles ready.

For the first time I realize he's doing this. He's really doing this. He's really going to kill them. In cold blood. He's going to shoot them all.

I don't stop to think. I run down the stairs. "General, general." My voice is shrill, and he turns, face darkening, his body expanding as he sees me.

I should keep quiet. But I won't be able to live with myself if I don't at least try. I drop my eyes. Don't antagonize him. Don't antagonize him.

"What?" He thunders. "What now!"

"General, please. You can't kill a whole family because of their father. It's wrong. You know it is. It's inhumane. Send them away. Send them to the Mainland. You can't kill that baby." Don't cry, I order myself. Do. Not. Cry.

He jaw juts as he barks. "Don't be hysterical, girl. This is in the interests of national security. You don't want one of his family to assume the role of High Priest, do you? Do you want to revert to the days of Prospiroh worship? Do you want them to get revenge on you for killing their father? I'm sure Haldus would be pleased to punish you. He was publicly shamed when you refused to marry him." He gestures toward Hal, who is facing the wall while a guard ties a blindfold around his face. "I doubt very much whether he's the sort of man who would forgive a slight like that. Even the girl Cassie has it in her to lead a rebellion. She wouldn't let you off. You'd be the one standing down there, facing the firing squad."

Lucas stands slightly apart from the rest of the family. He's nearest the edge, just a few feet from the plinth. He's not looking at it though. He's not shouting or crying. He's silent, his eyes focused on the sea.

"What about Lucas? He's totally harmless. He can come to Greenhaven and take Victor's place."

Major Zungu snorts. "Lucas Poladion? Not only harmless but useless too."

The family are lined up now. Everyone is blindfolded. The baby's thin wail drifts across the yard. I bite my knuckle so hard, I taste blood. He's really going to do it. The bastard. He's really going to kill them all.

"Ready..." Major Zungu yells, and the row of soldiers

lift their rifles.

"Aim..."

I don't care what the consequences are. I grab the general's arm and force him to turn, to look me in the face. "Stop! If you don't let them free, the deal is off. I'm not growing any more food for you."

He gestures to Zungu, who pauses.

The soldiers look up expectantly. General de Groot glares through narrowed eyes. "I'll remember this," he snarls. He pauses, then growls, "You can choose one."

Only *one*? I have to pick *one* person to save? Who will it be? Cassie, who was my friend? Hal, who I fell in love with? The baby? I really must take the baby. Her mother is facing the army just like my mother did. If she dies, I'll never forgive myself. Never ever. I'll take her. I'll bring her home to Greenhaven and give her the life I never had.

But then I see Lucas, who risked everything to save me. Who could also see my ancestor Clementine and her little boy. Who drew a map for me so we could escape.

I'm relieved the others are blindfolded. I could not bear to see the desperation in their eyes.

"Lucas. I pick Lucas."

Major Zungu shouts an order, and a soldier pulls Lucas away from the wall, ripping off his blindfold.

He stands alone on one side, facing his family. Twenty-one people, backs to the wall.

"Ready...aim...FIRE!" yells Major Zungu.

I cover my ears as the shots echo across the yard and back again.

Then silence.

When I open my eyes again, the bodies lie crumpled on the ground. I turn away and vomit, spewing out the despair that lies in a bloody heap in the courtyard, the pure evil that stands next to me, stiff-jawed and unmoved.

Mr. Frye steps forward. "General, I think I should take Miss den Eeden home. We'll take Lucas Poladion too, if that's not an inconvenience."

The general shrugs. "As you wish, Frye."

"This way," Mr. Frye says gently. He leads me down the stairs flanked by the stone lions. I keep my eyes away from the bodies, from the spray of blood across the wall. But when I see Cassie's feet in her pretty gold sandals, I throw up again.

Lucas stands alone, staring over the sea. Mr. Frye pats his shoulder. "Come along, Lucas. You're going to Greenhaven."

Lucas's eyes are huge in his battered face. Huge and vacant.

The moment Lucas sits down in the carriage, he falls asleep. The coachman flicks his whip and the horses set off at a canter, away from the offices, the courtyard, the remains of the massacre. I never expected it, but I'm alive. I'm going home. *Thank you, thank you*, I whisper to the Goddess.

For once, Mr. Frye is quiet too, his face drawn as he leans against the velvet cushions of his carriage.

I wince at the blood stain on my sandal. How many more people is the general planning to kill?

"Mr. Frye?"

He opens one eye. "Yes, dear."

"I didn't mean it, the thing I said." Is Lucas listening? I don't want anyone knowing the words that came out of my mouth in the dungeon. He hasn't reacted, his head lolling against the window. "I would never...I would never betray..." I stop, the words jammed in my throat. I'm too ashamed to continue.

"Shhh," he mutters. "We can talk about this another time."

I watch Mr. Frye's frown relax as he falls asleep, and wonder about his life, his relationship with the High Priest and the Poladion family. How quick was he to swear allegiance to the general?

There's a knot in my stomach I can't loosen. How do I ever tell my Sabenzis that I also swore allegiance to our enemy? I have never kept a secret from any of them, but this—they might find this unforgivable. And if they ever find out that I offered to tell the general everything...

At last the rumble of the carriage lulls me to sleep, and I don't wake until the horses stop and the coachman opens the door. We're home and Isi waits on the stoep.

The moment we get out of the carriage, she runs not to me but to Lucas, jumping up to rest her front paws and head on his chest, whining softly—almost like she knows him. Aunty Figgy goes straight to Lucas too and reaches out to hug him. "My poor boy! What have they done to you?"

He winces, and instantly she steps back. "Come inside," she says. "Let me find some ointment for your face."

They go inside and the carriage drives off. For once, Isi doesn't chase it. She stays by my side, and her tongue sweeps across the birthmark on my hand.

Does she sense how upset I am? She follows me into the house, staying right on my heels.

In the kitchen, Aunty Figgy clucks around Lucas, putting him into the chair nearest the fire, chopping fresh rosemary to make him a soothing tea. Letti beats eggs and cream together in a jug. I need to tell them about the execution, about the baby, about Cassie, but not here. Not in front of Lucas.

Aunty Figgy gives me an armful of linen to take

through to the yellow bedroom.

I take the linen into the bedroom next to the sitting room. It has faded yellow wallpaper, an old but beautiful oriental carpet, and threadbare curtains that must have been grand once with their pattern of birds and flowers and swirling leaves. The bed is large and comfortable— he will be able to get a good night's sleep. I put the linen on the armchair, and get started on making the bed. My shoulder burns inside the sling. The jolting of the carriage has made it ache, but how can I complain after what I saw today?

"Food's ready," Letti says, taking the pillow from me and stripping off the case in one movement. A few days ago Aunty Figgy collected all the old pairs of spectacles in the house and made her try them one by one. Finding the right pair has made her so much more confident and determined. Fez is teaching her to read. He wanted to start with some of the picture books in the library, but she's insisted on starting with a book about medicine. "I'm not interested in puppies and butterflies," she says. "I want to know how to heal people." And she's sounding out the Latin names of plants, syllable by syllable. "We can finish this just now," she says, picking up the pile of dirty linen.

"Letti..." I need to tell her, to tell someone what I saw. "I..." But then I stop. She's only known life inside the bunker. What I want to tell her is so far from her experience that she won't understand. It will upset her too much. If only Micah were here. He would know exactly what I was feeling. I brush away a tear with the palm of my hand, wishing it was the end of the day.

"What, Ebba?" she turns to me, her eyes soft. "Is your arm really sore? Let me find you something for the pain."

"It's nothing. I'm just tired."

I want to crawl into my bed and sleep until the throbbing ache in my shoulder is gone and the nightmare playing in my head is over. The pile of bodies. Cassie's gold sandals. The baby, held so tightly in her mother's arms. And Hal...How will I ever get the images out of my head?

The food is ash in my mouth. I play with my slice of frittata, picking out the courgettes, the peas, grouping them in sections on the plate. Lucas doesn't eat either. When he looks up at us, he doesn't see us, doesn't see anything except the horror replaying inside his head. How will he ever heal after what he's been through?

"So what happened with the general?" Jasmine asks. "Were you in trouble?"

"We thought...well, I thought," Letti begins, frowning behind her new spectacles. She pauses then the words rush out, "I was scared you weren't coming back."

"What did happen?" Jasmine asks. "Did they interrogate you?"

"I thought they were going to..." I stop. I can't mention the jail cells, the execution, not in front of Lucas. The guilt shifts inside me as I remember the words I said to Mr. Frye. Major Zungu must have heard them. How will I ever make it up to my Sabenzis? To Leonid, the Resistance, to Micah, if he comes back?"

"So tell us," Fez says, eyeing my plate. "If you're not going to eat your food, can I have it?"

I push it over to him. "Help yourself." I look around the table at the curious faces, cowering inside at the inevitable response. "It was the last thing I expected. The general wanted me to join the Table Island Council."

Instantly, Leonid's face darkens. "You didn't agree, did you?"

"Wait..." Jasmine's eyes narrow as she reads my face. "I know you. You didn't have the balls to refuse."

My cheeks burn. "What could I do, Jasmine? I didn't have a choice. And at least it gives me some power. I got him to agree to let fifty girls out of the Colony, and I can find out what happened to Micah, and..."

"You complete idiot!" Leonid bangs the table so hard the crockery jumps.

Lucas recoils. His eyes flicker around the room, checking the doors, the windows.

I grab the papers from my pocket and wave them in the air. "I did more than that. None of you need to worry about being arrested. We're all Citizens now. Even you, Shorty."

I hand them their papers. Fez, Letti, Shorty, Jasmine. They stare at them— turn them over, then Jasmine points to the paper left in my hand. "Who is that for?"

"Micah..."

Leonid's chair screeches as he pushes it back. He walks out, slamming the door behind him.

Jasmine jumps up and sticks her face in mine. "You bitch. Your own half-brother, and you didn't think to get him made a Citizen too. And Aunty Figgy? Did you ever stop to think about *her*?"

I stare at the shocked faces around me, and realize what I've done. Aunty Figgy—how could I forget her? She's like a mother to me, and I didn't even think to ask for her citizenship. She could be safe, free to come and go as she likes, no need to carry a passbook. She'd even be allowed to own land. After everything she meant to my great aunt. Once she would have been free to live on the island, where she liked. I could have given her that power back. Given her part of the farm, built her a house...What oh what have I done?

"Aunty Figgy," I say. "I'm—I'm—"

She leans across the table and squeezes my hand. "Don't you worry about me," she says. "I don't want to be a Citizen. Your aunt could have arranged it if she wanted to. But I told her no. I'm a boat person, and I will be till the day I die."

"Does this mean we can stay in the house?" Letti asks brightly. "If so, claiming the room with the pink curtains."

"I want the blue one with the bookcases," Fez says.

I remember how, when I first came to Greenhaven alone, straight from the Colony, I imagined having my Sabenzis in the house with me, each with our own room. And now it's come true.

"Where will you sleep, Jaz?" Letti asks. "You needn't share the lodge with Aunty Figgy anymore."

"There's the yellow room," Fez says.

"Lucas is in the yellow room," I say, and instantly regret it.

"Actually, you know what?" Jasmine snarls. "I don't want your stupid citizenship. You can keep it. And your ugly yellow room. I'm going to remain one of your servants, like Leonid. And I'm going to move down to the coachhouse and share his room."

"Please stay with us," Letti pleads. "Remember how we always talked about living in the same house one day?"

"Don't be so blind, Letti," Jasmine snaps. "Ebba's given the last room to a member of the High Priest's family. She's made her choice."

Lucas's eyes are fixed on his untouched plate. Only his right leg jiggles under the table, faster and faster, and the gray energy swirls around him, sucking us all in.

Suddenly he gets up and walks out into the passage.

I run after him. "Lucas, stop. Please stop. They didn't mean it. You're very welcome, I promise you."

I follow him down the passage, out through the open front door. "Please, Lucas," I beg as he strides across the meadow. "Don't go."

But he ignores me, and soon his tall frame is swallowed by the forest. I want to run after him and bring him back, but I can't. I must talk to Jasmine. I have to get her to see that I made a genuine mistake. I wasn't trying to be hurt-ful. All I can hope is that maybe, someday, she'll believe me.

Chapter Four

Letti, Fez, and Shorty are almost finished eating. Jasmine has gone.

"Aunty Figgy went to talk to her," Letti says. "Come and eat something."

Tears sting my eyes but I'm not going to cry in front of them. I'm not. I tie an apron around my waist and collect the dirty dishes.

"Thank you for making sure we're safe. We really appreciate it," Letti says. "Why don't you go to bed? We can sort out the rooms in the morning."

Shorty brings a kettle of hot water from the stove. "I can wash up. It's no trouble."

I wipe my nose with the side of my hand. "It's fine. I want to be by myself. You've had a long day too."

They troop off, leaving me alone in the silent kitchen. Letti and Fez are very sweet, but they don't really understand why what I did to Aunty Figgy and Leonid is so hurtful. They haven't been here long enough to know what advantages there are to being a Citizen of Table Island City.

I watch the water swirling in the basin. The level rises, covering the pile of plates, just as sixteen years ago the sea drowned most of the city. And I think that right now, I am drowning too. Drowning in the things I have to do just to keep the farm running. Drowning without Micah to give me advice. But at least I'm...at least I'm still here. Just a few short months ago, Cassie and Hal were in this house, eating Aunty Figgy's bread, laughing and joking, and full of life. And now they're dead.

Then Isi lifts her head and gives a small bark. The door opens. Micah stands there, arms held out for a hug, the familiar lock of black hair falling over his forehead.

The relief knocks me backwards. I burst into tears. "You're back. You're back."

"Shhhh. Don't cry, babe."

It's so good to be in his arms again. "Are you injured? I've been so worried...I thought...I thought you must be dead."

"I'm fine," he murmurs. "What's been going on here?"

I sit on the table and tell him about the Poladion family, about Hal and Cassie. About Lucas and the baby. "I should have saved the baby," I say. "I feel so terrible about it."

"That tiny baby didn't have a chance without its mother," he says as he fills the kettle and puts it on the stove. "Even if you had saved it, it would probably have died. You haven't got any way to feed it, for one thing."

"I could have sent it to Boat Bay. I'm sure there's someone there who is breastfeeding a baby. I could have paid them to look after her."

"Babe, I know the Boat Bay people. They're not going to accept one of the Poladions, no matter how young." He rinses out the teapot and spoons fresh tea leaves into it. "You did the right thing. Lucas saved you—saved all of us by giving you the keys to the prison. It's right that you repaid him."

"But he's gone off into the forest. Everybody started to fight about..." I stop, remembering he doesn't know he's a Citizen. What if he's furious? "But where have you been? I thought you were dead. I really thought you were dead. We watched them chase you up the mountain, and then they came after us."

"They didn't catch me. I found another cave higher up, and hid there, and watched the soldiers go into the cave where you were hiding, and seriously I thought it was the end for you four, especially when I heard the gunshots. But then they came out again looking pissed off. They were poking around between the rocks, arguing with each other, and when they gave up and went back to the base, I knew you'd found a way to escape."

"So where have you been?"

"I know a path over the mountains—it took me a while, but I finally got back to Boat Bay. And then with the coup, security was so high there was no way back into the city. I've been hiding out, waiting for a chance to get back here. Back to you, my love." And he leans over and kisses me.

All the weeks of fear melt away. Then the kettle starts to whistle, and I realize that any of the others might be back any minute and tell him about the citizenship. I'd better bite the bullet and tell him the truth.

"Um..." I begin. "I have other news."

He turns around quickly, trying to read my expression. "News?"

"We're legal. We don't have to hide our love anymore. I got you papers—you're a legal Citizen, like me."

For a second he goes rigid, and I know I've blown it. He's going to be as acid as Jasmine. But then he exhales loudly, and a smile breaks across his face.

"How did you manage that?"

I push down the rush of guilt. I can't tell him the truth. I don't even know what the truth is. Did the general make me a Council member because I said I'd tell them everything? Was I really about to be thrown into jail? Or was Major Zungu throwing his weight around and trying to torture me for a bit of fun?

"General de Groot made me part of the Council because he wants me to grow more food. I told him I would if he made you and the Sabenzis and Shorty legal. But I forgot about Leonid." I bite my lip, remembering how furious he and Jasmine were.

"*You're* on the Council?"

I tense, waiting for the reaction, but instead he shakes his head slowly, his smile stretching into a grin. He cackles. "That's clever, Ebba. Very clever. We need to know what they're up to. We can use this to our advantage."

"I totally forgot about Leonid, so he's not a Citizen, and Aunty Figgy too. Leonid and Jasmine are furious. I don't know how to make it right with them. Will you talk to them? Will you tell them I'll ask for Leonid's papers next time I go to the meeting?"

"Of course. I'll go down there now. You coming?"

I shake my head. I don't want to face any of them tonight. "I'll finish washing up."

Giving me one last kiss, one last, "I love you," he leaves, carrying his mug of tea and a handful of rusks. I settle into finishing off the cleaning. It's just been fifteen minutes, but everything has changed. Everything. I have hope again.

When Aunty Figgy comes in a few minutes later, she's already heard the news.

"So he's back safe and sound." Her voice is dry. She begins to stack the soup bowls on the dresser.

"I can't believe it. I couldn't believe it when he turned up out of nowhere. I was so terrified he was dead. I never want to let him out of my sight, ever again."

"Ebba, my girl, you need to keep your distance from him so you can focus on your sacred task. It's not long till the equinox. Find the amulets, save the planet, and then you can have all the romance you want."

"Ag, Aunty Figgy," I snap, throwing the washing up cloth in the sink. "Can't you just be happy for me?"

Her lips are squeezed tight as she picks up the pile of plates and bangs it onto the dresser shelf.

"I'm going to bed," I say. I'm not going to hang around here with her in one of her moods.

Later, as I'm closing the bedroom shutters, I hear the rush of water and fling open the window. It's raining, pelting down. We've needed the rain for so long and at last it's here. The earthy fragrance rises up from the ground and mixes with the smell of wet thatch and it's just wonderful. Micah is back and being on the Council is going to help the Resistance. The rain has arrived. This is a new beginning for Greenhaven. For us.

I don't know what Micah said to the others, but the next morning, everyone has calmed down. I'm collecting eggs in the hen house when Jasmine arrives to help.

"It's okay," I say, a little awkwardly. "I can manage."

She digs in the nesting boxes and brings out a pair of brown speckled eggs. "I want to apologize for what I said last night," she says, not looking at me, turning the eggs in her hands. "And I know Leonid is sorry too. I thank you for making Letti and Fez legal. It's a big relief."

"I seriously didn't leave Leonid out on purpose. I'm really sorry. I'll get him papers at the next Council meeting." *If I can*, I add, in my head. *If the general is in a good mood.*

"That's okay. We all make mistakes. And Micah is back, and that's what really matters. And you saved Lucas, and that's excellent because he saved us." She hugs me, and I squeeze her tight, grateful that we're friends again.

"It's the Festival of the Boats today," Jasmine says as she searches through the hedge behind the hen house. The big brown hen likes to lay her eggs deep in the hedge.

"Tadaaa!" she calls, crawling out backwards. She holds up an egg. "Got it."

"What's the Festival of the Boats?"

"It's a big party to celebrate the establishment of Boat City. Apparently, it's twenty years today since Boat Island was made and everyone moved there. There will be music and food and dancing. It sounds like such fun. Let's go."

Then her face tightens, and I realize that my status as the boss has come between us again. She has to ask my permission to take the day off work. It's humiliating for her, for Leonid.

Can we afford a whole day off from the farm? There will be fifty more mouths to feed soon. We must get planting. But they'll hold it against me if I say no. And it sounds like fun. I'm dying to see Boat Bay.

"Of course we'll go," I say, brightly.

Back at the kitchen, Micah is stacking wood next to the stove. "Jas has had a brilliant idea," I say, as he slings his arm around my waist and kisses me. "Shall we go to the Festival of the Boats?"

Leonid is toasting bread in the oven. He looks up quickly from under his eyebrows. I know what he's thinking—I'm not welcome in Boat City because I'm a den Eeden.

"Why not?" Micah says. "I can't wait to see the guards' faces when they have to let us through the border post without our *dompasse*."

"We can't all go," Leonid grumbles. "Who will look after the farm?"

"Don't be grumpy," Jasmine laughs, punching Leonid playfully. "I want to meet your family, or is it too soon? Shall I stay at home in case they think we're serious?"

"We are serious," Leonid says. "My mom's been asking to meet you."

He glares at me again, and I'm sure he's thinking that

I'll be an embarrassment. That his mother doesn't want to meet me, her husband's illegitimate daughter. I should stay behind and take care of the farm. But Alexia might be there—my half-sister and my only other living relative. I am longing to meet her.

"You should go too, Aunty Figgy," Shorty says. "Letti and I can stay here. There's no room for everyone in the carriage."

I grin. He's so transparent. He's been following her around since she arrived. And I've seen her watching him. She definitely likes him. I'm not going to stay behind and ruin his big chance.

"That's decided then," Micah says. "Shorty and Letti look after the farm. We should leave right after breakfast."

I'm too grateful to have him home to care that he's the one making the decision, not me. It's a beautiful day. The rain has washed away the dust. The sun is shining. Outside the kitchen window, a sunbird is flitting around the honeysuckle, its iridescent green feathers catching the light. Micah is home, and everything is going to be okay.

———

The landscape fascinates Fez as we leave the farm and begin climbing up the road that leads to the pass. Jasmine and Leonid sit up front, and Micah, Fez, Aunty Figgy and I scrunch together inside the carriage, bouncing with every pothole we hit.

"And this is all Greenhaven?" he exclaims, as we drive past the vineyards and fields that hug the left side of the road.

"The farm runs all the way to the mountains over there," Aunty Figgy says, pointing to the range of peaks that dominate the skyline behind the fields on the left.

"What's on the other side of them?"

"It used to be a town called Fishhoek—an old-fashioned seaside place. When I was a child, our whole family used to take the train down to Fishhoek every New Year's Day. The beach was always packed—there was hardly place to put down your umbrella. But we didn't care. We'd swim and make sand castles and decorate them with shells. At lunchtime, my daddy would go buy fish and chips for everyone. They tasted so good, those slaptjips, covered with salt and tomato sauce, and the crispy batter around the fish...It was like heaven." Her shoulders fall and she's quiet for a moment. "When the sea filled the whole valley, it was like the incoming tide that used to wash away our castles. Everything was gone."

I can't imagine what it must have been like. The fear that must have loomed over everyone and everything, the terror that you and the people you loved, that everyone you knew could be wiped out. That everything you knew, like the trips to the seaside with your family, like going to the shopping malls or the movies, even going to school and planning a career—it was all coming to an end.

The mountainside gets steeper.

"Some of you must walk," Leonid calls from the front. "It's too tiring for the horses to pull all of us."

Micah, Fez, and I jump down. The right side of the road is shady, bordered with trees and thick undergrowth. Is this where Lucas is hiding out?

"Your great aunt planted all of these, Ebba," Aunty Figgy calls from the carriage window. "She started buying this land thirty years ago as people left for the Mainland and the government started with their new laws. Everyone said she was mad."

"She wasn't mad," Micah says. "That was incredibly crafty. I'm amazed no one else thought of buying the land. And now it's all yours, babe." He tickles my ribs. "She made you rich."

"So this forest is young? What used to be here?" Fez asks.

"Rich people's houses. They had big gardens, swimming pools, horses even, although they were just a hobby. Everyone had cars to get around in. The houses are still there, some of them. They're tumbled down by now of course. Miss Daisy didn't care about the houses. All she wanted to do was plant trees. She must have planted close to a million in her lifetime."

I peer into the forest, trying to catch sight of one of the ruined houses. I hope Lucas has found one to shelter in. Maybe he found some blankets and warm clothes and has made himself comfortable. There might even be furniture left there, so he isn't sleeping on the cold ground.

Hot and out of breath, we finally reach the top and pause to rest our aching legs.

"This is all your land?" Fez asks, pointing to the bowl shaped valley, running from our feet down to Greenhaven and the sea, across to the Silvermine mountains on one side and Wynberg Hill on the other. "You could plant right up here if you had the labor. How many people would you need to clear the land and do the planting? Ten? Twenty? And you'd have a crop to sell in what, three months? Or you could get more animals—ostriches maybe, or more goats. Shorty will know. I'll ask him when we get home."

Micah also looks down over the mountainside, but he's focused on Greenhaven, beyond the fields, the house and outbuildings, the meadow where the goats and sheep graze. Past the strip of forest that runs down to the granite wall that encircles the island. His head turns slowly—he's tracing a route—from the break in the wall, around the bay, past the point that Aunty Figgy calls Muizenberg. I follow his eyes as they continue up the Silvermine sound. I know what he's doing. He's calculating the distance from

Greenhaven to Boat Bay, the center of the Resistance.

Finally we climb back into the carriage at the top of the hill, and as we round the pass Fez is captivated by the view down the Longkloof. "So it's a—what did they call them again in the old world—a fjord?" He points at the narrow strip of sea that lies below us, bordered by cliffs on three sides, and topped with the granite wall that surrounds the whole Island.

"It's underwater now," Aunty Figgy says. "But before the Calamity, this was a valley with roads, houses, schools, sports fields. When the Council kicked everyone out who wasn't a Citizen, people built floating homes, and they moved them here to be safe from the storms. Leonid's father had the idea of joining them together to form the island—you'll see it in a moment."

"So there's actual houses under the sea?" Fez exclaims. "With furniture and cars and computers and stuff?"

"People took what they could, but yes, they left most of their possessions behind. Remember, back then Cape Town was part of the Mainland. At least ten million people lived here. But as the sea started rising and the storms got fiercer and fiercer, they had to find new places to live."

We've reached the border post. The guards see me and wave us through. Word must have got out already that I'm on the Council.

Leonid drives the carriage past the harbor and around the mountainside to the fjord's entrance. This is the port, where the boats berth. Some are dhows—the fishermen use these when they go to sea. We watch a long boat coming into the harbor, rowed by ten men on each side. As it approaches the jetty, six or seven people emerge from a shed carrying brown sacks on their backs.

"Hey, those are from the Colony." Jasmine calls, taps on the front window to get our attention. "See that?" She points to a man heaving a sack into the long boat.

"Those are the sacks of dehydrated vegetables we used to send to storage," Fez says, leaning out of the window. "I wonder how long they'll be able to keep that up. They were running out of growing medium last time I looked."

"Then it's up to Greenhaven to grow enough food for everyone," I say, my stomach tightening into a knot.

Aunty Figgy is sitting opposite me, and she leans over and pats my hand. "Ebba, the Goddess controls everything that grows and flourishes. She's made Greenhaven super abundant, and since you arrived, the crops are growing even faster. You've got the gift, so just trust her, and it will all be all right."

"But I don't have the amulet," I say. "I've lost my powers. I've lost Clementine."

"There are other amulets," she says firmly. "You must find them."

It's easy for her to say it, but I've just been looking at how enormous my farm is. There's zero chance of finding them on my own. And who is to say all the amulets are somewhere on Greenhaven land anyway?

Leonid stops the carriage under a tree near the entrance to the port. Micah opens the carriage door and jumps down before he's even tied the reins to the post. "I'll see you just now, babe," he calls. "I've just got some business to attend to. I'll find you on the island now now."

"We'll have to walk from here," Leonid says, as Jasmine ignores his outstretched hand and springs off the perch. "You coming, Fez?"

"Sure."

They're gone. A boy brings water for the horses, and he stares at me as though I've grown extra legs and arms. I look for Aunty Figgy—she's greeting a group of older women. They're laughing and hugging each other. She waves to me to join her, but I'm shy—the rich girl from the city, Darius Maas's illegitimate daughter. The Council member. Surely they'll see me as the enemy.

But then I hear someone calling my name, and a girl is running toward me. She's got short curly hair, a turned up nose, and a wide smile. She stands on tip toe and gives me a smacking kiss on the cheek.

"Ebba! My big sister Ebba. I'm Alexia."

I see myself in her—the square jaw, the shape of our eyes, but hers are hazel not green and her hair is brown instead of ugly red. She takes my hands in hers and beams at me. "I have been dying to meet you."

My self-doubts vanish. She's so warm, so welcoming, so...so genuine. She's the sort of person you like instantly. It's hard to imagine she's related to Leonid.

"Come on." Taking my hand she pulls me toward a path that leads past the first row of houses on the mountain-side. "Let me show you around."

I look up, past the rows of houses, built of anything and everything—planks of wood, shipping containers, old boats that have been turned upside down. The breeze brings the smell of the sea, mingling with the pungent aroma of the dried fish hanging on poles at the front of some of the houses.

"How huge is this!" I exclaim as we round a corner and find a battered white structure as tall as the Greenhaven barn. It sticks out into the pathway and we squeeze our way past. "Is it half a ship?"

"It's part of a luxury yacht," Alexia says. "It must have belonged to one of the super-rich in the old world. It washed up on the beach and my uncle and aunt found it when they were out fishing. It took them weeks to get it up here."

"We saw one of these in a Kinetika once, when I was in the Colony. They even had a swimming pool, and these huge soft chairs and sofas and massive TV screens, and they just had to push a button and someone would bring them a drink or snacks or whatever they asked for.

"Greenhaven must be like that. You must think this is really basic."

Seriously? Is that how she views me, like the super-rich in the old world? Sitting around relaxing all day while servants bring me food? Is that what Leonid has told them?

I peer through the window. It looks cozy, with bunk beds and wooden lockers. I feel a pang for the old days, when our Sabenzis slept close together like this and dreamed of escaping one day.

But she's gone on ahead, running down the path.

"What are these for?" I ask, pointing at the nets that hang like curtains between two wooden houses.

"It's foggy here in the mornings. The nets trap the water in the mist and it runs into the barrels. Come on," she says, jumping down the last stair onto a wide wooden deck that runs the length of the fjord. "Let's cross over to the other side of the bay."

Is this island really made out of plastic barrels lashed together? It doesn't look like it. A thick layer of soil covers the island. Fynbos has sprouted in patches—I can see geraniums and wild rosemary and there's even some grass. I bend down at the end of the walkway and peer into the water. There they are—the blue barrels packed together in rows with ropes binding them together.

"Come on." Alexia pulls me onto the island. "What are you waiting for?"

"Won't it sink? There are so many people on it."

"No, silly. We keep the weight balanced. See? Everyone is grouped in the middle sections. It's perfectly safe."

It's milling with people. I expect it to feel wobbly, but apart from a faint motion, it's firm, and I soon forget the sea is beneath me.

We weave across the island while she introduces me

to everyone—"my sister..." and "This is Ebba, my sister."

An older woman lifts a lock of my hair. "Mooi hare," she says. "Pretty." Then she pinches my cheek and says, "Jy lyk 'n bietjie soos jou Ouma."

"She says you take after our granny," Alexia says. And then she's off, through the crowd, heading for the far side of the fjord, where more houses cluster against the mountain, and faded laundry flaps in the wind and people stand in doorways, their clothing flashes of color against the scrubby backdrop.

"Where are we going?"

"I'm taking you to meet my mother."

I stop. It's the first time she's mentioned her mother. The woman my father was married to when he had an affair with my mother. "She doesn't want to see me...."

She smiles, and grabs my hand. "Of course she does. Come on."

I follow her through a small vegetable garden where tomato bushes straggle together and stumpy pepper plants fight against the wind and up a dirt path to a white painted cottage set into the mountainside.

"Our dad built this, when Leonid was a baby. It's a shipping container. You'd think that would be too hot to live in, right? But he lined it with wood inside and out and dug it into the mountainside." The first room is the kitchen. There's a table and four chairs. Pots and pans hang on the wall above the wood stove. A battered sofa stands under the window. Through a doorway I can just make out a double bed and small cupboard.

A woman drops the clothing she's washing in a bucket, and comes over to greet me, drying her hands on her apron.

"Ebba," she says formally, holding out her hand. "I'm pleased to meet you. I am Natasja."

I can see Leonid in her—she has the same serious face,

the same strong eyebrows. I draw back a little, waiting for her to say something about me, about my mother...

"I must thank you for giving my boy work," she says. "Work is scarce here at the harbor."

I feel myself blushing. "Th...thank you," I stutter, wishing Leonid saw it that way.

"And Jasmine too," she says. "They were just here. Such a lovely girl, and you got her out of the bunker. I'm sure she's so grateful. It can't have been easy for you."

Alexia tugs my sleeve. "Next time you're looking for staff, will you consider me? I'm nearly sixteen, I can cook and sew, and I can make things out of just about anything."

"Alexia, you're my half-sister. You can't be there as my servant. Leonid was already working there when I arrived, but you're different."

"It's the only way I can live in the city," she says. "Please say yes. I'm dying to leave here, and Leonid says Greenhaven is awesome. And it means one less mouth for my mom to feed."

Her mother is looking at me expectantly. I glance around the cottage again, at the sparse possessions, at her mother's ragged clothing. There's not much money coming into this house. And I have so much. "Of course," I say. "You can come home with us today if you like?" Then to cover my embarrassment, I say with a grin, "You can keep an eye on Leonid and Jasmine for me. Make sure they don't get up to mischief."

Down on the island, a horn blows and a cheer erupts. "The food's ready," Natasja says, taking off her apron. "Let's go and eat."

The cottage is high up the slope and we have a wide view over the island. I pause on the doorstep, searching the crowd for Micah. He's not among the group dancing. He's not chatting around the fires where some men are turning fish on the braais. I let my eyes sweep the whole island. Has he left without me? What sort of business did he have to do? Suddenly I see him. He's standing downhill from me, half hidden behind a rain tank, talking to a girl. She's tall, with a body like a model from the old world. Her long neck is shown off by the bright cloth wound in a turban around her head. She turns slightly, waving her hand as she makes a point, and I see her high cheekbones and flashing smile. Who is she?

Should I call him? Run down and introduce myself? I'm scared—she looks like Bonita Mentoor, the prettiest girl in the Colony. Bonita was beautiful, but she had a tongue like a knife and she wasn't scared to use it. Once in the recreation room, the girls were all together watching a Kinetika about animals, and when it was finished she said, "I heard that people with red-hair are orangutans." Everyone laughed, except for Jasmine and Letti.

"Let's take it up to level 1 and lock it in one of the animal cages," Bonita said.

I shrieked as she and her friend Vanessa grabbed me, chanting, "Rangutang, rangutang." The guards just stood there watching, grinning. The girls had dragged me almost to the stairwell when Rifda, another Year One, shouted, "Leave her. I heard she's got witch's powers. She'll turn us into frogs or something."

They paused, then Bonita scoffed, "She's a witch-ape," and gave me a shove before she and Vanessa walked off. I heard the others laughing as she said, "She's not even human. They meant to dump her at the zoo but they got the address wrong."

I know this girl isn't Bonita but...now I have to walk right past her. Maybe I should pretend I haven't seen them.

I'm about to set off down the hill when she leans forward, and kisses him on the lips. Not the way he kisses me, not like girlfriend-boyfriend, but still there's something so intimate about the way they're standing a bit too close together that I feel like the hillside has dropped away from under me.

Alexia turns back and calls out. "Hey. You coming?"

I want to tell her what I've seen but I don't know her well enough. So instead I fake a smile. "Sorry, no. Just fixing my shoe. It had a stone in it."

As we approach, Micah saunters out from behind the rain tank and takes my hand. "Here you are. You hungry?"

"I'm starving."

Maybe it's nothing, I think as we head for the row of potjies and join the queue. Maybe kissing on the lips is something they do here as a sign of friendship, nothing else. Maybe...I don't know, I just know I don't want to believe anything bad about Micah. He's the one person I can rely on.

I thought he'd spend the rest of the day with me, but everyone wants to talk to him. Every now and then he turns to me and smiles, or murmurs, "You okay?" and I nod and say, "Of course." But I can't get the pretty girl out of my mind.

I wish Micah and I could sail away in a yacht like the one Alexia's aunt and uncle live in. We could travel right around the world, just the two of us, with no beautiful girls trying to steal him away from me, no Resistance demanding his attention.

Everyone is dancing now. The vibration of the beat and pounding feet makes the island rock gently against its tethering posts as if it's dancing too.

"Come on," Alexia calls. "It's fun."

Her enthusiasm is infectious. I copy her moves, and soon they're automatic and I'm lost in the beat, one of the crowd, having the best time.

That's when I see the girl near us. The one who kissed Micah. She's dancing in the middle of a ring of people, swaying her hips and moving like a snake to the beat of the music. All the men are watching her, and she loves it, tossing her long dark curls back and lifting her chin higher.

"Who's that?" I call to Alexia.

"Oh HER," she sneers. "That's Samantha Lee. Can't stand her. She's so in love with herself."

Is she also in love with my boyfriend? I think, not daring to tell Alexia what I saw. "Where does she live?"

Alexia points across the island to a faded red wooden house close to the water's edge. "She lives there with Uncle Chad and his family."

"Chad the maintenance worker for the city?"

"That's him. He adopted her when she was a baby. Micah lived with them too for a long time when he first escaped from the bunker. He's been staying there again lately."

The girl looks across and catches my eye. She lifts one eyebrow, as though she's saying, "You don't stand a chance with Micah."

The music drains out of me. The way she lifts her chin, the way she stands with her shoulders back—she knows she's gorgeous. And she's right. I don't stand a chance.

Chapter Five

We're all tired as we set off for home in the late afternoon. The day is drawing in and long shadows thrown by the wall shroud the road with gray. There's a chill in the air. Autumn is coming.

Micah sits opposite me, still for once. I watch his face, the high cheekbones, the nose that once was straight but now has a lump on the bridge where it was broken, the eyes that are as bright and black as a mossie's. He's as quick and busy as a mossie too—they love the kitchen garden, and if we don't cover the gooseberries with netting, they'll eat the fruit on the bush before we get a chance to pick it.

What is going on inside his head? What made him come to Greenhaven? Why would he want to work as a farmhand when he's got so much to do at Boat Bay? Was it just because he knew I was there? How did he get the job anyway? Did Lucas appoint him on behalf of the High Priest? If he didn't come because of me, that means he is using me, using Greenhaven...

I don't want to think about it. The Micah I've known since I was a child would never act like that. Never.

Letti and Shorty appear through the kitchen garden, covered in dust and grime.

"We cleaned out that old shed," Letti says, when Leonid has introduced Alexia. "There was a hole in the roof and a broken floorboard, but Shorty mended them."

"I want to use it as a laboratory," she says. "I'll start with making medicine from the plants on the farm, and maybe we can sell them at market."

It's getting late. Micah gives me a quick kiss and leaves to bring in the horses. Jasmine and Leonid fetch more wood for the stove and fill the water barrels. Aunty Figgy disappears into the kitchen to start dinner.

"What shall I do?" Alexia asks.

It still feels wrong, having my sister work for me. I don't like Leonid, so it's easier not to think of him as family, but Alexia is warm and funny, the little sister I always wanted.

I give her a tour of the house, the Jonkershuis where the farm offices are, the barn, the rooms over the coach house where Leonid, Shorty, and Micah live, even the wine cellar near the gates, which hasn't been used for years.

She thinks her bedroom is wonderful. It's the same room in the laborers' cottages that Jasmine complained about when she arrived, but she's just thrilled to have her own room, and not to have to share a bed with her mother anymore. Even when we end up back in my room, she doesn't grumble about the difference between her small, dark room and mine. She climbs on the bed, draws her knees up, and hugs one of my pillows. "Can I ask you something?'

"Sure. Anything."

"Is it true you're part Goddess? That's what Leonid heard."

I turn away, pretending to tidy the dressing table so she won't see me blush.

"Is it true?" she persists. "Is that why you're so beautiful?"

I snort. "No one's ever called me beautiful before."

"Oh, but you are. You're so tall, and your hair is the color of fire. I'd die to have hair like yours. And you're the richest person in the world. That's what Leonid says, and the most powerful. He's a bit in awe of you."

"Leonid is in awe of me?" I turn around and check to see if she's joking. But she's serious. "I thought he hated me."

"Of course he doesn't. He just looks grumpy most of the time. My mom says he's like the gray cloud that covers the mountain when the black Southeaster blows."

"I'm not the richest person in the world," I say. "It's not like I've got a bunker filled with supplies for another hundred years. I've got more land than anyone else in Table Island City and it's the only land on the island where you can grow food. But unless I use it well, it doesn't make me any money. And I still have to pay taxes, and wages..."

She ponders this for a minute, frowning slightly. Then she looks up, twirling one brown curl around her finger. "But is the other bit true? Are you part Goddess?"

"Wait here." I fetch the Book of the Goddess from the library and open it up. "It's all in here. Apparently, this mark on my hand is the Goddess sign—that's what Aunty Figgy says. I don't feel like I'm a Goddess. I'm scared most of the time, and out of my depth, and worried..." I'm about to add "about Micah" but I stop. I haven't told anyone what I saw. I haven't even asked him what they were doing hiding behind the rain tanks. "I don't even know if anything written in the book is true. But apparently the Earth Goddess Theia was my great-great-a-million-times-great-grandmother."

She looks from the book to me with wide eyes. "Can I read it?"

"Sure. If you're really careful. Aunty Figgy will kill me if it gets damaged."

She bounces off the bed and gives me a peck on the cheek. "Thank you for letting me work here. It's going to be great. I can just feel it."

———————

The next morning, I call a meeting in the farm office. We're all there, all nine of us crowded around the old yellowwood table where Shorty sits taking notes. I begin: "As you know, the general is assigning fifty girls to work on the farm. I have to give him the list tomorrow afternoon." Before I've even finished speaking, they're all telling me what to do.

"We need help in the kitchen if we're cooking for fifty people," Aunty Figgy says.

I'm struggling to hear her over the rumpus, but I nod to Shorty to add one extra cook to the list.

"Wait, I thought I was helping with the cooking," Alexia says.

"Get one anyway," Fez suggests. "We can sort it out later. And you're going to need some stone masons."

"Stone masons?" Jasmine scoffs. "What, aren't Leonid and I good enough? Didn't we do a good enough job on the gable?" She and Leonid scowl as though we've insulted them.

"Stop taking it so personally," Fez says. "The extra produce will mean more wagon loads, which means wear and tear on the road. If we can't get the produce to market, we can't sell it. We'll need someone who knows what they're doing to repair it."

"I don't care who you get," Letti says. "Just don't get that girl Watheeqah. She's a miserable cow, and always tries to get out of work." She starts to tell Shorty about the time Watheeqah told Ma Goodson she was sick when she wasn't, and Letti had to work a double shift so they didn't fall behind.

"I think we should just go with the most easy-going girls," I say. "Let's choose the ones who do as they're asked and never cause trouble."

Once again they start shouting me down. I take a step back. Now I'm almost up against the wall, and they've got me trapped, all arguing and insisting and trying to force me to listen to them only. "One at a time," I beg. "Please just talk one at a time."

But no one is listening to me. Now Alexia and Leonid are fighting because she's told him to stop bullying me, Jasmine is talking down my ear, warning me about Bonita and Vanessa, like I'd even think of choosing them, and even Micah is saying something I can't make out. I take another step back, Jasmine bumps against me, and I put my left hand up against the grandfather clock to steady myself.

Instantly, a strange woman is standing there. She's cloudy, semi-transparent, but her voice is clear enough in my head. "Oh for heaven's sake," she snaps. "Don't be such a little mouse. Take charge, girl. Take charge."

I blink. Who was that? She's gone now, but her words still sting. "Don't be such a little mouse….Take charge."

"Be quiet, all of you," I shout. "Everyone just be *quiet*."

There's instant silence.

"Thank you. If you all talk at once, I can't hear you. Now let's start with the most important. Leonid, how many girls do we need to work in the fields?"

He and Jasmine discuss it briefly. He's adding up on his fingers and then he nods and says. "Thirty minimum. Plus someone to work with the carthorses."

"Write that down, Shorty," I say. "Any suggestions on who the thirty should be? They have to be from the growing chamber, obviously."

"Just get the biggest and strongest," Leonid says. "It's hard work in the fields. Harder than they'll be used to."

Letti starts to tell him he knows nothing about how hard everyone works in the Colony, but I hold out my hand to silence them. "Right. Next item. What else do we need?"

"You need to get the produce to market," Fez says. "You'll need someone to sew sacks. And a weaver."

"They'll have to be the same person," I say. Shorty makes a note of it.

By the end of the meeting, we've agreed on stone masons and carpenters to help with the maintenance around the farm, some poultry workers, two girls to work with the goats and pigs, and then Micah, who has been largely quiet until now, says, "We should get some engineers. The only person who can fix anything around here is Leonid, and it's good to have a backup. What about Camryn?"

"No way," Fez exclaims. "She's trouble."

"She was moody," he says, "but that's okay."

"In the last three years, she got more than moody. She got really surly," Jasmine says. "I swear that girl hates everyone and everything."

"Robyn is a better choice," Fez says. "She's easy to work with too."

"But she's half the engineer Camryn is," Micah insists. "Camryn could fix anything. We could really use someone with her skills."

I sigh. Now everyone is arguing about engineers, even Leonid and Shorty who've never met either of them.

I must regain control. "OK," I say, banging on the side of the filing cabinet. "Let's take a vote. Everyone who wants Camryn, put your hand up."

Micah's is the first hand that goes up. I put mine up too. She's difficult, but she'll be working under Leonid, and I'm certain he will be able to handle her. Alexia raises hers as well.

"So that's three people in favor, and six against," Fez says. "It's a no."

"The last thing," I say, avoiding Micah's eyes. "I have to go into the bunker tomorrow morning to select the girls. Who is coming with me?"

Secretly, I'm hoping we'll all go—Jasmine, Fez, Letti, me...and Micah. All five of us returning to the place we grew up, standing together, showing them how life can be on the outside, giving fifty girls a chance to join us in the sun and open air, knowing freedom.

Fez shakes his head. "I'm not risking it, sorry. I'll be thinking of you, but I'm staying here."

"No way," Jasmine says. "I'm not going back there. And Leonid's not going either."

"I...I will," Letti says, but I can see from her face that it's the last thing she wants to do.

"You're staying right here where I can keep an eye on you," Shorty declares. "What if they never let you out?" Then he points to Micah. "You should go with Ebba. Make sure she comes home safely."

But Micah shrugs before flashing a smile at me. "Sorry. Too risky."

Not a single person will go to the bunker with me? I'm going to have to go alone into that dark hole in the ground? But Alexia smiles and says simply, "I'll go."

I take her hand and squeeze it. This is what a sister is meant to be. Someone who has your back.

———

That evening Micah and I are bringing in the horses for the night. The weather is changing—there's a nip in the air and the wind is picking up.

"Can you smell the rain?" he asks as we fetch the halters from the fence. "When I first came out of the bunker, I thought it was amazing that you could smell rain."

I sniff the air, thinking about going back underground

to that rock bunker where you never see the sky. Thinking about all the years I longed for him and missed him, how he came back to me, and how I'm not sure he loves me, even though he says he does.

"Why didn't you say you'd come with me to the Colony?" I ask. "You're a Citizen now. Nothing can happen to you."

He shrugs. "Why put myself in unnecessary danger?"

To protect me, I think. *To make sure I'm safe*. Why can't he see it like that?

"Is everything okay between us? You're not angry with me about something?"

He's unlatching the gate, but he glances up at me from under his fringe.

"Everything is fine. You'd be fine going into the bunker alone anyway. You're on the Council."

"Where did you live when you escaped from the bunker?" I ask him. In my head, I'm seeing him sharing that small faded red cottage with Samantha Lee and her adopted family.

"Here and there. With Chad Loubscher, then I moved to Silvermine Island and lived in the caves there. I was on the Mainland too for a while, in a training camp."

"A training camp? What kind of training?"

He pats Ponto, the big black stallion's neck. "Come on, boy," he says, ignoring me.

I hear my voice becoming petulant and I hate myself for it. "What kind of camp?"

"Just a camp."

But I can't stop seeing him with Samantha Lee. Why was she kissing him? Why is he downplaying the time he lived with them? I'm sure she's about to steal him away from me, and she could have any man in Boat Bay. I know I should keep my mouth shut, but I can't. I have to know.

"I saw you with someone—a girl. Sa...Samantha Lee."

He lifts one eyebrow, his body stiffening. "You were spying on me?"

"I was not! I was coming down the hill from Alexia's house and I saw you behind the rain tank." I shuffle my feet. It seems so petty now. I should just have kept quiet. But I've started, and the words are burning me up. "And... I saw her kiss you."

"For god's sake, Ebba," he snaps, throwing the halter over Ponto's neck. "Don't start getting all jealous on me now. Really. If there's one thing I can't stand, it's paranoid girlfriends. She's my friend, right. She's like my sister. And she works for the Resistance."

"So...so why hide then? Why not talk to her in the open where everyone can see you?"

"Because..." His eyes have narrowed as he turns to look me full in the face. "Because there are spies everywhere, reporting everything that goes on to Major Zungu."

My stomach lurches. What does he know? Has he heard that I offered...? I'm too ashamed to even think about what I said in the dungeons when I thought I was about to be imprisoned. Am I any better than an actual spy?

He hands me Ponto's reins. "Take him in. I'll fetch the rest."

He stalks off and I'm left holding the reins of a horse I'm still nervous around. Why did it have to end like this, in a fight? Why couldn't he reassure me? Give me a big, wrap-around-the-body hug? Say he loves me and I have nothing to worry about in regards to Samantha Lee? I'm anything but reassured. Isi pushes her nose into my hand, her body warm against my legs. What is she trying to tell me?

I take Ponto into his stall. I would rather Micah take care of him, but I have to show that I'm not the weak girl I was during the tour of the dungeon.

Chapter Six

The next morning, Aunty Figgy checks my shoulder and pronounces it healed.

"You needn't wear the sling," she says untying the knot behind my neck, and letting my arm free for the first time in weeks. "But be careful. No sudden movements, and don't lift anything heavy."

Her fussing is irritating. I stroke Isi in her basket, trying to absorb her calmness. "I wish you were coming with me, girl," I murmur, and she thumps her tail against her crocheted blanket. Her amber eyes are warm and understanding as she looks into mine.

"I made you some padkos," Aunty Figgy says. "There's a flask of herb tea for pain, if your shoulder gets jolted on the drive. Now you look after Ebba, Alexia. Make sure she comes back safely."

Leonid is ready with the carriage and we set off down the driveway, Isi running alongside until we reach the farm gates. The world looks magical in the early morning light. The mountains glow salmon pink, and the sea is a striking cobalt blue. Somewhere, in the depths of the forest, Lucas is camping out. I wonder what it would be like to live in the forest alone, away from all the bickering and demands and people wanting things. Just to live simply and quietly, in peace with nature.

We're halfway there, driving past the Newlands security village, when a man in servant's uniform runs into the road. Leonid stops the carriage.

"My apologies, Miss den Eeden," the man says coming over to my window. "Mr. Mavimbela would like a word."

Mr. Mavimbela from the Council? Pamza's father? Why does he want to see me?

"Do you want me to come with you?" Alexia asks, and without hesitation, I say, "Yes."

I'm not thinking straight. Not thinking about this mixed-up, cruel, elitist society. Another servant opens the front door, bows to me, and says, "Welcome, miss."

Alexia follows me inside, but he waves her away, and says rudely, "Back door."

I go hot with embarrassment. Should I go to the back door too? I can't let them treat her like this.

"I'll wait in the carriage," she says quietly.

"Ebba, dear Ebba!" It's Mr. Mavimbela, both arms open wide as he comes out to greet me. He takes my hand in both of his. "Forgive this interruption in your busy day. Could I have a moment, please?"

I try to remember what I know about him. He's really wealthy. He lives here, but he owns farms in the Mainland. He's the biggest ostrich farmer in the world, and part of a syndicate who grow mealies and wheat in the Boland. What does he want?

He takes me into the sitting room. It's the center of the house and the other rooms lead off it like spokes on a wheel. I catch a glimpse of Pamza in the kitchen. "Pamza, your friend is here," her father calls.

I take a step toward her, but when I call her name she doesn't turn around, and I notice her shoulders are shaking with sobs.

It's Hal. I know it. She was in love with him, I'm sure. The way she used to look at him during Shrine services, how she watched him climbing the Ficus tree when they came to lunch at the farm, how she said she wished his father would hurry up and decide who he was going to marry. How sad she looked that awful day at the Shrine when the High Priest tried to force me to marry him. I want to give her a big hug and tell her how sorry I am, but her father gestures toward an open door.

Three men stand up as we enter his office.

"My colleagues, Mr. Siningwa, Mr. February, and Mr. Joubert," he says. "Please." He pulls out a chair. "Please, sit down."

"But first, some refreshments," Mr. Mavimbela says, going to the door. "Pamza, some refreshments for our guests please." He takes a comfortable chair opposite mine and continues. "Now Ebba," he says. "Your farming production is increasing rapidly, I understand. The extra crops you planted when you arrived at Greenhaven must be coming up for harvesting. And soon your production will increase enormously. You're going to need some help getting your vegetables to market. You're going to need a middle man."

"The general is taking care of all of that," I say, wondering where this is going.

"And he'll take a hefty cut, no doubt. Now Ebba." He sits forward on his chair and speaks like we're old friends sharing a secret. "Do you want to give the general more power than he's already seized for himself?"

If only Fez was here with me. He's brilliant with business.

"I don't want to annoy the general," I say, twisting my fingers in my lap. "I think we should stick with the arrangement he's already made."

Mr. Mavimbela sighs. "Don't be short-sighted now, Ebba."

Pamza comes in with a jug of cordial on a tray. She stops in front of the four men, and they each take a glass. She's about to reach me. I'm about to get up, to say quietly that I'm sorry for her loss, but she walks straight past me, and leaves the room. Her father jumps up. "Pamza," he roars.

She comes back, and stands in the doorway, glowering.

"Don't be rude, my girl," he snaps. "Give Ebba her drink."

Dragging her feet, she brings me the glass of juice. The hatred when she finally makes eye contact makes me flinch.

"Thank...thank you."

She ignores me, and I sit down again, twisting my fingers in my lap. Images of Hal and Cassie lying dead in the courtyard flash across my brain. The general is ruthless. He didn't even blink when the whole family was shot, even the baby.

"Ebba, as I was saying," Mr. Mavimbela says, and I shove the dark memories to the back of my mind and try to concentrate.

I try to listen, but her father talks so fast, it's hard to keep up. Mr. February, the short man with a heavy five o'clock shadow keeps interrupting with figures and projections.

They're talking access and profit sharing and setting up a company together, but I can't concentrate because I'm trying to work out what I've done to upset Pamza. Is it just that she's heartbroken about Hal and Cassie? But why direct it at me? I didn't have anything to do with the execution. I begged the general to stop it.

"I don't know, gentlemen," I say when there's a pause and they're all looking at me expectantly. "I've made a deal with the general. I really shouldn't break that."

Mr. Siningwa, an older man with gray hair, has said nothing so far, he's been busy writing in a notebook. Yet I get the feeling that nothing is escaping him.

"One additional benefit," he says. "I've heard from Fergus Frye that your business manager, young Fezile, is brilliant for his age. I'd be happy to take him under my wing. Teach him everything I know."

"Absolutely," shouts Mr. February. "Me too. One hundred percent correct. Everything we know. He'd be an expert in under a year."

Mr. Mavimbela taps his index finger on the table. "Let's say this is part of the deal. Young Fezile will get one day a week training from one of us four, on a rotational basis, until he has a solid working knowledge of everything there is to know about running a successful business."

"And running a farm," Mr. Siningwa says.

This will be so good for Greenhaven. And after all those years in the Colony, this is Fez's chance to grow his talent. Fez, who is so clever, who is desperate for more knowledge, who in the old world would have gone to university and built his own company.... But what will the general say if I renege on the deal? He's the only one with the power to release the two thousand. He might decide to take revenge and refuse to release any more.

I don't know what to do. And I can't make any decisions until I stop worrying about Pamza.

"Excuse me," I say. "I want to focus on what you're saying, but there's something I need to do."

I walk out, across the sitting room to the kitchen, where Pamza is slumped at the table, her head in her arms. She doesn't look up.

"Pam, what is it?" I say, sitting opposite her and leaning forward. "Please tell me what I've done to offend you. I didn't have any say in the general's decision to..." I flinch at the memory of the family standing against the wall, facing the firing squad. "I tried to stop him."

"You know what you did," she snaps, lifting her head slightly and glaring at me under her eyebrows.

"You could have saved any one of the Poladion family. Any one. You could have chosen Cassie or..." She pauses and when she speaks again her voice cracks. "...Hal. Why did you have to choose Lucas. Why. WHY?" And she pushes past me and runs out of the room. I hear a door slam.

The last place I want to go is back into a meeting with the four men, but I have no choice. I just want to get out of here now. I'll ask them for the proposal on paper and discuss it with Fez and Shorty. Tell them I'll let them know my answer in a week. Or just say no. That would be best. Keep things as they were.

"We were just outlining the profit projections," Pamza's father says, as I go back into the room. "It's a good opportunity, Ebba, it really is."

"Thank you for the offer, gentlemen. It is very attractive, but I have already agreed in principle to the general's proposition. He is giving me fifty girls from the Colony, and in return he will transport my produce for me. I think I'll stick with what's already in place."

Mr. Siningwa snorts. He and Mr. February exchange glances.

"You really believe he will let anyone out of the Colony?" Mr. February says, widening his eyes. "He is playing you. You should know by now you can't trust a word he says. We're all farmers—we need to work together."

They could be right. What guarantee do I have that he will follow through on his promises to start preparing the Colonists for the outside world?

"You can't trust him, Ebba," Mr. Mavimbela says gently. "Look what he did to the Poladion family. You think we're not all just commodities to him? Just a way to feed his army? He can turn on you in an instant."

I look at these four men sitting across from me and I wonder if I can trust them any more than the general. One thing I know for sure is that everyone wants something from me, and I can't just do what seems a good idea before I've thought through all the pros and cons.

"It's getting late. I need to get going." I start to stand up. "I'm going to think about this, and get back to you."

Now the man who has been silent the whole time, Mr. Joubert, finally speaks, his voice high and girlish. "'Tell the general I'll do everything he says. I'll tell him everything I know. Just don't let him kill me.'"

His words chill my spine and I break into a sweat. Those are my exact words. How did he hear about this? Why is he bringing this up now? All four men are still, watching, like cobras ready to strike.

"I'm sure your boyfriend would like to know that you offered to betray the Resistance." He raises one eyebrow. I swallow hard.

Mr. Mavimbela pushes some pages across the table toward me. Mr. Siningwa hands me his pen. "Just sign at the bottom of each page."

My hand shakes but I do what they say. They've got me cornered.

Back in the carriage, Alexia says nothing as Leonid flicks his whip and we set off again toward the Colony.

"I'm so sorry about what happened back there. I should have remembered they'd treat you like that."

"It's not your fault," she says. "It's fine."

I'm ashamed to be a Citizen, ashamed to be on the Council, ashamed that even though we share a father, we can never be equal. Ashamed that I've just signed a document that is going to cause more trouble.

Who told them what I said in the dungeon? Mr. Frye? He's on the Council with them, but surely I can trust him? Major Zungu? One of the guards perhaps?

If there's one thing I've learned since I was elevated, it's this: everyone is out to get something from me.

I'm going to go with my gut instinct. Micah has been my hero and protector since I was a baby. I'm going to trust him. I'm going to get him to trust me so thoroughly that even if he does hear what I said to Mr. Frye that day in the dungeon, he'll never believe it. He must trust me like I trust him.

At last the road begins to zigzag up the mountain side toward Cableway Road. Alexia surveys the huge flat-topped mountain above us, covered with a layer of white cloud that Aunty Figgy calls the Tablecloth.

"I've never seen it from this side. My mom says that in the old days, there was a cable car. It took people from here to the top of the mountain in a tiny cabin hanging on wires. There was a restaurant up there and everything."

I look up at the monolith of pink-gray rock, imagining dangling over that cliff on a thin cable that could break at any minute.

"I wouldn't want to go in that," Alexia says. "Unless you went with me. You're really brave, Ebba. It's incredible what you do, running the farm, dealing with businessmen, being on the Council...and now you're getting fifty girls out of the Colony."

If only she knew that most of the time I feel as though I'm dangling over a cliff waiting for the cable to snap.

Leonid stops the carriage at the bottom of the flight of stairs—the same stairs I walked down with Mr. Frye the morning I was elevated out of the Colony. I remember how terrified I was by the feel of the wind, by how far I might fall, the open space around me. For a second, I'm choked by the same fear and my heart starts to race as it did that morning. But I pause, and drink in the view over the sea to the Mainland, where the Hottentots Holland Mountains are layers of blue and purple against the sky. A goshawk swoops overhead, a flash of orange on its beak, and I watch its flight, grateful for the fresh air, that my Sabenzis are all safe, that I have Micah and Aunty Figgy and Isi. And that this lovely girl who thinks that I am brave, who is so forgiving, is my sister.

———————◆———————

Major Zungu is waiting in the glass-fronted room where I first saw the city, and the fact that they'd lied to us nearly exploded my mind. I linger at the window, reluctant to re-enter the underground world I hated.

When I lived here, everyone looked down on me because I was the girl with the red-hair and no history. Their parents were all high achievers. Letti and Fez's mom was a professor of mathematics. Jasmine's mom won sixteen gold medals at the Olympics for gymnastics. Micah's parents were famous architects. All two thousand kids were gifted genetically, and then there was me, the youngest in the Colony who came from who knows where?

And now I'm coming back with the power to choose who to save, who to bring to the surface to a lifetime of sunshine and sky and fresh air.

"Come on," Alexia whispers. "Let's get the job done."

I take a deep breath. "We'll start with the livestock level, Major."

Major Zungu raps an order to the soldiers standing next to the elevator. They put their shoulders to the huge wheel and the doors slowly open. I force myself to step inside the small wooden box. Major Zungu's bulk fills most of the space and Alexia and I squash against the walls. When the soldiers close the door, it's pitch dark and I grab Alexia's arm, my body shaking as we start to move downwards. The Major could reach over with those huge hands and strangle us and we'd have no way to escape. I shrink into the corner as far from him as possible, my nostrils filled with the smell of his sweat and power.

But then the lift shakes and jolts and stops and the

doors open and we step out, into the gloomy Colony. It's worse than I remember it—the monotone walls and floors, ceilings all carved out of the same gray granite. The air is stale with the smell of the animals kept on this level. There's no sun, no wind. It's like being buried alive.

We turn the corner and there are the banks of cages that line the walls. The first thing that strikes me is how skinny and raggedy the chickens are. They have never known what it's like to scratch in real dirt for worms, never left these poky cages, never felt the breeze ruffle their feathers or taken a dust bath.

The second thing that I notice is that nobody is surprised to see me. The six or seven boys cleaning the cages barely look up as we enter. Did they know we were coming? Why are they so listless, barely able to wield the brooms as they sweep the chicken droppings into the chute that carries them to the compost heap on the second bottom level? Like the chickens, these boys are scrawny—much thinner than they were when I left the Colony four months ago.

In the next section, some Year Twos are washing the eggs and packing them into plastic trays. They're moving slowly with none of the chatter that used to fill the room. One looks up at me and smiles. It's Isabella, the girl who knows everything about poultry farming. If she can still get eggs from these miserable chickens, she'll do wonders with the Greenhaven hens. I'd like to see her with color in her cheeks and full of the energy she had when we were small and she was the champion at hopscotch.

Alexia consults the list Shorty wrote out neatly. "We need four poultry workers," she says.

"Isabella," I say. "Would you like to come with me?"

Her face lights up. "Thank you, thank you. When they told us you were coming to see us, we were so excited. I can't believe it's safe to go Above at last. I can't wait to find my family."

How do I tell her the Island only has about one thousand Citizens, and none of them sent their kids to the Colony? How do I tell her that she and all the Colonists have been betrayed and abused? I can't here, not in front of the Major. So I just smile and nod and say, "Can you choose another three girls to come too? You'll be working with my poultry."

They crowd around her, shouting out, pulling her tunic, begging to be chosen. The guards step closer, raising their sjamboks, and I want to intervene, but Alexia taps the list.

"Come on, Ebba," she says. "Let's get going. We've still got to pick girls to work with the goats, pigs, and rabbits."

We carefully work through the rest of the farm level, then move down to the growing level. I go straight to the section our squad used to work.

She pauses in the doorway, trying to take it all in. "This is where you spent twelve hours a day?"

I look at it through her eyes—at the tired girls turning the handles so the huge planters can revolve, giving each layer access to the light coming through the system of mirrors and tunnels. I see what remains of my squad —there are only fifteen doing the work of twenty. Their skinny shoulder blades stick out as they lift the buckets of solution for the plants. Nobody should ever have to live in conditions like this. I've got to persuade the general to let them all out soon.

Bonita sees us first and comes running over with a huge fake smile.

"Ebba, it's fabulous seeing you again. You look so gorgeous—we've missed you so much, haven't we, Vanessa? They said you were coming to pick fifty girls, and we were so excited, weren't we, Van?"

Her friend Vanessa is all smiles and hugs. "I love your new haircut," she says. "I can't wait to see the outside world. We've made a list of who you must take."

Apparently, they assume I'm going to pick them because they were in my squad. For a minute, I'm tempted. They like me at last.

But I remember the years of bullying and I turn away.

Their smiles grow more brittle as we walk through the chamber, selecting the girls I know are hard workers. By the time we come back to them, their smiles are fixed and their eyes hard.

"That's it," Alexia says, ticking off the list.

"You're not taking us?" Bonita snaps. "What is wrong with you?"

Alexia taps her pencil on the paper, "That's the quota. We've got everyone we need."

Bonita raises one eyebrow and looks Alexia up and down like she's pig dung. "And who might you be?"

"She's my sister," I say, taking Alexia's arm. "And no, I'm not picking you."

Her face blanches. "Wait," she shrieks, but we move on toward the workshop area.

We choose masons, carpenters, weavers, and seamstresses. Then we reach the engineering workshop. I stop in the doorway and watch the engineers at work. Camryn is on her haunches with a spanner adjusting something inside one of the treadmills. She's fit and muscular and she moves with a confidence that says she knows exactly what she's doing. Robyn is battling to refit the belt, her face red with effort. Camryn leans over and unbolts a metal plate. The belt slips back into place.

We really need her because she can fix everything. But we took a vote. When I pick Robyn, Camryn watches me from under her fringe, as prickly as a porcupine, and I can feel her hostility swell as Major Zungu says, "Is that everyone?"

Micah wanted her. I know we voted, but he really

wanted her. Maybe I should change my mind.

"Are you ready to move on, Miss den Eeden?" the Major snaps.

"Not yet. I want to greet Ma Goodson," I tell him. Surprisingly, he nods.

Alexia and I set off down the corridor to the sleeping cells. It's so dark down here, we can barely make out the path.

"They're running out of electricity," I tell her. "The treadmills are wearing out, and there's no way to replace them. Did you see the plants in the nursery? So weedy and pale, like they could fall over any moment? There's not enough fertilizer, and they're not getting enough light."

"And nobody's getting enough to eat by the look of it," she says. "They're all so thin."

"That's where Micah slept," I say quietly as we pass one of the sleeping cells. "Until one morning we woke up and he wasn't there anymore. He'd asked one too many questions. They threw him out of the ventilation shaft, but he survived."

She shudders. "Serious? Onto the rocks?"

"Same place they were going to throw me. I cried for weeks when he didn't come back. I thought he was dead."

And now he's out there, leading a revolution against the very people who kept us as slaves in this terrible place.

We've reached my old cell. I stop just inside the door, looking around. When it was all I knew, I didn't question it, but now it feels like the dungeons where the Poladions were locked. It's squashed and airless. There's a bad smell from the bathrooms. Something has gone wrong with the sewage system. The linen on the beds is ragged and worn into holes. At the end of each bunk is a single locker. Everything we owned was inside it. One change of clothes. One worn down toothbrush. One frayed towel as hard as sandpaper.

"Seriously, you grew up here, when you should have been at Greenhaven?"

"There's my bunk in the corner." I point to a stripped mattress in the far end of the cell. "I shared it with Jasmine. The twins were next to us. It didn't seem so bad at the time—it was the only thing I'd ever known."

Ma Goodson runs out of the storeroom.

"Ebba, Ebba," she cries, grabbing me in a bear hug. "I'm so happy to see you."

I lean against her, remembering her comforting smell and softness. She is the closest thing to a mother I've ever known.

"You're quite the fancy lady, all grown up in your pretty robe," she exclaims, standing back to examine me. "Not so pale anymore. And who's this?"

"My sister, Alexia. Fez and Letti are safe too, and Jasmine. They're all Citizens now and live on my farm."

"Oh thank Prospiroh!" she exclaims. "I thought the twins were dead. I heard they'd been caught. So you've got a farm now, and you're very rich? I always knew there was a reason you'd been saved. Everyone always said you were just a little scrap of nothing, but I knew. There was something about you. Even when you were a little girl..."

She chatters on, but I'm distracted. Major Zungu has grown tired of waiting and he's come to hurry us up. He's standing with his hands behind his back, his face impenetrable, but I know he's listening to everything she says.

"Ma Goodson," I interrupt. "Are the memory boxes still here? Can I have mine?"

"Come with me." We follow her into the storeroom. "Here it is," she says standing on a footstool and feeling at the back of the top shelf. "Although there's not much in it. Just your baby clothes and your blanket. Funny little scrap you were, bawling your eyes out, with your red-hair and big feet."

"Can I have Jasmine and Letti and Fez's too? And...and Micah's. Is it still here?"

"Micah?" Her face softens. "He was a good boy. Spirited. A born leader. But he didn't take easily to authority, and they didn't like that down here."

"He's with me on the farm," I whisper. "They threw him out of the shaft, but he survived." I want to tell her more, but Major Zungu's boots ring on the floor as he paces up and down, up and down. I don't want to give him any reason for anger, any reason to decide that he's not going to let me out again.

Soon I have all four boxes, neatly packed into two ragged pillowcases. "Give them my love and tell them I miss you all every day of my life," Ma Goodson whispers as she hugs me. She holds me close, keeping me against her as though she can't bear to see me leave again.

What must it have been like for adults like Ma Goodson to leave their families and friends on the outside world and come into the Colony to be parents to two thousand babies and toddlers? She gave up having children of her own to care for us. "Thank you for everything you did for me," I murmur in her ear. "I'll never forget you. And if you ever leave here and need somewhere to stay, come to the farm. There will always be a place for you."

"Miss den Eeden," Major Zungu snaps before Ma Goodson can begin talking again.

"Go, go," she smiles, chasing us out of the storeroom like she used to when we were toddlers, looking for mischief. "Come back soon. Next time stay longer so we can have a proper chat. I want to hear all about your new life. Everything, everything."

A memory hits me as we go through the door into the dining room.

Jared in Year One was bigger than anyone else on the

Colony, and the biggest bully too. Everyone was scared of him. One day he cornered me—he was about thirteen, and I must have been eight. It was recreation time, and Letti and I were playing a board game quietly in the corner when he came up to us, kicked over the board and said, "Hey, runt, your family dumped you because you're so ugly."

His friends started to chant, "Runt, runt, runt."

Letti whispered to me, "Just ignore them. You're pretty, you're really pretty."

But I was stung. Micah was playing cars close by with two of his friends. He was much smaller than Jared—not as muscular and two years younger. He saw me crying and came over. "You know what?" he said loudly so everyone in the room could hear. "When they circumcised Jared, they threw away the wrong bit."

The older kids doubled up laughing—everyone except Jared. I didn't know what Micah was talking about, but Letti and I joined in. We laughed even more when Jared stormed off to lie on his bunk.

Micah has been my protector as long as I have known him. This is my chance to repay him.

"Stop, Major," I say, as we reach the corridor leading to the lift. "I need to make a change. I need to go back to the engineering workshop."

He sighs. "Ma'am, is it necessary? A girl is a girl."

I bite my lip. He's glaring at me but I think of Micah's face when he sees Camryn. And she really is the best engineer. "It won't take a minute, please."

He purses his lips, but I've already turned back and am hurrying down the passage to the stairs.

Camryn, when I find her, doesn't seem keen. "Whatever," she says. Her long fringe covers her eyes, and she can barely be bothered to toss it back. In the corner, Robyn, the girl I had to turn down, is quietly crying.

"But we took a vote," Alexia whispers. "You can't go against that, can you?"

"It's my farm. I can do what I want."

She shakes her head. Is that disappointment? Or just resignation? "Come on, Ebba," she says, tugging my arm. "Let's get out of here. This place creeps me out."

Camryn has already turned back to her work. I dither for a minute. Maybe the others are right. Camryn is trouble, and I have enough troubles of my own without importing new ones. But Micah...I need him to believe in me. And yet...Robyn is crying so hard...

"Wait," I mutter. "I'm not sure..."

Major Zungu scowls, his fists clenching against his thighs, as he snaps, "No more changes, Miss den Eeden. This way, please." And he marches us smartly along the passage to the elevator.

A few minutes later, we're back in the glass room where I first saw the world. Major Zungu opens the door and I step out into the winter sunshine and stop, closing my eyes, feeling the warmth and the cool wind on my cheek, and breathing the fresh air deep into my lungs.

Alexia is quiet until we reach the bottom of the stairs. Then she turns to look up at the cliff, shaking her head. Tears shine in her eyes. "That is a terrible, terrible place. Those poor people aren't living—they're just existing, just trying to get through each day."

And judging by their jutting bones and dull eyes, their days are running out. We have to get them all released. We just have to.

Chapter Seven

There's a weird atmosphere at supper. Maybe it's because I've got a guilty conscience, but it seems as though the three across the table from me—Letti, Fez, and Shorty—are colder. Closed off. Glancing at each other when I speak. Alexia must have told them that I chose Camryn. I'm used to Leonid and Jasmine being grumpy, but these three? Luckily Micah is super friendly. His leg presses against mine, reassuring me that I can rely on him, just like I always have.

"I've got good news for you, Fez." We're halfway through dinner before I realize that I may have a way to unfreeze the atmosphere.

Fez looks up quickly. "For me?"

"I had a meeting with a syndicate of businessmen—Mr. Mavimbela, Mr. February and a few others. They're going to give you business training so that you'll be an expert, like you went to study at a university."

Letti peers at me, frowning behind the owlish spectacles. "Shorty knows business. He's already teaching Fez."

Now I've doubly offended Letti, and even Shorty looks pissed off. It's like they're looking for things to be offended about. I'm trying my best here, I want to say. Just cut me a bit of slack.

"I thought you were only going to the Colony," Jasmine snaps. "We've been waiting for you to get back so we could eat."

So now I'm responsible for the late meal too. "Well,

sorry you had to wait ten minutes for dinner. I didn't ask for a meeting. They stopped me as I was driving by."

There's silence for a short while. Then Micah says, "Is that all they stopped you for? To offer to teach business to Fezile?"

"Um..." How can I put a spin on this, so it doesn't sound so bad? It will be best just to launch straight in and get it over with. "I'm making some changes. They're taking over the transport and distribution of our produce."

Fez raises his eyebrows. "What exactly does 'taking over' entail?"

"I'm not sure. I just signed the papers they gave me." As I say it I realize how lame it sounds. But I can't tell them what really happened. That they tried to blackmail me.

Micah's jaw is clamped like he's trying to keep the words in his mouth. He pushes back his chair and gets up. "A word, please, in private," he snaps, pointing to the back door.

"Ebba," Aunty Figgy says, catching my arm as I walk past her. "He shouldn't speak to you like that. You don't have to go. He works for you."

But I do have to go. Although my stomach is clenched in a knot and my mouth is dry, I have to do as he says. I need one person on my side, and it has to be him.

He points to the wall around the duckpond, and I sit down, practicing what I'm going to say. The ducks are asleep, curled up with their bills tucked under their wings. Micah looms over me, pacing up and down like Mr. Dermond used to do in the Colony when he was getting ready to shout at us. I wish I could tuck my head away like a duck so I didn't have to listen.

"How could you make that kind of decision without consulting anyone?" The words come out, hard as bullets. "We talked about it, remember? We agreed that you'd run all your business decisions via me and Shorty."

"Did we? I don't remember that." I'm wracking my brains, but coming up blank.

"Of course we did, just last week, in the office. Remember? You were showing me the books."

I bite my cuticles. "I'm sorry, Micah. It slipped my mind. It's just that Pamza was so upset about Hal and Cassie, and she blamed me for not saving them...She was crying and crying, and I wanted to do something to show her I cared."

"Didn't you think that maybe her father arranged it like that so she could manipulate you? Why didn't he order her to stay out of the way? Why didn't he come and see you here? It's because he wanted to take advantage of you. He knew you would buckle under the pressure."

He takes my face in his hands and looks me in the eye. "Listen. You were brainwashed in the Colony. We all were. It took me years to recover once I'd got out, and you've only been out a few months. It's impossible to see things clearly when your mind has been poisoned. The poison still has to work its way out of your system. That's why you need me to make your decisions for you."

He sits next to me and takes my hand in both of his. "We both know what it's like to live in a bunker being watched and controlled twenty-four hours of the day. We've been slaves, killing ourselves with hard labor to make other people rich. People like the Syndicate. They're not on your side. Believe me. If they were, they'd have been professional today and not let you sign something when you were upset."

"Okay," I sniff.

"We'll sort out the mess in the morning," he says, getting up. "Good night."

I was hoping he'd spend the evening with me, but he's gone, heading for the barn, without even a kiss or a squeeze of my shoulder.

When I go back to the kitchen, only Alexia's there, kneading the bread for breakfast. "What happened? Did he shout at you?"

I shake my head, trying to stop the tears from rising. "I wish he had. He showed me how they manipulated me —how stupid I've been. I feel like such an idiot. He says I must run all my business decisions by him and Shorty."

"Ag, Micah! He thinks he's a god."

She covers the dough with a tea towel and pushes it to one side of the stove. "I'm finished here. You need to relax. Let's go and listen to some records."

It's illegal. She's not allowed to socialize with me, only to work for me. But there's nobody here to see, so we take the candles to the sitting room and take turns choosing records and winding the gramophone. Isi hops onto the sofa next to me and rests her nose in my lap.

"She can sense you're upset," Alexia says. "Have you noticed that? She stays by your side if you're sad. She's like a mom, comforting you."

I shrug. "I never had a mom. The best I had was Ma Goodson, but she was housemother to twelve of us. She just didn't have enough arms to go around."

"Maybe that's what went wrong with Micah. He didn't get enough loving."

It hurts too much to talk about him. "Tell me about your mom," I say to change the subject. "She seems like a fantastic mother. Don't you miss her?"

"I do. But life is really hard in Boat Bay. She's always struggled. Her family had worked for generations in the fish factory, but she got a chance in life. She won a scholarship to study computer coding straight from school. That's where she met my dad—our dad."

"He was a coder?" I sit up. "I thought he was an activist."

"He was. First he was a coder. Then when the government changed and the world started going to shit, he began to use the internet to organize secret protests. But anyway…" The record is scratching in the last groove and she leans over to lift up the needle. "There wasn't much call for coders after they blew the world up, and that's her story. She's had to survive for the last fifteen years which-ever way she could. So it really helps her if she doesn't have to feed me and Leonid."

I wish I could get Natasja to Greenhaven. But with fifty new mouths to feed, it's going to be a stretch as it is. I watch Alexia lying on the sofa waving her foot in time to the music. She's so forgiving. So positive. With Micah, I always seem to get it wrong and I just don't know how to fix it.

Micah doesn't come in for breakfast the next day.

It starts to rain, big drops pelting down, and I want to go back to bed and stay there for the day. Have I re-ally jeopardized the safety of everyone remaining in the Colony? I've got myself in a huge mess, and there's nobody I can talk to about it without explaining what I said in the dungeon. We're all tense—the fifty new girls are arriving today after breakfast and I need to find something for them to do.

I toy with my bread, pushing it around my plate, cut-ting it into smaller and smaller squares. At last everyone has finished. I help Aunty Figgy tidy up, hoping he'll come in, hoping that maybe he was just delayed with the animals. Finally, I grab a raincoat and run after Leonid. I catch him on the path to the stables.

"Leonid, is Micah still in bed? Have you seen him this morning?"

"Left last night." He gestures toward the forest.

"He's gone? Where?"

"Boat Bay." He brushes the rain out of his face, stony-faced. "That all, miss?"

"Sorry. Leonid, get out of the wet."

He jogs off and I turn toward the forest, my heart aching. Right this minute he's with Samantha Lee, and she's tossing her hair back, all sparkly-eyed and having another secret meeting with him, but this time they're probably meeting in Chad's house, maybe in her bedroom, and he's...

Just stop it, I tell myself. He's not like that. Don't torture yourself.

But the thoughts persist. He's sick of me already. He's heard something—if the Syndicate know what I said in the dungeon, it's probably reached him too. He might never come back.

But once I'm in the forest, the soft greenness soothes me, as it always does. I choose the path to the river, listening to the gentle pat of the rain on the trees, the drip drip as it filters through to the forest floor. I reach the clearing and run across the grass to the holy well. Someone has started repairing it, fitting some of the stones together that form the wall. It's Micah, I think with a flash of hope. He's doing it to surprise me. But I brush aside the thought. He's focused on one thing only. Could it be Leonid and Jasmine? Alexia perhaps?

When I see the bare footprints in the mud, I know. These long, narrow feet can only belong to Lucas.

On the far side of the well, carefully arranged on the stump of the milkwood tree, I find a clean saucepan with a lid and a blue and white striped plate. Aunty Figgy must be bringing him food. But where is he sleeping? Is he warm enough and dry?

I follow the river downstream, turning over stones and pulling aside the bushes that grow along the bank, searching for more signs of Lucas, for the brown amulet.

The further down toward the sea I go, the greater the destruction from the earthquake. There's a swathe of fallen trees. They'll be good for firewood. I must remember to send Leonid to cut them into logs. I pass the pond where Micah and I swam, where I lost my necklace and he found it for me. I stop and lean against a tree. I'm not going to think about him, about Samantha Lee. It gets me nowhere. Instead I try and focus on the Goddess, summoning up the statue in the kitchen window. "Theia," I mutter, letting my mind's eye run over her tall figure, the green robe falling in folds, the necklace complete with all four amulets, around her long neck. "Goddess of all that grows, Goddess of the planet, please listen to me. Please," I beg, "send me the amulets. Show me where to find them. And… send Micah back to me."

I beg with everything I have, but she doesn't answer. She doesn't send me a sign, or an amulet blinking in the mud, or Micah's cheerful whistle coming through the trees. Nothing.

This is what the Dark Forces have done, I think, breaking off a twig and snapping it into tiny pieces. They've rolled over the Earth like a tide, and blocked the Goddess from the planet she created. That's why everything keeps going wrong.

Round one more bend, I reach the wall. It's still standing, but the earthquake has shifted the iron grille over the culvert so there's a gap big enough to crawl through. The wall has been breached and the island is open to the outside world. If the general finds out, he'll send his guards to seal it up. I must remember to tell Leonid to keep the girls and their guards out of the forest in case they report it.

The high arched footprints in the mud are Micah's. He's gone through the culvert. Left the island. I sit on a rock listening to the waves washing onto the shore. Rain drips down the wall so it glistens silver. Weaver birds are chattering in their nests hanging low over the river. I wish I could break down the wall. I wish the Resistance had done its work already, and that the island was free. Then Micah and I could be together, and I could be his first and only love, more important than politics.

Chapter Eight

The girls have arrived. Fifty of them, standing in rows in the rain, dripping wet and miserable. The guards pace alongside them, making sure nobody moves or talks. I count ten guards, as sour-faced as they were in the Colony.

"You can't stand out here getting wet," I exclaim, running over. "Come inside where it's warm." I'm about to take them into the house when I remember it's illegal. I can get arrested for that.

"Come in here." I lead them across the yard to the big barn where we store the farm equipment and where Leonid has his workbench. They crowd inside, shivering, peering around wide-eyed, confused by what they're seeing as I was when I was first elevated.

"Leonid, can you light a fire?" I call. He's at the back of the barn, working on the big wagon we take to market.

"In here, miss?" His tone is scathing and Camryn picks it up immediately. A slow smile crosses her face. "With the thatch roof and no chimney?"

Damnit. I'd forgotten about the thatch. The girls are huddled together, trying to get warm. They're wearing the tunics and pants that were perfect in the Colony where the temperature stayed constant and it never rained.

"Stay here with them," I say and hurry over to the house. Aunty Figgy is sweeping out Letti's room, but I push past her to the wardrobe and start pulling out clothes and throwing them into a pile on the bed.

"What are you doing?" She drops the broom and picks up a cream-colored jersey with a fancy pattern around the neck, holding it to her chest like it's her most precious possession.

"Those girls are freezing cold and wet through. If I don't get them warm, they'll catch pneumonia."

"But these are your aunt's clothes."

"Aunty Figgy, it's hardly like she needs them anymore. And anyway, they're mine now, and I can give them away if I want to."

She tightens her lips, picks up the broom, and starts sweeping like the carpet has done her wrong and she's going to punish it. I go through all the cupboards and pull out fifty pieces of clothing that I hope will fit. Soon I have a motley collection of dresses, jerseys, and jackets, enough for every girl to get at least one.

Letti helps me carry them across to the barn. I drop them in a pile in front of the rows of girls. "Here. Put these on."

They mob the pile at once, pushing and shouting and grabbing.

"One at a time," I yell. "One at a time."

Prava, one of the seamstresses, gets knocked over. I help her up and somebody elbows me in the eye. "Hey," I yell again. "Stop it, all of you. Just stop it."

Camryn and Kirsten from the plant nursery are fighting over the cream jersey. Kirsten is clutching it. Camryn has one end and is pulling it. "Give it here, bitch," she yells and slaps Kirsten in the face.

"That's enough!" I yell. "Camryn, give that jersey to Kirsten."

"What are you going to do?" she sneers. "You're just a Year One."

She's forgotten who I am. Where she is. That the guards have guns. Shots ring out and there's instant silence.

The girls fall back into line. Most have their clothing—everyone has something except Camryn who has lost the battle of the jersey. Kirsten is pulling it over her wet tunic with a triumphant grin on her face.

A guard picks up the last remaining garment—a heavy yellow dress with big purple flowers splashed over it. He hands it to Camryn. "Put it on."

She looks around, glaring, daring anyone to laugh. It's way too big, coming down to her ankles, and it is the ugliest thing I've ever seen.

Kirsten giggles. Camryn goes for her, eyes blazing. She's about to attack her when a guard digs her in the ribs with his rifle and she stops dead. Then she notices Letti.

"What is she doing here?" she demands. "How did she get out?'

"Shut up," the guard commands.

She's glaring at Letti like a scorpion about to sting. The rest of the girls examine each other, fascinated. For the first time in their lives, they're seeing each other not in a uniform but in individual garments like their parents and grandparents might have worn. They're seeing what life was like when you could be your own person, make your own decisions, and choose the kind of life you wanted.

When one of the guards comes in with a crate of enamel plates and mugs, I realize it's almost time for lunch, and somehow I've got to find food for fifty people. I look through the rows, trying to remember who I picked to help out in the kitchen. Ah—Frieda, the Year Three. I gesture to her, and she follows me up to the house.

Letti follows us. "I can't believe you brought Camryn," she says quietly. "We voted no. Why did you do it?"

I shake my head and sigh. "Because I'm an idiot. Because I forgot how much trouble she causes. Be..."

"Because Micah wanted you to," she interrupts. "Why did you listen to him?"

"I don't know," I say. "I don't know."

He's gone anyway, leaving me with a major headache and a broken heart.

———◆———

While Aunty Figgy and Alexia sort out the meals, I go across to the farm office. I've got to find something for the girls to do when they've finished eating. They can't sit all day in the barn. They're used to being busy.

I stop in front of the big map of the area that one of my relations must have stuck on the wall. Someone has drawn a red line around the farm and labeled the buildings. Homestead, Jonkershuis—that's where I am now. It used to be the house where the young men of the family lived in the early days. Now it's our office and storerooms. I locate the barn, the shed, the coach house, the old laborers' cottages where Aunty Figgy lives, and right down near the gates, the wine cellar. Once this farm grew mostly grapes, and was famous for its wine, but the wine cellar is standing unused now. We might be able to turn it into an extra packing shed once we're ready to harvest the new fields of vegetables.

A second line shows how the farm has expanded westward up toward the mountain, and a thick black line on the east side must be the wall built just before the Calamity. Someone has taken a blue crayon and colored in everything below the wall to show how the sea has swallowed most of the land that once stood there. Was it my mother? Did she look forward to farming this land one day, or did she feel as overwhelmed as I do?

I need to develop some new fields. We're going to need hoes to clear the weeds and prepare the soil, and spades to dig ditches around each field so we can pump water to them from the windmill. There's an old car standing behind the stables. Maybe the engineering crew can melt it down in the forge and turn it into spades and hoes.

Out the window, I can see Alexia, Frieda, and Aunty Figgy coming down the path with trays of food. A few minutes later there's shouting from the barn. Is that Camryn yelling? I hurry across and find her standing at the front arguing with the guard.

"What's the problem?" So much trouble already, and it's only the first morning.

"What is this food?" Camryn shouts at me. "We don't eat this. It's not proper food."

"Camryn," I say calmly, though I'm quaking inside. "Just try it. It's not protein pellets and vegetable stew—but it's just as good. Better in fact. We don't have dehydrated vegetables and pellets up here."

The girls gathered around her shake their heads. "How do we know you're not poisoning us?" Prava asks. "Frieda says you're eating different food—you and Letti and Jasmine and Fez." She almost spits out the names.

"You think you're better than us," Camryn snarls.

Aunty Figgy spins around, hands on her hips. "I have never met such a bunch of rude, ungrateful young women," she snaps. "If you don't like the food, don't eat it. There are plenty of hungry people in this world who would be very grateful for a healthy, home-cooked meal like this. Now sit on your bottoms and eat your food before I count to three. After that, the food is going, and you'll have nothing till dinner time. AND," she continues, "you lot should be extremely grateful to Miss Ebba for rescuing you from the Colony. If you're not, you're welcome to go back. Leonid can hitch up the wagon right now and have you there by nightfall."

She glares at them and they take a step back.

"Sorry, ma'am," Prava says, taking her plate of food and

spoon. She sits down meekly, and the others follow suit. Everyone calms down except Camryn. She's hunched over, watching me from under her fringe as she spoons the food into her mouth, as though I'm about to spring some other dirty trick on her.

Back in the office, I sit down at the old wooden desk and sink my head in my arms. How can I be the boss to fifty girls, especially ones who knew me back in the Colony? They're all older than me. They've looked down on me all my life because I was the baby who got dumped in the Colony, instead of being chosen. Why didn't I think this through? What made me think I'd be able to handle fifty more farm workers when I can hardly cope with the ones I have?

I push down my fear. I'm going to make a plan. I'm going to survive. I have to find another amulet so that Clementine can return. I open the top drawer and scratch through the old papers, ballpoint pens, balls of string and random keys with labels on them—Storeroom Spare, Coach House, Back Door....There's nothing valuable here. I pull them all open one after the other. Nothing. Finally I reach the last drawer. It's tightly wedged, and I pull too hard. The whole drawer falls out onto the floor. Great. One more thing for me to fix. I pick it up and push it back onto its runners. It's stiff. It goes in a little and then jams. I give it a good shove with the back of my hand. Still jammed. I'll have to pull it right out and straighten it. Grabbing the handle with both hands, I give it a sharp tug. It gives suddenly, and I fall backwards.

There's something there, taped to the inside of the desk. I peel off the tape and unfold an old brown envelope, folded up small around something hard. My heart speeds up—the missing amulet. I've found one of them.

Unfolding the envelope, I lift the flap. I'm going to hang

the amulet on my necklace right away. Clementine will come back. She'll guide me, help me. I won't feel so alone. I tip it into my hand.

It's a key. Damnit. Just a stupid key!

I'm about to toss it back into the drawer when footsteps clip across the floor and a pair of navy blue shoes stop next to me. Legs in beige stockings. A knee-length navy blue skirt, white blouse tied at the neck in a bow, and then a stern face looks down at me, over a pair of glasses. I scramble up, brushing my hands down my robe. It's the lady again, but this time she's much clearer.

She's wearing a white coat with a name tag on it. I sound out the letters in my head. "Dr. Iris den Eeden." She's an ancestor. But she didn't live as long ago as Clementine did—her clothes are from the twentieth century. I glance at her hand. There it is—the birth mark.

"Wipe your eyes, girl," she says in my head. "No use sitting here feeling sorry for yourself. We have work to do."

She's so bossy, I dare not argue. Clutching the key, I follow her out of the door. But as soon as we cross the threshold, she disappears. I go back into the office and she's standing there, tapping her foot. But as soon as I step onto the narrow stoep outside, she's gone. I try three times, and each time her frown deepens, her lips tighten, and she taps harder.

"It's not my fault," I tell her. "I can't follow you if you keep disappearing."

"Good heavens," she snaps. "Excuses, excuses."

Then her collar moves slightly, and I notice the necklace. She's got two amulets—the brown one that the High Priest stole from me and a blue one that shines as the light hits it.

Aunty Figgy rings the bell to call us for lunch and I'm about to put the key back in the drawer but Dr. Iris still stands there with her hands on her hips. What does she want?

"I'll try it again later, okay?"

Her lips tighten like Aunty Figgy's laundry wringer. I'm hungry and tired of her ordering me around. I need to think. I slip the key onto the empty chain around my neck. It's comforting to have something hanging there again. I'm a step closer to finding one of the lost amulets.

Later, when the girls have gone home for the night, I come around the corner unexpectedly and hear my Sabenzis gossiping about me. My Sabenzis, the three people I thought would always have my back. They don't see me half hidden in the shadow of the water barrels.

"She's not one of us anymore," Jasmine says. "She's one of them. The Citizens."

"We're all Citizens too, remember?" Letti says. "We've got the papers. Maybe things are changing."

"We're only Citizens in name," Fez says. "The papers are just a convenience."

"She doesn't behave like we're her equals." Jasmine's voice is harsh as steel clanging. "We voted, but she over-rided us and chose Camryn. She doesn't care. She just thinks about herself now and what she wants. Now she's incredibly rich, she can do what she wants."

"She didn't do it to be nasty or to show her power over us, I'm a hundred percent certain," Letti says. "She did it because that's what Micah wanted."

"He shouldn't count more than us," Fez declares. "We took a vote. If she wasn't going to stick to the results, she shouldn't have called for a vote at all."

"I miss the old Ebba." Letti sounds sad, not angry, and that's worse. I feel like a shit.

I go to my room and crawl under my duvet. Isi jumps

up next to me and her soft breathing is like the murmur of the waves beyond the wall. I know I'm making mistakes in this complicated new world, but she still sees the me that is underneath it all.

Just relax, she seems to say. *It will be all right.*

I've just fallen asleep when my door opens and a voice whispers, "Ebba."

Still groggy, I sit up on my elbows, trying to see across the dark room.

"Are you awake?"

My heart swirls. Micah's back. I light the oil lamp and smile up at him as he leans over to kiss me. The light is catching his high cheekbones, showing the sparkle in his black eyes. "How are you?" he asks, sitting down next to me. "I'm sorry I had to sneak away. I've been to Boat Bay."

"What were you doing there?" I pull him down and snuggle up against him, breathing in the delicious smell of his neck.

"I can't tell you. It's better if you don't know."

"Why?" I ask, rolling onto my back. "Because you don't trust me? Because I'm on the Council?"

He chuckles and pulls me back to him. "Of course not. Because I don't tell anyone. The fewer people who know our movements, the safer for us all."

"But Samantha Lee knows."

"Oh Ebba." His voice is exasperated but amused. He pinches my cheek softly and gives it a little shake. "Of course she knows. We're co-leaders. We don't do anything without discussing it first."

The old sour feeling rises in my chest. He's choosing her. She's going to take him from me forever. I'm going to lose him, just like I lose everyone I love.

I shove it away. I'm not going down that road. I'm going to trust in him. I'm going to make him trust me.

"Hey, babe," he whispers, his breath warm on the shell of my ear. "I wish you knew how much I love you and only you."

I lift the duvet and he slides underneath it. Isi gives a grunt and jumps off the bed. I lie against him, feeling his body with every atom of mine. The energy tingles between us and as his hands run across my skin, my body ignites and glows like the coals in the woodstove. I can feel his hunger. I want to give him what he wants, what I want so desperately too. His kisses grow deeper, hungrier, and he begins to lift my robe over my head.

Aunty Figgy throws open the door. "I've left your dinner in the oven," she snaps. "Come and get it before it dries out."

I sit up, pulling the duvet up to cover my shoulders. "Is there enough for Micah too? He's come back."

"I see that." She squeezes her lips and gives him a dirty look. "You should not have a boy in your bedroom, Ebba. You're only sixteen. Your mother would be horrified."

Reluctantly, I swing my legs over the edge of the bed, pulling down my robe. "Come on," I say, smacking him with my pillow. "Time to go."

"Make sure it doesn't happen again," Aunty Figgy scolds. "And Micah, you're an employee here. You're taking liberties and that is out of line."

"Sorry, Aunty," he says, getting off the bed.

She huffs off down the passage and Micah grins at me. "Bossy old lady. Anyway, I'm hungry. Let's go and eat."

Chapter Nine

I find Letti in the kitchen garden the next morning soon after sunrise. She's the last person in the world I want to hurt. I need her to know that I haven't changed, that I'm still the same girl even though our lives have drastically altered.

"What are you going to do with all this thyme?" I ask. "Can I help you pick?"

"That would be great. I need to harvest a basket full before the sun gets too hot. We're going to try out the essential oil still."

She found the copper still under the workbench in the barn a few days ago. The big boiling pot just needed a good clean, but the copper pipe that leads from the coned lid was broken off. Fez found a book in the library with a picture of what it should look like, and he and Alexia have been trying to repair it with a piece of old piping from the pile behind the barn.

The bees are here already, humming around the small pink flowers. Letti eyes them warily. "I still can't get used to the creepy crawlies up here. I know the plants need them, but there are so many, and they get into everything."

"I'll do the picking if you like."

"Thanks, Ebba." She flashes me her bright smile, and we're back where we were, comfortable with each other. "I'll get the fire going and fetch the water for the still."

The girls will be here soon and the atmosphere on the farm will change. But for now, with the sun warming my back, the soft coo of the pigeons in the dovecote, the lemony fragrance of thyme, and Isi snuffling for lizards in the cracks in the wall, everything is peaceful. *I was over-reacting last night*, I decide. *They were upset with me, but it's going to be okay.*

The guys are coming up for breakfast when Letti's scream cuts through the calm. I leap up. Is it a cobra? She's leaped up onto the wall of the duck pond. "Letti, what's wrong?"

"It's a...a..." She's pointing at the ground next to her. "It's green and slimy. It's a.... Ugh, it's jumping. Ebba!" She screeches as it springs onto the wall next to her.

"It's just a frog, silly," I laugh. "It won't hurt you."

"It's horrible. It's going to bite me."

I'm laughing so much I can hardly get the words out. "Frogs don't bite. I promise you."

"Shorty!!!!" she shrieks. "Shorty!"

When he hears her screams, he sprints as fast as his short legs can carry him. He scoops Letti up into his arms, and carries her across to the water cask. "Sit here," he commands.

She perches on top of the cask as he runs back across the yard, picks up the frog—that makes Letti shriek once more—and disappears behind the house.

He's back a few minutes later, wiping his hands. "There, my darling. It won't frighten you anymore." He tries to lift her down, but she shudders.

"No, no wash your hands. You touched it. It's disgusting."

"You're so brave," she says, as he washes his hands. "Those things give me the creeps."

I swear I can see his chest puffing up.

Would Micah save me in the same situation? Fat chance. He'd say, "Push through the fear. It won't kill you." He'd leave me to fend for myself.

I know his way is better in the long run, but sometimes I just want someone to protect me, to love me like Shorty loves Letti.

A few days later, I'm in the office early, planning what everyone will do now that the weather's clear. Jasmine is going to take the planting girls into the fields and show them where to start weeding. Leonid has the engineering and carpentry staff under control. Letti has agreed to organize Isabella and the poultry girls and Micah will look into ways of expanding the livestock with the girls who used to work with the pigs, sheep, and rabbits. Everyone has something to do, and I'm going to go over the books with Shorty while Fez works on the business plan.

Shorty comes to the office door, shifting his weight from one foot to the other. "Excuse me, Miss Ebba..."

"What is it, Shorty?"

"I was wondering. Could I please take the day off?"

"The day off? What for? Aren't you well?"

"No, it's not like that, miss. It's just...it's just...it's personal."

For once he's at a loss for words. His face is bright red, right to the top of his huge forehead. I'm dying to know what it is that is making him so embarrassed. How can I refuse him?

"That's fine," I say.

"Thank you, thank you, miss. I'll make up the time, I promise you." He skips off across the yard on his stumpy legs and I turn back to my list, wondering what he's up to.

Whatever it is, Aunty Figgy is in on it. She's got her recipe book out, and when I go through an hour later to get a cup of peppermint tea, she's tying a muslin cloth across the top of a tiny pudding basin. There's a pot boiling on the stove and she lowers the basin into it, muttering under her breath.

"What are you doing?" I ask.

"Nothing. Praying."

It is something though. She looks guilty. But no matter how much I press her, she won't tell me any more.

Later I set off for the fields to see how the girls are doing with the weeding. They're in the top field, getting the rows ready for the cauliflower and cabbage seedlings we've been propagating in the greenhouse. They're calm and happy. The sun's shining and they're chatting quietly to themselves. Roxie and Tia are looking up at the mountain with the same awe I felt when I was first elevated. When I came out, I had nobody except Isi. They're lucky to have their friends to share it with.

Isi is running ahead of me to the dam and I follow to see what the water level is like. She disappears into the bushes at the bottom of the wind pump. I follow her right up to the edge of the dam. Shorty is standing there, legs apart, clutching a rod.

"Shorty! Whatever are you doing?"

He turns quickly. "Nothing. I mean, fishing, miss."

"You wanted a day off so you could fish?"

"Yes, miss. I mean, no, miss." He's stuttering, his face red under his floppy sun hat. "I mean, it's complicated, Miss Ebba. I want...I want to make a surprise for Letti."

My heart warms to him, standing there all alone, trying so hard. "Are there even fish in here?"

"I think so. I mean, I hope so. I mean, there might be... Wait, here's something." His voice rises to a squeak of excitement. He reels in his line. On the end is a little silver fish, as big as his hand. "There," he beams. "Caught one. See this, miss? I got one."

I stride across the field, checking the weeding the girls have done. They're standing in the shade under the oak trees that line the field. Micah is talking to them, explaining something while the guards sit at a distance, watching. Since he got back, everything is back in control. He knows how to talk to the girls, how to get them to co-operate. He's told me to leave them to him, and I'm more than happy to because...because it makes my life easier, that's why.

Everything is good this morning. The sun is shining. The world is beautiful. I have enough labor to expand. Micah is home. All is good. All is amazing. All is—

The girls leave at 5:00, their feet squelching in puddles as they march down the driveway. I find Shorty near the water barrels, busy with a knife. He's gutting the tiny fish.

"Is that all you caught?"

He looks up and blushes. "It's enough for Letti. You won't tell her, will you, miss? It's a surprise. Could you do me a huge favor? Could you keep her away until I'm ready for her? For about half an hour?"

"Of course." The more time I spend with Shorty, the more I love him. He's so...what's the word? Sincere. That's it. Everything is on the surface with him. He's incapable of guile, doesn't know how to manipulate people.

Unlike Micah...

The thought pops into my head. Immediately, I push it down. It's disloyal. They're totally different people. Shorty is a team player, a follower; Micah is a leader. He has to be cunning because of the Resistance—because thousands of people depend on him being able to keep secrets, to make plans, to strategize. Shorty wouldn't be able to strategize himself out of a grain sack. He's totally transparent. Whatever he thinks, he says.

I find Letti and Alexia at the washing lines next to the laundry. They're taking down the sheets and duvet covers and folding them. How am I going to distract Letti? They won't take long to bring in the clean washing.

"If we'd stayed in the Colony, I'd never have met Shorty," Letti says, dropping a peg into the pocket of her apron. "Here, can you take the other end?"

Alexia takes the two far corners of the sheet and she and Letti walk backwards until the sheet is taut between them. "I heard they gave you drugs so you wouldn't think about sex," Alexia says, bringing her corners together. "Wasn't that weird?"

"I suppose so," Letti says. "But we didn't know what it was like to be normal. They showed us Kinetika—at least, until the machine wore out and they couldn't fix it. We would see kids like us in the old world, before the Calamity, so we knew we were different, but we couldn't feel like they did because we didn't know what it was like without the drugs. They kept us so busy in the Colony anyway. It wasn't interesting work, like it is here. We did the same thing every day. Those twelve hours felt like they went on forever. And after that, we had to run on the treadmills to make the electricity. I was so tired all the time. If I'd stayed, I would have been sacrificed. But Jas and Ebba saved me—and Micah, of course."

Alexia pauses, and raises one eyebrow. "I don't know about that one. He's too smooth. I don't trust him."

Letti tugs her end of the sheet and brings the edges together. "Really? I like him. Shorty does too."

"Maybe I'm wrong. How much do you know about the sacred task?" Alexia and Letti walk forward and meet in the middle. Alexia takes the sheet, smooths it with her palm, and drops it into the basket.

"I don't really like all this religious stuff. I think it's a way of manipulating people—just look what they did to us in the Colony. I reckon you can only trust science— if you can see it, it's real. If you can't prove it's real, I'm not interested."

"I've just finished reading the Book of the Goddess." Alexia's hands dart along the line, unpegging the smaller items and giving them a swift shake so they flap like the coots that skim along the dam. "It's serious stuff."

"Uh huh?"

"If she doesn't complete her task by the winter equinox, there will be a second Calamity worse than the last one."

Letti stops. "Another sea level rise? How is that possible?"

"It will be worse than that. It will be the end of the planet. There's a war between the Goddess and Prospiroh, and he will win it if the Goddess can't come back to Earth by the equinox."

"We'll all be dead? We could all be dead in...what... about three months from now? Do you have proof?"

Alexia shrugs as she drops the last peg into the peg bag and picks up the basket. "Only what's in the book. And the necklace. That book is hundreds of years old, and it talks about the birthmark—Ebba has that—and the necklace. It's definitely still the same necklace. So I think we should take it seriously just in case it's right. And for Ebba."

"Anyway, I'm going to find Shorty," Letti says, pushing her glasses up her nose. "I haven't seen him all day."

Damnit. We have to keep her away from him. I undo the clasp, and take the key off the necklace. Letti may not believe in the Goddess, but she loves a good mystery, ferreting away at any difficult puzzle long after everyone else has lost interest.

I saunter over, holding it out to them. "Can you two help me? I found this key. I think it's linked to the amulets, but I don't know what it unlocks."

Letti takes it and turns it over in her hands. "I don't think it's meant for a door to a room. This one's quite delicate, so it probably opens something smaller."

"Like a box?" Alexia's face lights up. "Maybe there's a box somewhere with all the amulets in it. Or a drawer that's locked? Imagine if all the missing amulets are inside it, and we find the one that the High Priest stole, and the Goddess returned and restored the world, and...and... can you imagine it?" Her eyes shine as she says, "The seas rolling back to where they used to be, and everything restored, fresh and green and beautiful. A new start..."

Letti's opening her mouth to argue and I shake my head to warn her off. Let Alexia dream—somebody has to. It can't all be destruction and danger and damage.

"Letti," Shorty calls across the garden. "It's time for your surprise. You must promise not to peek. Okay?"

"I promise," she says, laughing as he folds a tea towel into a blindfold and ties it over her eyes. "Where are we going?"

"It wouldn't be a surprise if I told you..." He takes her arm and leads her toward the garden gate.

"They're going around the side of the house," Alexia whispers. "Let's follow them. I want to see what the surprise is.'

"No, man. We can't."

"Come ON. You know you want to." She's already halfway across the garden. "They're on the stoep," she whispers as we round the last corner of the house. We huddle behind the Plumbago bush that grows outside my bedroom window.

"Look what he's done," she whispers.

He's gathered all the candles and lanterns in the house and arranged them on the stoep in the shape of a heart. Letti is standing in the middle, still blindfolded, while he lights them. Behind her is a small table laid for one person. There's a barbecue lit in an old drum, and he's roasting mealies and butternut.

Letti's nose wrinkles under the blindfold. "Hurry, hurry," she shrieks. "I'm bursting with excitement."

"Just a moment, my love," he says. He pulls a piece of

paper from his pocket, unfolds it, smooths out the page, and starts to read.

"Letti, my love, if we were living in the olden days, I would give you a house with brand new furniture and hot water that just came running out of the gold taps in the bathroom. I'd fly you to Paris in my personal jet to buy you all the clothes and shoes and handbags you deserve. I'd work hard all my life long to give you everything you wanted. We would go to Switzerland and see snow and eat chocolate, and eat real pizza in a restaurant in Italy.

"But the olden days are gone. I haven't got a car or jet or clothes. I'll never be able to give you a brand new house with a hot tub and an electric oven. All I have to give you is one thing. One small, unworthy thing...my heart."

He takes off her blindfold and she gasps as she takes it all in, the candles, the table, the pretty tablecloth and the fancy wine glass.

He pulls out her chair. "Sit down, madame," he says, flicking out her serviette and putting it on her knee. "Dinner will be served shortly."

"He's so sweet," Alexia whispers. "I hope she doesn't think he's giving her pizza or chocolate."

Shorty takes the mielie and butternut off the fire with the tongs and places them on a plate. Then he carefully lifts the tiny fish off the grid and arranges it as the centerpiece. "Your dinner, *madame*," he says, placing it before her with a flourish.

She looks at it curiously. "What's that in the middle?'

"It's a fish. I caught it myself."

Alexia stifles a giggle. "It's barely more than a tadpole," she whispers. "If it comes from the dam, it will probably taste of mud."

"Try it," he says, beaming.

Letti takes a bite and her face changes. She puts her hand to her mouth and spits the food out.

"Don't you like it?" he asks.

"Bones," she says, taking another one out of her mouth. "It's got lots of bones. Apart from that, it's delicious."

"Darling!" he exclaims. "I'm so sorry. You could have choked. Here. Allow me." He takes her plate. Carefully and slowly like a surgeon in a medical Kinetika, he dissects the fish and takes out all the bones. There's not much left by the end. Just a piece of gray skin and some little flecks of beige flesh.

He piles the fish onto her fork and says, "Open wide. Tell me this isn't delicious. I caught it myself, just like my granddad used to do for my gran. Every anniversary he made a lekker braai for her, and he cooked her a fish he'd caught himself, and then he'd make her favorite dessert in a potjie and she'd be so happy and he'd..."

"There's dessert?" Letti's face lights up. "What kind?"

"It's a surprise, but you're going to like it, I promise you. Everyone likes it, it's the best ever. It's a family recipe."

He turns his back to check the fire, and Letti slides the rest of the fish off the plate onto the floor. Isi runs over to eat it. Alexia nudges me and we have to cover our mouths to keep in our giggles.

At last she's eaten the butternut and mealies, while he hovers next to her watching every mouthful and asking, "You do like it, don't you, darling? You're not just pretending to? I didn't get it quite right. The fire may have been a bit too hot, but it's the thought that counts, isn't it? And I thought of you every moment of every second of every minute I spent making this."

"I know you did," she exclaims, reaching her hand out to his. "You are the best. This is much better than chocolate and pizza, I promise."

Alexia snorts, but they're too wrapped up in each other to notice.

"I'll just take your plate," he says, "—unless you'd like

some more? There's no more fish, but I can catch you another one tomorrow. You ate this one so fast, you must have loved it."

She coughs. "No more, thank you. I'm keeping space for the pudding."

He disappears into the house with her dirty plate. Letti sits there, humming and admiring the sky turning pink and orange as the sun sets. Isi leans against her knee, and Letti strokes her head.

I think of the times in the Colony when we imagined life on the outside. The house we wanted to share, the food we drooled over in the family recipe books, our dreams of one day finding love. We have the big house. Although our food isn't as luxurious as the food we saw in the Kinetika, it's fresh from our own farm and so much better than protein pellets. And Letti has found someone who will do anything to show how much he loves her. Someone uncomplicated and loyal and honest. Just what she deserves.

A moment later he emerges from the front door, and places a plate in front of her with a bow. "Your dessert, *madame*."

This time her excitement is genuine. "Oh wow, it's a little steamed pudding like they used to serve at Christmas! Is it all for me?"

"Of course," he says. "All for you."

Alexia looks at me with a grin. It's a standing joke at meal times, how much they both love food, especially bread and honey. "Poor Shorty," she whispers. "That's real love for you—giving her all the dessert."

"It's good, isn't it?' Shorty says as she digs in. "You like it, don't you? It's my Gran's recipe. It's got raisins and nuts in it. Aunty Figgy had to change the recipe a bit because she didn't have some of the ingredients, but she did a good job, didn't she?" He's rocking on his feet, hands locked behind his back, talking non-stop as she wolfs it down. He's watching every spoonful, checking the remains of the pudding. He's up to something...

Then she stops eating. She's staring at him, making a funny sound. It's getting darker and I can't see exactly what's going on, but Alexia whispers, "She's choking."

Shorty is still chattering away and Letti's body is rigid. She jumps up, making a gurgling sound.

"We must help her," Alexia hisses, but I pull her back.

"She'll never forgive us if she knows we were spying on her."

"But look at her. She could die."

Finally Shorty realizes something is wrong. "Oh dear," he exclaims. "Oh no, no, no, what do I do now?" He's standing there frozen, but Letti seizes his arm and points to her back. He grabs her in a hug from behind, and punches her in the stomach. She coughs and something shoots out of her mouth.

She doubles up coughing, but Shorty is on his hands and knees scrabbling in the cracks on the stoep floor.

"What's he looking for?" Alexia cranes her neck over the plumbago. "What's going on?"

"What was that?" Letti gasps, her voice hoarse. "What did I swallow?"

"Ah, found it," Shorty calls.

"What is it?" She's scowling at him, hands on her hips, but he's too busy scrabbling in the dirt to notice.

"This." He holds something in the air. "It was this, my darling." He is kneeling at her feet and he shows her something small that glistens in the candlelight.

"It's a ring," Alexia hisses. "That's so adorable."

"Letti, will you do me the honor of becoming my wife?"

"Yes," she shrieks. "Yes, yes, yes!"

Chapter Ten

For the next few weeks, everything is calm. We've settled into a routine with the girls and they don't seem as confused and unhappy anymore. Even Camryn has stopped glowering and seems to be—well, if not enjoying, at least tolerating the challenge of keeping the farm equipment running. The other girls steer clear of her, and she's often alone at the workbench in the barn, hands covered in grease, taking apart some machine she has never seen before, whistling between her teeth as she searches for the malfunction.

The new lands are planted at last, and the seedlings are growing fast. Micah stays on the farm with me. He doesn't leave once, and I almost stop thinking about Samantha Lee.

Aunty Figgy keeps a close eye on us though, making sure he doesn't sneak into my room or do anything—as she puts it—inappropriate. She's spending every spare moment searching for the amulets. She's got Alexia emptying every cupboard and drawer in the house, and she even makes Leonid open up the bunker under the house one afternoon so that we can search it from top to bottom. I've tried the key in every possible lock in every cupboard and drawer, but nothing has turned up. Micah shakes his head when I mention it. "Poor old lady is delusional. You can't believe what she says. But do what you need to keep her happy."

"But...but I'm sure my ancestors helped me escape

from the dungeon. I've seen them."

"It's called the power of suggestion. You were in a desperate situation and your subconscious gave you an idea."

I want to argue but he presses his lips on mine and kisses me until I feel as though I am melting inside. He breaks away finally and says gently, "Babe, I've been here longer than you. Your brain is still susceptible to brainwashing—it's trained to accept what the authorities say, and Aunty Figgy is acting like a cult leader, not letting you think for yourself. Trust me. I'm always here for you."

Letti and Shorty are so happy together—there's no friction, and it's not just because they're in love. They seem to slot together like two parts of a machine that turn in tandem. Everything works smoothly. Micah and I, on the other hand, don't have it so easy. It's like our gears grind against each other, and I have to keep finding ways to adjust. My wealth keeps getting in the way. If only he owned the farm, not me. It would be so much easier if I wasn't his boss.

One afternoon he comes to call me. It's been drizzling on and off all day, and I've told the guards to take the girls back to their quarters so they don't spend all day in wet clothes.

I'm in the greenhouse checking on the seedlings when he appears in the doorway. "Come with me," he says. "I want to show you something."

I untie my muddy apron and shrug on my raincoat. "Where are we going?"

"To the wall."

"Why? What's there?"

"Shh," he says, putting his finger on my lips. "Stop asking questions."

We set off through the forest, hand in hand, following the course of the river. When we reach the culvert Micah wades into the water and gestures to a pile of fallen rocks. "Come on," he says. "The thing I want to show you is out here."

The wall must be three meters thick. It used to arch slightly over the river leaving a gap covered by the iron grille. Now it's cracked and half fallen. It's still too high to climb over though. But someone has been working here, opening the culvert, shoring it up with fallen rocks to create a passage under the wall.

"Come on." He points to the opening. "We have to go through here."

Green slime covers the rocks and drips down into the murky water, but I follow him. Holding my breath, I crouch in the shallow water, and crawl through the dank tunnel.

I'd imagined that the beach would be like the beaches we saw in the Kinetika—golden sand, blue sea with waves, and foam and shells. The sea smelled good in the Kinetika—the aroma that piped through the speakers was salty and fresh. You wanted to be there, playing on the beach, kayaking in the surf, having fun while children dug sandcastles and old people sat in deck chairs enjoying the view.

But this beach is brown and littered with debris—plastic bottles, broken shoes, rusty appliances half buried in the sand. The further we walk, the stronger the bad smell grows. We reach a rocky outcrop and there's a dead seal, part of its face torn away, its teeth displayed in a macabre grin. A bird stands on its back, ripping away the flesh. It gives a guttural squawk and flaps away as we approach.

"I don't like it here. Let's go home."

Micah squeezes my hand. "You can do it. Come, I want to show you what's around the corner."

"Why? What's so important that I have to see it?'

"Ebba, you can't hide from reality like a child. You need to see what really happened with the Calamity. Not the people who survived, like the people from Boat Bay, but the people who could have been saved but weren't. Then you'll understand why our work is so important. Why the work of the Resistance is more important than ever."

I follow him because I don't want him to think I'm childish. We wade around the rocks, the sea lapping sullenly at our feet

"Do you remember in the Colony how we showered?" I ask him. "How we lined up and soaped ourselves, then stepped under the shower, and the water turned on just long enough to wash the soap off our bodies. And the water was freezing."

"I remember." He grins. "I remember you without your clothes on."

I smack his arm. "You've got a dirty mind. Whenever we watched people in the Kinetika in water—in a swimming pool or the sea, I'd wonder what it was like to be under-water like that. To be floating in that blue emptiness, with your hair swirling around your face, weightless. The coral, the fish, the sea anemones..."

He nods. "I used to wonder what it would be like to swim out to sea. Even now, I'd like to get in the ocean and swim all the way to those mountains." He points to the horizon and I imagine us both swimming away, to start a new life, just the two of us in some distant place where we have no troubles. Far from the Resistance, the general, the girls from the bunker and Camryn's sulky face.

"Here we are," he says as we step around the last rock. We're in a little bay, surrounded on two sides by high boulders, and overshadowed at the back by the wall that runs around the island. It's gloomy in here and I shiver. A small sailboat is pulled up onto the sand and he checks the rope, mooring it to a concrete block.

"Are we going in the boat?" I take a step back. I'm not sure I'm ready to venture out to the sea, especially not in something so small.

"No, not today. I wanted you to see this." He points up the beach to the tumbled down buildings, the debris of lives long gone. "This is what happened because of the wall. The people who lived here could have survived, but the wall cut off their access to water and food. That's why we fight the government. Why your parents fought. For justice. For fair access to food and water and a safe place to live."

I shiver. I'm picturing this place when it was a thriving neighborhood with houses and families and happy children playing in the gardens. So much was destroyed in the Calamity. And if I don't find the amulets soon, as Aunty Figgy keeps reminding me, another one is coming.

A ruined house stands at the back right up against the wall, and he leads me up the beach toward it. "People tried to keep living here after they built the wall," Micah says.

I try to imagine what it was like in those days when people were preparing for a disaster they knew was going to happen. What it was like to be cut off from the city you'd known all your life.

"They couldn't have survived for long," Micah says. "They'd have had to fetch all their water from the river, and it runs low in summer. And where would they get food?"

"Stockpiled?" I suggest.

"Not everyone could afford to stockpile food," he says. "And once you had a stockpile, you'd have to guard it from thieves."

We've reached the house now, and I try the door. It doesn't budge.

He puts his shoulder against it and the brittle wood cracks and gives way. Inside it's desolate. An old lounge suite, faded to nothing, rots on the rags of a carpet. A Kinetika lies cracked on the floor and faded photographs hang askew on the wall, covered with dust. I go closer and wipe them with my sleeve.

A smiling family looks out at me—a mom and dad lying on their tummies with two small boys lying on their backs. They're happy and well fed. In the second photo, the children are older. They're standing in the garden. Behind them is the outline of the mountain and I realize with a shock that it was taken from outside this house. The back garden, as it once was before they built the wall, before the sea washed in. I can even see the roof of Greenhaven in the distance.

Micah pushes open a door leading off the passage. It's the kitchen. Rusted tins of food line the shelves. There are cups and plates in the sink. A half-finished bowl of something gray stands covered in dust on the kitchen table.

"I wonder what happened to them," I say. "Why would they leave behind all this food?"

It's when he doesn't reply that I realize he's standing in front of a half-closed door, almost as though he's blocking me from it.

"What's in there?"

"You don't want to go in there," he says grimly.

But I push open the door and look inside. A double bed has collapsed. It lies at an angle, the mattress rotted and full of holes. The windows have blown out, but somehow the mattress has barricaded the front of the room, keeping back the pile of sand that has half filled the room. At my feet are white bones, half covered in tattered wisps of faded clothing. Two adults, two children. The family that once lived here.

"They're dead," I gasp. "They died here?"

"Come out of here," he says, pulling me back and kicking the door shut. "They must have died of a disease. The germs may still be here."

I follow him out of the house, shaking. I just want to

get away from the death house as fast as possible, away from this black, gloomy, sunless beach. "Couldn't they get help? The old world had every kind of medicine. They could fix everything."

"Of course the Citizens had medicine that could have helped this family, and millions of others. The storage bunkers under the security villages were packed to the roof with medicine, food, bottled water, designer clothing, luxury goods. They employed private doctors—I've heard they even had a bunker that was set up as a hospital ward with operating theaters and everything, but it was for the Citizens only. The wall kept everybody out. That's why we have to push forward with the Resistance. To undo the wrongs. To give everyone a chance to share in what is left of the resources. To give everyone a say in the government and its decisions."

We wade through the surf, around the rocky outcrop, past the grinning seal and hike up the beach to the culvert. I can't stop thinking about the family. No wonder people gave their kids up to the Colony. It must have been heart wrenching, but Jas's parents, Micah's, Letti's, Fez's parents—they must have guessed what was coming. They must have known that their chance of survival was almost nil, so they trusted their babies to the High Priest, to the Colony, to keep them safe.

And not one of them foresaw that they would grow up to be slaves.

As we walk home, I can't get that family out of my mind. How terrible to die alone in that house, squashed between the wall and the sea, to be ill, knowing that on the other side of the wall there were bunkers with medicine, food, and fresh water.

I keep seeing their bleached bones, jumbled up on the floor, sprinkled with sand. And the words of the prophecy run relentlessly through my head:

"In the sixteenth year after the first Calamity, a young woman will arise from the Earth. She will bear the mark of the Goddess upon her left hand. To her will fall the task of reuniting the sacred amulets before the year is out. She must open the gateway to Celestia, so the Goddess can return to heal the Earth."

When we reach the Holy Well Isi is there, front feet up on the rubble, snuffling in the reeds.

"What are you doing here, girl?" I ask. "Are you looking for the amulet?"

I run my fingers through the reeds, opening them up. Maybe the amulet is caught there.

"Are you still looking for that trinket?" Micah asks. "You said you were going to stop looking."

"Did I?" I really don't remember that. Why would I say that?

"Of course. The other day. Surely you remember?"

"Um...no."

"Please, Ebba." He kisses the tip of my nose. "Of course you remember. We decided that poor Aunty Figgy is delusional, and..."

"But...the Book of the Goddess says it's true."

"Babe, that book is from the middle ages—it's all superstition, you know that. This is a political battle and that's all. No spirit stuff. No gods and goddesses interfering on Earth. That is all just a distraction. A distraction from the important stuff—the Resistance."

He pauses, his hands on my shoulders as he looks me in my eye. "You're so fixated on this Goddess stuff. You have other ancestors, you know. Your parents were both leaders of the Resistance. Why can't you follow their example? They didn't listen to old wives' tales. They were practical—made a difference to real people, in the real world."

Isi presses herself against my leg as Micah leans over

and kisses me. "All I'm saying is that you are very powerful. You keep making silly mistakes, but if you let me guide you, tell you exactly what to do with the general and the Council, your role could be even more vital than mine or Samantha Lee's. Anyway, I'm off. I've got things to do."

As I turn back along the path that leads to the house, I wonder if he's right. Life would be much simpler without amulets and ancestors and dark forces. But it's not just the amulets. I do believe in the Goddess. There's my birth-mark, which appeared so suddenly, and matches the one my ancestors have. There's the way I make plants grow so fast, there's Dr. Iris bossing me around, Clementine and her little boy. I would swear they are all real, they *feel* real, *it all feels real.* But maybe Micah is right. Maybe Aunty Figgy is crazy, and I believe her because I was brainwashed in the Colony.

I search the trees for signs of Lucas. I wish I could talk to him about the prophecy and the amulets. *He* saw Clementine and her little boy in the dungeon. He'd have a clearer perspective, I'm sure. He'd be able to tell me what's true and what isn't.

Then it strikes me—Isi might know where he is. She must know every inch of the farm. She'd know where he'd be hiding. Crouching down, I take her head in my hands and look into her eyes. "Where's Lucas? Find Lucas."

Her ears prick up. A quiver runs through her and she's off, down a path half hidden behind brambles. It leads away from the well, away from the house, into the depths of the forest. I've never been along this path before, but there are signs that the pathway has been used recently—some overhanging twigs have broken off and the brambles are cut back where they grow too close to the path.

She leads me uphill, through the trees, right to what was once the boundary of Greenhaven—the road. The farm wall has given way to fencing here, and she takes a running leap and flies over it. Then she's across the road and into the forest again—the forest that my great aunt planted when she bought up the neighbors' land. I can see that this was once a suburb—potholed roads break up the forest floor, hard under my feet as I follow her up the slope. A creeper winds up a lamppost, a rusty car lurks under the fallen roof of a garage. Behind it the house has half-disappeared behind shrubs. The front door hangs from its hinges, pushed aside by a sapling.

I remember Aunty Figgy saying that this used to be one of the wealthiest suburbs in Cape Town. The houses were grand with lawns and swimming pools and flower-beds. The Citizens lived here, rich enough to abandon these houses and move to the security villages where the houses were designed to be comfortable despite the grow-ing heat as the climate grew hotter. All clustered together, they could defend themselves more easily against thieves after their stockpiles. Against people like the poor family who died in the cottage on the beach.

Isi keeps running, looking back to check I am follow-ing, doubling back to nudge me along when I stop to peer inside windows, looking for clues about the people who lived here just twenty years ago. Didn't they feel guilty about their selfishness? Was it worth it in the end? I've probably sat next to them in Shrine, shaken their hands, been welcomed as one of them. Urgh.

I turn away. My parents were right—somebody had to challenge the Council. Someone had to organize the Resistance. It cost them both their lives, but the Resistance didn't end. And now it's in Micah's hands.

I find Lucas's shelter by accident. Isi has snuffled around the doorway, half-hidden behind a boulder. Then she's off, nose to the ground, her ears pricked up and tail wagging. I stoop and peer inside. It's constructed of saplings set in a circle. They've been bent inwards and tied at the top to form a small dome. He's woven branches and twigs between the trunks, to make solid growing walls. Somebody planted these saplings in this circle. They're at least ten years old, maybe more. Somebody trained them to bend, tied their crowns together when they were young and supple, cut back the branches that intruded on the inside. My great aunt? But why? Who would want a shelter like this in the forest? I'm not even sure it is Lucas's hiding place until I spot the quilt that used to lie on the bed in the yellow room. Aunty Figgy must have brought it for him, and the pillow.

A pile of books is stacked on a small shelf. Natural history—plants and insects. I didn't know he was interested in that. Or maybe they belonged to the person who made this living dome. I want to scratch more, but I don't want him to find me poking around behind his back.

I crawl out through the low doorway and glimpse Isi's white fur in the distance. She's running westward, along a narrow path that goes deep into the forest. Quietly, I pad along after her and stop when Lucas comes into view, on his haunches on the edge of a stream.

He's so thin, his long arms scrawny as the reeds he is clearing. But his posture is less closed in, his face less haunted. I watch him a while, pulling out the plants that are blocking the flow of water. Isi stops next to him, and he strokes her ears. A bird sings overhead and as he looks up at the tree, a shaft of sunlight catches his face. I see how he has his own kind of good looks. He's not conventionally handsome like Hal, but there's a quiet thoughtfulness about him that is just as appealing once you see it.

I consider going nearer to say hello, but I don't want to disturb him. He's looking more peaceful than I've ever seen him. I'll just ruin that. I turn around quietly and go back to the house.

Chapter Eleven

The next morning I join Aunty Figgy and Alexia in the orchard. I'm enjoying the morning sun on my skin and the plump citrus fruit against the intense green of the leaves. I watch Aunty Figgy reaching into the tree, breaking off the lemons with a quick twist, and dropping them into the bag hanging across her shoulders. She's working swiftly but methodically, her sharp eyes never missing a single lemon. If Micah could see her now, he wouldn't be able to say she's mad. Yes, she's irritating, but she's also the most down-to-earth, wise person on Greenhaven. She's been here for decades, she knows every inch of the farm and its history, and she and my great aunt loved each other. She wants only what's best for Greenhaven, and for me because it's my family home.

"Please tell me more about Laleuca," I say, looking around to check that Micah isn't within earshot. "You told me about how she was born to Theia and the woodcutter, and her older sister Bellzeta tried to kill her and she was hidden away by a wise woman. And when she grew up, she married my ancestor, someone den Eeden."

"Adam den Eeden."

"Adam den Eeden. What happened next? How did the family end up here in Table Island City?"

"Well," she says, reaching through the leaves for a lemon deep in the branches, "Laleuca grew up and became a Wise Woman, like her foster mother."

"What's a Wise Woman?" Alexia asks.

"Wise Women are healers. They look after people's bodies, but also their hearts. Laleuca was famous for her healing power. She helped women in childbirth, made the dying more comfortable, made poultices and infusions to deal with infections and diseases. People came from all around to consult her. She married Adam van Eeden, a man from the town, and they had two children—a girl, Emilie, and a boy, Adam. Emilie learned all her mother could teach her and in time grew to be as wise as her mother. But people in the town were jealous of Laleuca and Emilie's abilities and reported them as witches to the church authorities."

"Witches!" Alexia exclaims.

"Witch trials were common at the time. The authorities didn't want anyone outside of the church to have power, particularly not women. Laleuca and Emilie were proclaimed witches and burned at the stake." She shudders. "Imagine that. Burned at the stake."

"It's the same now, with the Citizens. They don't want women to have any power either," Alexia says. "But at least they don't burn people alive."

I shudder as I recall the Poladion family facing the firing squad, their bodies fallen against the wall, Cassie's bloodstained sandal. He may not burn people alive, but the general is just as cruel as the authorities were back then.

Alexia has filled her bag. She climbs down the ladder and empties it into a crate. "So how did Ebba get the necklace?" she asks, moving the ladder to the next tree.

"Before she was arrested, Laleuca took off her necklace with the sacred amulets and gave it to her son, telling him to hide it away. The poor child grew up, deeply scarred by the loss of his mother and sister. He kept the necklace hidden from everyone. He was a middle-aged man when he heard about the new country that his homeland had colonized. It was the chance to make a fresh start, away from this country that had damaged him so badly. He packed up his possessions, took his wife and children, and set sail for the Cape of Good Hope.

"Now Jan van Eeden had three daughters, but one of them, Clementine, bore a striking resemblance to his mother, with the same auburn hair and birthmark on her hand. One day on the long journey across the sea, she was looking through her mother's jewelry case when she found the necklace. She slipped it around her neck. Also on board the ship was the newly appointed governor, coming to the Cape to take the reins. He fell ill with a fever, and was on his death bed. Clementine had brought with them a selection of unctions and tinctures, and she slipped into his cabin one day and fed him a healing tincture, drop by drop, and that night the fever broke. A few days later he called for the redheaded girl who had nursed him back to health. Jan was terrified when they were summoned to the governor's cabin. He fully expected the witchcraft accusations to begin again. But the governor was grateful for her help. He granted her father some land as a reward. No more staying up all night to bake bread. He was going to be a farmer, in a new land. A fresh start."

"Is it this land we're on now?" Alexia asks.

She nods. "Yes. Adam van Eeden and his sons built this house. It's been in the family for nearly four hundred years. And this tree is nearly as old as that. But there, I think we have enough lemons now. Time for Letti to get to work. Winter is starting and those poor girls from the Colony will be catching winter colds."

We spend the rest of the day sterilizing bottles and squeezing the lemons so that Letti can start boiling the juice with honey and buchu leaves. By mid-afternoon, it's bottled and packed away in the medicine cupboard in the passage outside the kitchen. Aunty Figgy makes a pot of tea and we sit at the table. Letti has found family photo albums in the library, and she brings one through and pages through it.

"I wish I could have an old-fashioned wedding," Letti sighs as she turns to yet another photograph of one of my ancestors. "I've always dreamed of one like our parents had. Look at this one. How lovely is this? Daisy and Edward den Eeden, 1985."

I peer over her shoulder. A white dog with black spots is lying at the bride's feet. "That dog looks just like Isi. She can't be that old."

Isi thumps her tail on when I say her name.

"Of course she isn't," Letti says. "Dogs don't live that long. It must be one of her ancestors too."

"But she's identical," I say. "Look, she's got the three big spots on her back and the one tiny one, and she's got the yellow smudges on her face." Surely it's impossible that there can be two dogs fifty years apart that look the same?

"Forget the dog," Letti says, turning the page to a photo of the bride standing at the front door to Greenhaven. "Isn't her dress beautiful? And look, here they are in a church, with flowers everywhere. I'd give anything to go back in time and have a ceremony like that."

"There isn't any reason why you can't have a wedding," Alexia says. "We could have it here."

"But there's no minister, no dress...no nothing," Letti says, turning the page wistfully. "We'll just go to the Council offices like everyone else and be entered into a register."

"I bet we can find a dress here somewhere. And who needs a priest? Aunty Figgy," I call as she passes the door, "You're a kind of minister, aren't you? Can you do weddings?"

Aunty Figgy pops her head into the room. "I can say a prayer and ask for a blessing."

"There you are then," I say. "Perfect. You can have your old-fashioned wedding at Greenhaven."

"There is a wedding dress in the loft," Aunty Figgy says, propping the broom against the wall. "It's packed away in a trunk. Shall we go and find it?"

We clatter up the staircase in the kitchen and through the low door into the loft. It smells strongly of thatch up here, and the walls are lined with shelves of dried fruit, nuts and biltong.

"Where's the dress?" Letti says, her face falling. "There's nothing here."

"Patience," Aunty Figgy opens a second door half hidden in the back wall and gestures us through. This room, with its long slanted roof and dim light, extends the whole length of the building. It's filled with old furniture, traveling trunks, suitcases and boxes.

Aunty Figgy searches for a while then points to a blue metal box with the initials DDE painted on top. "This is the one. Your grandmother Daisy's trunk. Help me pull it out."

Letti hops with excitement as Aunty Figgy clicks open the fastenings and lifts the heavy lid.

"Here you are. This should fit." She pulls out a white silk dress with a deep lace frill around the neck, puffy sleeves, and a gathered skirt. Folded underneath it is a veil and a pair of gold shoes. "It was the height of fashion in 1985."

"It's gorgeous," Letti gasps, pulling it over her tunic. "How does it look?"

"Just a little bit of taking in at the waist." Aunty Figgy opens the door of an old wardrobe so Letti can see herself in the mirror. "I'll shorten it a bit and it will be perfect. I'm sure you'll find some suits in that wardrobe in the corner. There must be one that will fit Shorty."

I turn away from the others. Alexia is pinning a veil into Letti's hair and I don't want to think of Cassie and Pamza trying on clothes in my room.

I look out of the window and see the same Ficus tree that Hal and Oliver climbed. It seems so long ago, but it's only a few months. I swallow hard, trying not to think of how Hal and Cassie begged me to save them.

But Letti and Alexia are laughing together, and Jasmine is picking out a suit for Leonid, and Aunty Figgy is excited that it will be a Goddess blessed wedding. I push the sadness aside and pick out a yellow polka dot dress and matching high heels, and a black tuxedo and shiny black shoes for Micah. Scratching at the back of the wardrobe, I find a yellow tie that matches my dress.

We're going to look like a pair of Kinetika stars, even if it's just for a single day.

Chapter Twelve

Everyone is up early on the wedding day and although it's chilly, the sky is clear after three days of rain. It's Sunday, the one day the girls don't come to work on the farm. I grab basket and secateurs and head for the wall around the orchard to pick ivy. Fez has just brought the horses out to the paddock, and he comes to help me decorate the swing. We weave the ivy through the chains until they're like thick green ropes. Fez carries out the side table and the wind-up gramophone ready to play music as Letti arrives, and I roll up the faded Persian rug in front of the fireplace, and bring it out to the meadow. Scattered with bougainvillea flowers it looks rich and luxurious, and this is starting to look like a wedding venue from the old world.

Fez heads for the kitchen garden with the basket to pick sprigs of lavender and rosemary for confetti. I wander down to the river searching for flowers for a bouquet. It's late autumn, and the summer flowers are mostly gone.

The forest is quiet. The morning sun casts lacy shadows on the trees, lighting up the mauve sorrel flowers that peep between the ferns. Isi runs ahead, disappearing between the trees to hunt squirrels and then running back to me, tail wagging, her mouth open like she's smiling. I rub behind her ear and she looks up at me and barks. "Go on, girl, go," I tell her, and she's off, running deep into a thicket. I know how she feels. The forest brings me alive too—the smell of Earth, the soft greens and browns that blend softly on the eye, the sense that all around me creation is alive—trees and shrubs and animals and insects are growing and flourishing. Most of all, I love the feeling of something wild and holy, larger than the forest, and ever present.

I spy a single St. Joseph's lily on the opposite bank of the river and wade through the water, flinching at the cold. A single spray of white lilies is perfect for Letti.

It's early afternoon when we gather under the tree. Alexia winds up the gramophone and the wedding march rings across the meadow. Letti comes out of the front door on Fez's arm, the white flowers and dress glimmering against her dark skin. She's always been pretty, but today she's shining and utterly beautiful. Fez's face is solemn as he walks her down the stairs, making sure she doesn't trip over the hem of her gown. He's blossomed since he came out of the bunker—his once skinny frame is filling the black suit he's wearing and he's now at least four inches taller than his twin.

Shorty stands at the swing, his round face beaming as he watches her walk slowly across the grass. As she approaches, his hand goes up to his heart as though It's bouncing with joy and he's got to keep it in his chest. It's hard to believe that we ever thought he was a spy. His heart is as pure as Letti's and they're a perfect match for each other.

I look around at the nine of us clustered under the tree. Jasmine and Leonid are hand in hand looking like they belong together. Aunty Figgy and Alexia are whispering together and Alexia is wiping her eyes with her sleeve.

I lean closer to Micah and take his hand. I may be the last member of the den Eeden family left alive, but these eight people are my family. We'll stick together until the day we die. Nothing must be allowed to tear us apart.

"Letti, do you take this man Shorty to be your husband?" Aunty Figgy asks, when Letti reaches the carpet and Shorty has taken her hand. "Will you love him and be faithful to him all the days of your life?"

"I do."

Aunty Figgy turns to Shorty. "Do you, Shorty, take this woman, Letti, to be your wife? Will you love her and be faithful to her all the days of your life?"

A tear trickles down Letti's cheek and Shorty leans forward and wipes it away gently with his thumb.

"I do," he says. "Letti, I will look after you until the day I die." And then he cries too.

"We're a pair of idiots," Letti laughs, wiping his tear with the sleeve of her dress.

Fez hands Aunty Figgy the ring that once belonged to Shorty's grandmother.

"Goddess, bless this ring. Keep their love pure and their hearts full of joy, and bless them with children to populate your beautiful world," Aunty Figgy prays, and there is so much love and happiness and hope surrounding us that it feels like the Goddess herself might be standing among us.

Shorty slips the ring onto Letti's finger. "I wrote you a poem," he says and starts to recite in a plummy voice that sounds nothing like his own:

"Roses are red, violets are blue,
Letti my darling
I'm saying I do
I'll always be true
I'll look after you when you have the flu
I'll even die for you 'cos you're my Letti-Lou,
We'll always be two 'cos I love you."

And by the end his voice has gone all squeaky. Micah snorts and I dig him in the ribs and hiss, "Stop it." It's a terrible poem, but it comes straight from Shorty's heart, and that's all that matters. Letti flings her arms around him and Aunty Figgy says, "You may kiss the bride," but she's too late.

Afterwards Micah and I are in the garden, eating wedding cake while we lounge on the swing. "It was a lovely day," I say dreamily. "So romantic. It's been so long since Greenhaven had a wedding. Till death do us part. I loved that bit."

"One day we'll be married," he says. "I promise you."

"Can't we get married now?" I ask nuzzling up to him. "We're old enough. We're both Citizens. And we love each other so much."

He lifts my chin with one finger. "Nothing would make me happier, but we have a struggle to fight. We have to focus on that for now. The moment we win the battle, I promise you, we will get married."

Chapter Thirteen

Two days later, the general calls a Council meeting, and I leave home feeling sick with anxiety. This isn't going to go well. Not if he's heard about my deal with the Syndicate.

"On the agenda today," he begins, and rattles off a list of things to discuss—road repairs, a conflict between two Citizens about leasing the grazing land on Devil's Peak that used to belong to Lucas's family.

"The fifty young women from the Colony are now ensconced at Greenhaven farm. Miss den Eeden, could you please report on how they're settling in?"

I wonder briefly why he doesn't just ask Major Zungu for a report, seeing as the soldiers go with them everywhere. But I smile politely and say, "It's still early days, but so far so good. They're clearing the grape vines from some of the fields so we can plant out the winter vegetables—cauliflower, broccoli, sweet potatoes, etc. We've already planted some and they'll be ready for market in approximately five weeks."

He looks at me coldly with those fierce metallic eyes. "Now for our next issue. Transportation."

This is it. He's going to yell. I twist my feet together and look down, tracing the lines and patterns on the marble table.

"Owing to Miss den Eeden appointing the Syndicate as sole purveyors of Greenhaven produce, we find ourselves in a difficult position. The army was relying on the extra income to cover the additional expenses of administering the new staff on Greenhaven farm. The only solution as I see it is to elevate a further one hundred youth from the Colony to work under supervision of Major Zungu."

How will that help? Why is he elevating one hundred more Colonists? He knows that's what I want—to get them all out. I sneak a glance at him. His body language is closed off, and he's like a snake, eyes glittering as he looks at me sideways.

"Um...what work will they do?" I ask, hoping he doesn't say, "Work at Greenhaven." We can't afford to feed another hundred people. Not yet.

"Transportation from Longkloof Harbor to Bellville Dock."

It takes a moment to sink in. Mr. Frye's plump fingers are tapping the marble tabletop and he's shaking his head in disbelief. Mr. Adams is frantically doing calculations in his notebook.

"Furthermore," the general says, "we will elevate a further two hundred fifty young men to join the army."

Mr Adams holds up his hand. "Excuse me, General," he says. "We don't need one hundred new transporters. What is that...?" He pauses while he calculates. "Er...eight teams of twelve rowers? Where will we find boats? What will they transport?"

My heart sinks. I see what the bastard is planning.

"What about the people from Boat Bay?" I say. "You're planning to take their jobs?"

The general leans back and fixes me with his iron blue eyes. "You ask me to elevate your friends from the Colony, Miss den Eeden, but when I do, you complain. I can't get it right with you, can I?"

"I'm sorry, General," I mutter, dropping my head. I get a flashback to the way he and the High Priest examined each of us that last day in the Colony when I was chosen for the sacrifice.

"That is settled then," he says. "This meeting is adjourned."

He stands up and we all rise as he leaves the room.

Mr. Frye doesn't say goodbye. "I'll come and see you tomorrow," he snaps as he pushes past me and strides off. "You've really done it this time, Ebba. What did I tell you about being impulsive?"

I'm terrified of telling Micah about the general's decision. He'll probably break up with me, disappear to Boat Bay, and stay there forever. Samantha Lee wouldn't do anything as impulsive as sign a document without talking to Micah first and considering all the options.

I come home from the meeting, tell Aunty Figgy I've got a migraine, and go straight to bed. Micah comes in later to see if I'm okay and I pretend to be asleep. I wake up in the middle of the night, with a sick feeling in my stomach. I'm going to have to tell him soon. He'll be even angrier if he hears it from someone else.

The next morning everyone is chatty at breakfast, but I sit hunched over my cup of tea, wishing they'd all shut up.

"What happened at the meeting yesterday?" Fez asks. "Any new decisions?"

I swallow, hiding behind my mug as I try to figure out what to say. "Nothing," I say at last. "Nothing important."

Fez is satisfied, but Alexia looks at me curiously. She reaches over and takes my hand. "How's your head today? You don't look well."

"Sore."

They leave me alone then. When breakfast is over and everyone is going off to start work, I call Micah. "Can you come with me? I need to...I need to tell you something."

Immediately his black eyes bore into mine. "What? Is it to do with the Council?"

"Just come, please."

I lead him into the sitting room, sit on the sofa and pat the cushion next to me.

"Micah, I..."

His face darkens. "What, Ebba? Why are you so edgy? What have you done?"

"Nothing. I didn't do anything."

He raises his eyebrows. "Nothing? It doesn't seem like nothing."

He's getting irritated, and that makes me even more flustered.

"It's..." I begin. "It's not me." I open my mouth to explain but I'm interrupted by horse's hooves.

He gets up and strides to the window. "It's Mr. Frye. What does he want?"

Oh no. He's here to talk about the general's decision, and Micah will go ballistic with rage. I can't risk him hearing it from Mr. Frye. I say the first thing that comes to mind. "He's here to help me with some legal documents."

"What kind of legal documents?"

Mr. Frye has dismounted, and he's tying his horse's reins to the hitching post. Aunty Figgy is outside greeting him. They're turning toward the house. I can't think fast enough. "I can't tell you." That's the best I've got.

He takes my shoulders and shakes me. "Of course you can tell me," he snaps. "What is he here for? What have you done this time?"

Grasping for an answer, I mutter, "My will. I'm writing my will."

"So why can't you tell me that?" His voice is cold. I know he doesn't believe me. I've got to do something drastic, give myself time to figure out what to do.

"Because...because I'm leaving everything to you. I'm

making you my heir."

His hands drop from my shoulders. "You're kidding me."

"No. You already said we'll be married one day. And I have to leave it to someone."

"But Leonid...Alexia..."

"They're not Citizens. They're not allowed to own land."

"Okay," he says, grinning. "In that case, great. Thank you, babe." He gives me a high five. "Don't see why you had to make such a song and dance about it, but that's great."

Mr. Frye is standing in the doorway now, his usually sleek face etched with worry. "Ebba," he says. "We have to talk."

"I know," I say. "Thank you for coming all this way to make my will. Micah is just leaving. I've told him he's the only—what's the word—beneficiary—so he can't be a witness. That's right, isn't it?"

Mr. Frye looks at me like I'm mad. "What?"

"Micah, can you go and find two girls in the potato field?" I say, ignoring Mr. Frye. "They need to go into the forest to collect firewood. Could you find them a saw, and show them the fallen milkwood near the river?"

"Sure, babe." He pecks me on the cheek. "See you, Mr. Frye."

I watch him walking off round the front of the house. There's a skip in his step.

I turn around. Aunty Figgy is still behind me and her face is like a storm.

The meeting with Mr. Frye is short and ugly. He's angry about the general, but angrier that I signed with the Syndicate without talking to him first. "There are going to be serious repercussions," he snaps. "Serious political ramifications. Without the transportation contracts, so many boat people are going to be hungry. And hungry people are desperate people. Really, Ebba. You've been very foolish."

I know it's true. Probably the stupidest thing I've ever done. But he's not finished yet.

"And now you want to leave Greenhaven to a boy you've only just met! Are you deranged? I cannot allow this, in all honesty, I can't allow it. He's got some sort of a hold over you."

"It's my farm," I mutter. "I can leave it to anyone I like. And he doesn't have a hold over me. And anyway, it's not like I'm going to die soon, so what does it matter? Please, just write up the papers for me. I've made my decision, and I'm sticking to it."

When he's finally left, after a long discussion with Aunty Figgy, I call Isi and go for a walk. I pick up a stick and whack the grass as I pass, knocking off the seedpods. Damnit. It's my farm. I can leave it to whoever I like. But what is really making me angry is that I've screwed everything up.

I have to tell Micah the truth. I need to do it away from Jasmine and Leonid. And I need to do it quickly.

Late afternoon I pack some sandwiches and fruit and a bottle of lemon cordial into a basket along with a blanket. Aunty Figgy ignores me as I potter around the kitchen. Her jaw is set tight, and her beady little eyes avoid mine, although the angry energy coming off her is all directed my way. I find Micah in the shed.

"I've made us a picnic supper," I tell him, trying to sound light-hearted. "Surprise."

"Where are we going?" he asks as we cross the meadow. The horses come running over to the fence, whinnying in greeting. I stop and give them each an apple. I can't believe

I was ever so frightened of them.

"To the pond."

"Ah." He twists his arm around my waist. "Are we going to skinny dip again?"

"Too cold. It's not midsummer anymore."

"Ah come on," he grins. "I love a skinny dipping girl."

I can barely raise a smile. Now the time has come, I can't find the courage to raise the subject. Instead, I begin to obsess about Samantha Lee. I bet she skinny dips all the time. Even in the middle of winter. The anxiety is gnawing my stomach. I know he's going to leave me. He's going to go back to Boat Bay and work full-time on the Resistance. I'll never see him again. He probably likes Samantha Lee better than me anyway. She's beautiful and sophisticated and at least twenty-one. He'll never stick with me, gawky, big-footed, red-haired sixteen-year-old me.

I can't stop myself. I know I'm being unreasonable, but as we stride down the path toward the river, the words just tumble out.

"Tell me about your old girlfriends. Was Samantha Lee one of them?"

"Ag, Ebba," he sighs. "Don't go there. We've talked about this. You have no reason to be jealous of her."

"But I want to know," I say. I can hear the needy whine growing in my voice and I hate it. "Alexia tells me you and Samantha Lee were together for years. She says she saw you with her just a few weeks ago—after you escaped over the mountain. She says you were staying at Samantha Lee's house in Boat Bay." My throat is so tight, I can hardly get the words out.

His hand tightens around my waist. Is that affection? Or is he tensing up?

"I'm sorry," I say, trying to gauge what he's feeling. "It just makes me so insecure."

He stops, turns to face me, and I'm expecting him to

yell at me, but instead he puts his hands on each side of my face and pulls me to him in a kiss. I gaze into his eyes, awed that they're the exact deep brown of the richest topsoil, and fringed by impossibly long black lashes.

"I love you, Ebba den Eeden," he says when we pull away at last. "You and you alone. Please don't worry about Samantha. She's nothing to me."

"I love you, too," I whisper. Inside I'm quaking. I have to tell him the truth. And I'm not so sure he'll be saying those words when he hears what I've done.

He strokes my cheek with his fingers. "You're beautiful," he murmurs. He runs his long fingers down my neck, pressing them into the hollow of my throat, and I can feel the energy rising from him. I know what he wants. If I sleep with him, he'll see how much I love him. He won't be so angry when he discovers about the general's decision. I want to do it, but...not like this. I want it to be something spontaneous, not a way of placating him up before bad news. But he wants it, so badly.

"Let's picnic here," I say as we reach a grassy patch near the river bank. I shake out the blanket and drop it on the ground. I'm going to do it. I'm going to prove my love for him.

But Aunty Figgy's words are stuck in my head as loud as if a thousand people were shouting them. "Focus on the sacred task. Time is running out."

"Rubbish," I think, imagining I'm saying what I wouldn't dare say if I were face to face with her. "You're jealous because you haven't got a lover. You're just an old lady. What do you know about love?"

Micah lies down next to me. His hand moves down from my throat, running across my chest bone, teasing downwards toward my nipple. I reach over and pull his tunic over his head, flinching as I catch sight of the network of scars on his back. He's survived so much—being beaten by the guards before they threw him out of the ventilation shaft, hiding alone in the mountains while he healed, with only occasional visits from Chad to bring him food and tend to his injuries. It hasn't made him bitter and angry. Rather, he's determined to overthrow what is unjust and cruel. He's put everything he suffered into working for the good of the Boat Bay community. That is really heroic. My parents would be proud of him. Would they be that proud of me? Making him the heir to Greenhaven would surely be what they wanted.

"Hold on," I whisper, pulling my robe over my head. I lie back down on the blanket, cradling my right arm behind my head. He sighs and rolls over so he's up against me.

"Your skin is the exact golden brown of the pecans in the orchard," I tell him, tracing my little finger along the curve of his top lip.

He runs his hand up my ribs, around the curve of my breasts, and stops at the little key hanging from the chain around my neck. I've put it there in case I find a lock I haven't tried yet.

"What's this?"

"It's nothing."

I reach up and cover it with my hand, and as my birthmark touches the key, a woman appears, standing squarely on the path behind him, hands on hips, glaring at me over small wire-rimmed spectacles.

"Who are you?" I sit up quickly, covering myself with my arms. But I know already. Only one person could be looking so strict. She's wearing sensible navy shoes, thick stockings, a gray knee length skirt and a white coat with a name tag: it's my ancestor, Dr. Iris den Eeden.

"Come along," she says, patting her gray hair to make sure nothing has escaped from the bun at the back of her neck. *"You're being manipulative. Tell him the truth and get on with it."*

Who does she think she is? I glare at her. Go away, I think.

Micah shakes me. "Ebba, EBBA! You're being weird. What are you staring at?"

I turn my back on the woman. "Sorry."

He starts to kiss me again, but I'm finding it hard to get back into the mood. There's her annoying high-pitched voice again.

"Come along, girlie. Tempus Fugit. There will be plenty of time to gallivant later. Tell him the truth and get it over with."

She's not going to go away. And much as I hate it, she's right. I just have to spit it out.

Sitting up, I pull on my robe and say, "We need to talk."

Chapter Fourteen

Micah is gone. His face went white as I told him the general's decision. He didn't ask questions, interrupt, or respond at all until I'd finished. Then he got up abruptly and said, "I have to go there. Now."

All night I toss and turn, worrying about the boat people. I get up before it's light, and go across to the office. I'm going to search the room again, every drawer, every cupboard, every filing box and shelf, and I won't stop until I find that amulet.

Just before seven Leonid goes into the pigeon loft to feed the birds, and to check if any birds have arrived with messages. A few minutes later, the door slams and he storms across the yard, yelling for me.

Isi puts her head on my lap and whimpers.

"What am I going to do, girl?" I whisper. "What am I going to say to him?"

Turns out I don't have to say much, because he doesn't let me get a word in.

"How could you do this?" Leonid rages. "It's your fault. You knew about this, didn't you?" He jabs his finger in my face. Isi growls and he takes a step back.

I want to lie, but I can't. "I... I...the general announced it at the Council meeting. I told him it wasn't fair, but he wouldn't listen."

"So you were there when they decided it, but you did nothing," Leonid storms. "You didn't care that hundreds of people will starve to death because of you."

A rock is lodged in my throat. I try to speak through it but my voice comes out like a squawk. "I did care. I told him he couldn't do it. He yelled at me."

"So you just buckled. You betrayed your own family, your own people."

"Stop it, Leonid," a voice says behind me. It's Alexia, come to see what the shouting is about. "You're being a bully. Whatever Ebba did, she didn't do it on purpose. Just give her a break."

"She and the Council have decided to release more workers from the Colony," Leonid spits. "They're going to Boat City to run the transport. All private transporters are banned. It's a new law. The army are running the transport to the Mainland now."

Alexia goes pale. "Everyone is losing their jobs?"

"And their boats," Leonid says. "The army has confiscated them all."

She sinks down into the office armchair. "That's awful. But Ebba would never have voted for that."

"I didn't," I say, trying not to sound whiny. "There wasn't a vote. The general just announced it as a new law. I told him it was wrong and I couldn't support him, and he said it was my fault because I wanted the workers released from the Colony, so I had to shut up."

"And you didn't think he'd get revenge for appointing the Syndicate to transport the vegetables. Are you a fucking moron?"

"That's enough now, Leonid," Alexia snaps. "What's done is done."

"Our father would be ashamed of you," Leonid snarls, punching the desk. "You're a fucking disgrace."

It's early evening, and the girls have gone back to the

army barracks, marching down the driveway four abreast, feet sending up a cloud of dust. I've been collecting kindling for the fireplace, and I'm about to leave the forest when the wagon comes down the driveway and stops outside the barn. Leonid is back from market.

I pick up my basket, ready to run over and help him unload the crates when she crawls out from the tarpaulin, shaking out her long curly hair, and brushing straw off her clothes. My heart slides down to my feet. She's here already. Micah's chosen her over me, and they're going to rub it in.

She stands there on the edge of the wagon with her big boobs and tiny waist and her chin lifted up like she's the Statue of Liberty before it fell down.

I want to march over there and demand to know what she's doing on my property. I'm summoning up my courage when Micah comes round the corner. He looks around quickly, but he doesn't see me between the trees.

She's laughing and waving and he holds out his arms and lifts her down. Is she kissing him? Kissing him on the lips! I grab the basket of kindling and storm over to them. She's gone too far. I'm not giving him up without a fight. How dare she just come onto my farm and steal my boyfriend and make out with him right in front of me.

She doesn't even look perturbed when I drop the basket next to them and stick my hands on my hips.

"Why are *you* here?"

Micah frowns and lets her go. "Ebba! What's going on with you?"

What's going on with me? It's them, acting like kissing on the lips is perfectly okay even if you're in a relationship with someone else. Maybe we're not in a relationship any more. Maybe he's chosen her. I take a step back. "I...I'm just wondering why she's on my farm?"

"Ebba," he says sternly. "Come on. Samantha Lee's one

of my oldest friends. I asked her to come."

Samantha Lee holds out her hand. "Pleasure to meet you at last," she says, flashing her perfect smile. She has a cleft in her chin, and her cheek bones are even more beautiful close up. She looks like a famous artist would have painted her in the old days, and they might even have carved statues of her and put them up in the public square. I'm painfully aware of my dirty work robe and my hair that needs a wash.

I blush as I shake her hand. Have I been an idiot again? What must she think of me? It was just an innocent kiss. Right?

I'm totally out of my depth. They're both much older than me. They've seen the real world. I've only ever known the bunker and life on Greenhaven. I'm making a fool of myself. And Micah has his arm around me. Thank the Goddess. His arm is around me.

"Sorry," I say, trying to steady my voice. He's showing her that I'm the one. That we're together. "Welcome to Greenhaven."

"Samantha Lee's come to help with some organization, babe," Micah says. "She'll sleep in the hayloft. Just for a few nights."

"I'll be gone by the end of the week," she says brightly. "Thanks a mill."

"Just keep it quiet," Micah says as Leonid drives the wagon into the barn. "The guards will arrest her if they find her."

Don't tempt me, I think. She saunters off after the wagon and her hips sway like she's dancing. *Just put one foot wrong,* I say to myself. *Just make one move on my boyfriend and I'll have the guards arresting you before you can....* It's a nice fantasy, thinking of the guards thrashing her and throwing her out of the City, but I can't report her. Micah will never forgive me.

He follows her down to the barn and I go back to the house to shower. At least Micah is being friendly again, I think. At least his temper has blown over.

But how long until I do the next wrong thing?

Chapter Fifteen

Dr. Iris won't leave me alone. I go into the farm office the next morning and she's there with a burning cigarette in her hand, her court shoe going tap tap tap on the floor. What does she want? What does that thing mean she keeps saying: Tempus Fugit?

I sit down at the battered old table opposite Shorty and try to ignore her standing next to the clock, glaring at me like I'm a lazy five-year-old who isn't running fast enough on the treadmill.

Shorty is adding up columns in the ledger. He pushes it over to me. "See here, Miss Ebba? This is our income from the market yesterday. And here's the average for the last six months. See how much our income has dropped?"

I pull the book toward me, trying to make sense of the column that his stubby finger is pointing to.

"It's because we're feeding an extra fifty people," he says. "They're eating up everything we used to sell."

I bite my pencil. I've seen the wagon going off to market. There are hardly any eggs left to sell. The milk and cream are all being used up, and we're spending a fortune on mealies and wheat for bread.

"Can't you feed them cheaper food?" he asks.

I shake my head. "I just can't. They have to eat the same as we do. It would be wrong to feed them cabbage soup day in and day out when we're eating scrambled eggs and cheese."

"How long until the new lands can be harvested?" he

asks. "Once the income is coming in from the vegetables, they'll be able to pay their way."

I sigh. "At least a month. Things grow slowly in winter."

He turns back to his ledger, and I stare out of the window. Out of the corner of my eye, I see Dr. Iris shaking her head and tapping her wrist watch. I roll my eyes. The last thing I need now is some deranged ancestor nagging me in Latin. I have no idea what she wants from me.

She goes over to the desk, opens the drawer, feels underneath it and pulls out the envelope with the key.

My hand goes to the key hanging around my neck. It's definitely there. But it's also taped under the drawer? This is crazy. She's got it clutched firmly in her hand. She crosses to the corner where the clock is standing behind a pile of boxes. She shoves the boxes aside with her shoulder. Shorty hasn't noticed a thing. Can't he see the boxes have moved? Or is this all happening in some alternative world in my head—one where an object can be in two places at the same time?

She reaches up to the clock face, takes each side of the wood and glass top, and pulls it forward. The cover comes off, and she puts it carefully on the floor. Then she opens the glass window that covers the dial. There are two holes in the center of the dial, and she's turning the key in one, with a loud rasping noise. I count thirteen twists. She takes it out and inserts it into the second hole and the rasping begins again. She finishes winding and puts the cover back on the top.

A moment later, Shorty looks up. "What's that sound?"

"Sound?" All I can hear is Iris's tap tap tapping as she strides across the office and drops the key back into the drawer.

"A ticking noise."

Then I hear it too. A regular soft tick, tick, ticking.

Shorty jumps up. "It's that clock. It's started—it can't

have. How can it just start again out of the blue like that?"

He pushes the boxes out of the way, fetches the chair, and pulls it over to the clock. He clambers up and stands there, staring at the clock face. "I never noticed this before. Look, Miss Ebba. There's a ship painted here, on the sea, and every time the clock ticks, the sails move."

I go over and peer at the dial.

"See, these are the numbers one to twelve," he says, running his finger in a circle around the letters. "They're Roman Numerals. The short hand shows the hours and the long one shows the minute. It's so exciting. How did it suddenly start working again after all these years? I can't wait to show Letti. She's going to love it."

I'm intrigued by the painting above the numbers. Shorty's right. That is a ship on the sea, but there's a mountain in the background, and it looks like—it is, it's Table Mountain. There's Devil's Peak on one side and the Lion on the other.

"It's so old," he says. "Look—the date says London, 1722. And there's something written here in Latin." He rubs his chin. "Tem...Tempus Fugit. Now what does that mean again?"

It can't be. It just can't be. Can it?

"Time...that's it. Time is Fugit—running. Time is running out." He beams at me. "I knew I'd get it. My granddad used to teach me Latin when I was a kid. I must go and call Letti. It might stop working again. She must see this. She's going to love it."

He runs off toward the house, calling, "Letti, Letti my love, come and see this."

I stand back, wondering what is going on. Is Iris telling me there's an amulet there? I get up on the chair and run my hands over the dusty top of the clock. Nothing. Carefully, slowly, I lift off the wood and glass case and put it on the pile of boxes. I check the dial. Nothing.

Unclasping my necklace, I take off the key.

Shorty comes back, his cheeks pink with excitement. "She's coming. Hey what have you got there?"

"It's the key," I tell him. Carefully I insert it into the two holes in the dial and turn, one after the other. The same rasping noise creaks out.

"There's another keyhole here, miss," Shorty exclaims. "Won't you open here so we can see inside?"

I pass him the key and he unlocks the door. Inside are two heavy brass weights on wire pulleys, and a shining brass thing like a plate.

"The pendulum," he says. "Will you take a look at that!"

Heart speeding up, I kneel down and feel inside the clock case. The amulet must be hidden inside here. My ancestor has shown me where the amulet is. I'm going to have an amulet again.

I feel everywhere, but there's nothing there. I check and recheck. There's nothing inside the clock case. I run my hand down the heavy cylindrical weights, look up to see if something is hidden where the pendulum begins. But there's nothing. Shorty helps me push the clock away from the wall and I check the back. Nothing.

Meanwhile Dr. Iris has lit another cigarette and is staring at me. Are you an imbecile? she says in my head.

I haven't got the faintest idea what she wants from me or where the amulet might be. I'm stumped.

———

A few days later I've gone to find kindling in the forest. I head along the path that leads to the holy well. I like going there, imagining that it's still whole, and that when I lean over the edge I can still see the sky and clouds reflected against the indigo blue base, and that the algae still makes a map of the world on the bottom.

I get there and find most of the Milkwood tree that fell during the earthquake is gone. Instead, there's a pile of firewood next to the stump. Leonid must have been busy. I sit on the ruins of the wall, taking a moment to watch the water trickling up through the broken stones.

Then I smell it. The cigarette smoke. Damnit. It's Dr. Iris, nagging me to get looking for the amulet. Can't she leave me alone?

But she's not here for me. Lucas comes through the trees, carrying an axe. So he's the one chopping wood and fixing the wall. Iris is with him. Not clearly. I can't see all of her. But that's the outline of her white doctor's coat and glimpses of her navy skirt contrast with the cream of his robe. A trail of cigarette smoke wisps up next to his face. What is she doing with him?

He sees me, and his face tenses. He opens his mouth as though he's going to say something, then shuts it again.

"Lucas," I call. "Thank you for chopping the wood. Did you fix the wall? Do you need anything? Have you got enough to eat?"

But he's turned on his heel and melted back among the trees.

I'm hoping Iris went with him, but she's right behind me when I go back to the house, her cigarette smell wafting behind my shoulder. What is *wrong* with Lucas? Why won't he just come inside the house to where he'll be comfortable and warm? We'll give him hot meals and he'll have company. It's not good to be alone all the time, especially when you're bereaved. Soon it will be winter, and he can't stay out there through the storms and rain. It's not safe. Why is he being so damned stubborn?

I'm piling the kindling outside the kitchen door when I smell cigarette smoke again, and lose my temper. "Just go away," I snap. "Take that filthy cigarette away and leave me alone."

Alexia's head pops up from behind the trellis where she's harvesting butternut. "What cigarette? Who are you talking to?"

"Nobody."

She comes over, rubbing her hands on her tunic. "You were talking to someone. You're really cross. Tell me."

"I told you. Nobody."

But she's not going to give up. "You were talking to somebody. Was it your ancestor?"

I sigh, and she seizes it. "I'm right, aren't I? It's your ancestor. Have you found an amulet?"

I tell her about the cigarettes, and Iris and the clock. "So you see, it's useless. I've checked the clock. There's nothing there. She's got it wrong."

She taps the knife handle against her teeth. "But this doctor lady—Iris—she's always there when you're in the office?"

"Always."

"And she disappears when you leave the office?"

"Except for her cigarette. I can smell it. And I sort of saw her in the forest."

"So the amulet is in the office. We need to search for it. Come on."

"Now? I was going to have a cup of tea."

"There's no time for tea," she scoffs. "Time is running out."

I roll my eyes at her. "Not you too."

"The only way to get her off your back is to give her what she wants." She grabs my hand and pulls me back to the office. The instant we go inside, Iris is there, smiling her tight-lipped smile at me. "Tempus Fugit," she says, just as I knew she would.

Alexia goes straight for the clock. The key is still in the keyhole and she unlocks it and swings the door open. "Light the lamp," she says, pointing to the oil lamp on the mantel piece.

I hand it to her and she holds it inside the clock case, peering right up to the workings of the clock.

"The weights are hanging on a sort of pulley contraption," she says. Her voice sounds hollow from inside the clock. "There's space to hide something small up there. Damnit, I can't reach it. I reckon we need to take the clock apart to search it properly."

"But it might break," I exclaim.

"Ebba! It's broken anyway. You said yourself it hasn't worked for ages. And look, it's stopped ticking now."

"That's because you bumped the whatchamacallit," I tell her. "The pendulum. I don't want to break it anymore."

"So we call Camryn," she says, blowing out the lamp. "You said she's a brilliant engineer. She'll be able to take it apart and put it together again. I'll go and call her."

She scampers off, pleased as punch with her plan. I'm not so sure. Why would the amulet be hidden inside the clock? Who would have put it there? I can't understand how these amulets work. Does each ancestor get one? Or did Clementine have four, and then Iris had one, so somewhere in the intervening years the others got lost? I try and think back to Clementine's necklace. I only saw it once, when it slipped out of the neck of her dress. I was so busy staring at the mark on her hand and the amulet like mine that I forgot to count them.

Alexia comes back with Camryn, who is wiping her hands on her tunic, and looks around with her usual sneer. I know what she's thinking—all this belongs to you, you spoiled bitch, and now you think you're better than us. I want to grab her and shout, "Of course I'm not better than you. I didn't do anything to earn it. It just happened, and it's not exactly easy, you know." Alexia explains that we need to take the clock apart.

"Why?" Camryn says, from under her black fringe.

Her eyebrows meet in the middle, making her look even fiercer.

"We just do," Alexia says firmly.

She must think we're deliberately hiding something from her. It goes against everything we were taught in the Colony. It's bad enough that she and the other girls have to be marched in every morning by the army. The least I can do is treat her with some respect.

"There's a family heirloom inside," I say.

Alexia digs me in the ribs. "A letter. It's not worth anything."

"A letter?" Camryn looks from me to Alexia, searching our faces. "Who's it from?"

"My mother..."

"Ebba's grandfather," Alexia says at the same time.

Camryn's eyes narrow. But she doesn't say anything. She goes up to the clock and begins to look at it from each side. Then she reaches up and lifts off the top case. How did she know to do that?

She unhooks the weights from the pulleys and puts them on the floor. Then she reaches up and feels at the back. She gives a grunt and next thing she's passing me the pendulum. It's heavy. I turn it over and look at it from all sides. There's nothing hidden here.

Next she lifts off the clock face. Behind it are a set of cogs and wheels, and for the first time, I see her smile. "You beauty," she grunts. She's on the chair, peering inside, gently turning the wheels with her oil-stained finger. Then she reaches down with surprising delicacy and pulls out something. "You're looking for this?" she says in her gruff voice, and she holds out the amulet.

"Give it to me," I gasp, reaching up for it. "Please."

Her eyes narrow again. "Why should I?" She jumps down from the chair, sticks it in her pocket and sneers at me. "Make me."

I open my mouth and shut it again. I can't make her. But Alexia pulls herself up to her full height and snaps, "You work for her and she's your boss. So hand it over now or I'll call the guards."

"Alexia!" I gasp. "You can't talk to people like that."

But Camryn tosses it over to me. "Stick it on your stupid necklace. I see you lost the other charm you were so proud of. Hope you don't lose this one."

And she swaggers off back to her friends, leaving the clock in pieces.

Alexia digs me in the ribs. "You can't let her get away with that! She has to come back and finish what she started. Go on, call her back."

I bite my lip. "Me? I can't."

"You have to. Come on, be the boss."

She's right. I sigh and go to the door. "Camryn," I call. "Kindly come back and finish putting the clock together again."

She's halfway across the courtyard. She doesn't turn, but I know she heard me because she gives me the finger over her shoulder. One of the guards happens to be drinking from the water keg and he follows her, sjambok swinging against his thigh. I hear a thwack, and then Camryn comes back, glowering worse than ever, with a red welt across her arm. She doesn't say a word, just puts the clock together and hands me the key. The guard is standing at the door watching, and I keep my head down, pretending to read the ledger. Why do they have to be so brutal?

When she's gone, I open my hand and at long last get a closer look at the amulet. It's silver, like the other one. A spray of water created from sparking blue stone lies across the center of the oval. The silver is detailed with a pattern of clouds and rain drops. I clip it onto the chain, and I hear a sigh of pleasure. It's Iris, and she's smiling at last...

Chapter Sixteen

It's exactly twenty-four hours. I have the amulet for one full day. Then it disappears. I've been working in the greenhouse all morning and I go to shower before Micah comes in for lunch. Now that Samantha Lee is hanging around all the time, I'm taking more care to look good—well, to look the best I can compared to her. I go into my bathroom, take off the necklace and put it on the windowsill, as I always do.

When I've finished showering and toweling my hair, I reach over for the necklace, and it's gone.

Panic floods me. Maybe it fell out the window. I pull on my robe and rush outside, not caring that my hair is wet and wild. I dig in the gooseberry bushes that grow high outside the bathroom window.

"What are you looking for?" Micah calls, coming round the corner.

"I can't find my necklace," I screech, pushing and pulling the branches as I search for that flash of silver.

"It's not there." I grab him, shake him. "It's gone. It's gone. What am I going to do?"

"Calm down." He takes me by the biceps and holds me at arm's length. "Where did you see it last?"

"I put it on the windowsill while I was showering." Why didn't I just leave it on? How could I be so careless?

"I'll check inside. You probably took it off somewhere else."

"I never take it off," I snap. "I'm not an idiot. I only take it off when I shower, and I always put it in the same place, on the windowsill."

"Okay, okay. Stay calm. Getting upset won't help you find it."

Tears are pricking my eyes. "Aunty Figgy is going to kill me. It's been in my family for five hundred years."

"It can't have just disappeared," Micah says. "Someone must have taken it. It must be one of the Colony workers, or an army guard."

Camryn. Oh Goddess. It's Camryn.

"First check with Aunty Figgy and Alexia," Micah says. "Then we'll do one final search to make sure you haven't mislaid it. If we still haven't found it, you'll have to call the guards and ask them to do a search."

Aunty Figgy is in the kitchen, stirring a huge pot of soup while Alexia slices a mountain of bread.

"My necklace...have either of you seen it?"

Aunty Figgy drops the ladle with a clatter. "Your necklace? Your amulet necklace?"

"I left it on the windowsill when I showered, and it's gone."

Alexia jumps up. "It's Camryn. She's taken it to get revenge. She must give it back. Come on."

"No, wait." I grab her sleeve. "We haven't got proof."

"We don't need proof," she says, waving the bread knife in the air. "She took it once already, and we know she's really angry."

"She didn't actually take it earlier," I say, though my doubt is growing. "She wasn't serious, was she? I mean what use would it be to her?"

"She could see how much it means to you," Alexia says. "She only gave it back because I threatened to call the guard. You're too soft on her—on all the Colony workers. They won't respect you if you let them get away with shit like this."

"Language!" Aunty Figgy snaps. "And Alexia is right. You can't let her get away with this. This isn't just any necklace. This is priceless. It's an heirloom."

"I'm going to call the guards right now," Alexia says. Micah comes into the kitchen then, and I look up hopefully, but his face says it all. He shakes his head. "It's definitely gone."

"She stole it," Alexia exclaims and storms off. I follow, burning with embarrassment. The girls are going to think I'm such a bitch. They're sitting in their rows on the grass outside the barn waiting for lunch.

Camryn is sitting by herself to one side, her face slumped in its familiar scowl. She looks up as she hears Alexia saying her name to the guard. She watches me following Alexia halfheartedly across the grass, and her face is filled with pure hatred.

"You!" the guard shouts. "Camryn. Get up. Where's the missing necklace?"

"What necklace?" she holds her hands out, palms up. "I haven't seen any necklace."

"The one you tried to take yesterday," Alexia says, back straight, voice firm.

Micah has joined us now, and Aunty Figgy, wringing her hands in her apron. We stand there, accusing, while the guard marches over, grabs Camryn by the right arm, and forces it behind her back. "Walk," he demands.

It doesn't feel right. I can't work out why she would take it? There's nothing she can do with an amulet. And she seems so genuinely outraged that I can't believe she's guilty. I stand close to Micah, finding comfort in his warm steadiness. He'll know what to do. I'll just do whatever he tells me to.

The guard marches Camryn up to us, and she stands in front of me, glowering at the ground. "Tell her," the guard orders. "Tell her where it is."

She says nothing. I try not to look at the forty-nine other workers sitting silently in their rows watching. Just a few months ago, I was one of them and if there was any problem, we took it to Mr. Dermond. Now it's me standing over them like the boss.

"Right," the guard says. "Take off your clothes."

"You can't do that!" I exclaim. "It's...it's..."

Micah tightens his hold on my hand, and I shut my mouth. A female guard comes over and rips off the ugly floral dress, her tunic, pants, and underwear. She stands there naked while the guard runs her hands over her body.

"I told you, I haven't got her stupid necklace," Camryn shouts, trying to cover herself with her hands. "She was wearing it last time I saw it."

The guard slaps her.

I'm ripping my cuticle, torn between wanting to make them stop and my need to find the necklace. I can't lose it. I just can't. My stomach is churning as the guard slaps her again.

Alexia steps forward. "Just tell us where it is, and you can get dressed again," she says, her voice kind. "I'm sure Ebba won't let them punish you. You can have a warning this time."

"That's right, Camryn." I'm pleading with her. "I won't let the guards punish you. Just give the necklace back. Please. It's really important to me."

Camryn's face is dark with rage as she pulls on her clothes. I'm mortified. Did I get it wrong? Did I have her stripped naked and humiliated in front of everyone, when she was totally innocent?

"She must have hidden it," Micah says. "There's a million places she might have put it. She probably wants to get it later."

"Like the old wine cellar," Camryn snarls. "Maybe I hid

it there. It's a good place to hide things, isn't it, Micah?"

Micah stiffens. "I saw you in the stables just now," he snaps. "When I came in earlier you were there, in the tack room."

"Rubbish," Camryn shouts.

The female guard slaps her. "Show some respect. What were you doing in the tack room?"

Her eyes are huge with fear. She opens her mouth to say something, then shuts it again. And suddenly she bolts toward the driveway. The guards lift their rifles and fire without a warning shot.

She falls.

There's a small circle of blood on her back, like a bullseye.

Alexia takes my hand. "Come inside, Ebba."

I pull free. Is she still alive?

"Come on," Micah calls, his voice hard. "Let the guards deal with this. It's not your problem."

He and Alexia make me go with them into the kitchen. I slump at the table, picking my cuticle. "It is my problem though," I say. "It's my fault she got shot. Tell them to bring her inside. She can have my room until her wound is healed."

Aunty Figgy comes in then, followed by Jasmine and Leonid. "She's gone," Aunty Figgy says, wiping her tears with her apron. "She died instantly."

The blood drains out of me. I stand up, clutching the edge of the table. "She's dead? What about the necklace? Where did she hide the necklace?"

Jasmine stares at me, aghast. "That's all you can think about? Camryn is lying outside the door, dead because of you, and all you can think about is where she put your stupid necklace? If you'd just listened to us and left her in the Colony, she'd still be alive. But no, you had to do what your boyfriend wanted. You had to do what you wanted.

And look where it's ended."

I stand there and no words come to my mouth. Everything she has said is true. I'm a murderer.

I turn around and go to my room. Isi is there, cowering under the bed. I lock the door, pull the curtains around my bed and crawl under the duvet. I've totally screwed up everything. I don't even know who I am anymore.

Isi jumps up onto the bed and lies with me. She licks my hand, then rests her chin on my birthmark and slowly I calm down. She loves me. Even though I'm a terrible person.

Late that night I'm getting ready for bed, and I go into the bathroom.

I lift my nightie off the hook behind the door and stop dead. My necklace is hanging there.

I sit on the edge of the bath, clammy and sweating. Oh Goddess. What have I done? Camryn dead when the necklace was here all this time?

But as my mind clears, I realize I couldn't have hung it under my nightie. I took off my nightie this morning, and I haven't moved it since. If I'd hung my necklace on that hook it would be on top of the nightie, not hidden underneath it. And I checked it, anyway. I searched the whole bathroom from top to bottom. It wasn't there earlier.

But it wasn't Camryn. She couldn't get into the house without a guard watching.

There's only one person it could be—Samantha Lee. She must have done it while the commotion was going on in the yard. She's trying to turn the workers against me. But I don't have any proof.

Chapter Seventeen

I'm standing at my dressing table worrying about how to tell everyone that I've found the necklace when a horse canters up the drive. It's Mr. Frye. I was expecting him today with the will he'd drawn up for me, but this early?

I finish dressing, tuck the necklace under my robe and go out to greet him. "This is a serious business, Ebba," he says, before he's even greeted me. "Very serious indeed. My servant woke me with the news about the girl this morning and I came straight over."

He takes a file out of the saddle bag and comes up the stairs, shaking his head. "We need to make a decision about the best way forward. Come now."

I follow him into the sitting room, twisting my hands together.

"Now why don't you tell me exactly what happened," he says, dropping the file on the coffee table, and pointing to the chair. I sit down and tell him everything while he paces up and down, hands behind his back, shaking his head as I reach the part where Camryn was shot.

"And you have no idea where the necklace is?" he demands when I've finished. "It's extremely valuable."

The blush rises up my neck and spreads over my face as I pull it out from under my robe. "I f...found it."

His eyebrows shoot up. "You found it? YOU FOUND IT? For Prospiroh's sake, Ebba. You mean to tell me that all this time it was merely mislaid?"

"No, of course not. Somebody took it. I swear. It wasn't

where I left it. Someone took it from the windowsill and then later they got back into my room and hung it behind the door."

Now it's just one eyebrow raised. "Who would do such a thing? Why would anyone want to do something like that?"

It's what I've been asking myself all night. What does Samantha Lee have to gain from deceiving me like this?

"Who?" he demands again. "Who do you think did it?"

Her name is on the edge of my tongue, but I can't say it. If I tell Mr. Frye she's on the farm, Micah will be furious. "Say it," part of me urges. "Say it and get her arrested. Nasty little bitch. She deserves to go to prison." But I don't dare. I know Micah. The Resistance matters more to him than anything else—even me. So I bite back her name and shake my head. "I don't know."

"Ebba, Ebba, Ebba," he scolds, wagging his finger at me. "You've got to stop being so impetuous. Every week it's a new crisis, and I have to scrape and bow to the authorities and beg them to have mercy because you're just a child. But their patience will run out soon. Perhaps it's time to pack up the house here and move to the city. You can live with me. Mrs. Frye will look after you and make sure you don't get into any fresh trouble. We can find a manager to keep the farm going. Yes," he says, stopping pacing at last. "That's what we must do. You go and pack your bags, my girl. I'm taking you back to town."

I jump up. "No, no, NO. Absolutely no," I yell. "I am NOT going to the city. I am NOT leaving Greenhaven."

Isi gets up too and stands between me and him, the ridge on her back bristling. He takes a step back, glancing from Isi to me and back to her. She's snarling at him, baring her teeth.

"All right, all right," he mutters. He pulls a handkerchief from his pocket and wipes his forehead. "You can stay. But the girls have to go then. The general must send them back to the Colony."

"No." But as I say it I realize what a good solution it will be. They won't be traipsing all over the farm six days a week. No more guards. Fifty fewer mouths to feed. And no embarrassing explanations about the necklace that has miraculously reappeared.

Just as quickly I see what will happen to them. Food is running out down there. The general won't let them back in. They can't be let out in the city. He'll kill them. The guards will take them back inside the Colony, straight along the ventilation shaft and they'll throw them out, one by one.

"No." My voice is squeaky, and I clear my throat and try again, forcing it to sound confident. "No, they can stay. They must stay. I've got fields of cauliflowers and potatoes that need harvesting. I can't manage without more labor."

He tightens his lips, his eyes narrowing. "I'll give you until the end of the month," he says at last. "Meanwhile, I'll be keeping a closer eye on you. And no more rash decisions, do you understand? I'm deadly serious. No more rash decisions. We'll tell everyone that Camryn stole the necklace and hid it, but you found it. No use letting people know you'd simply misplaced it. It will cause untold repercussions. Untold."

I want to yell at him that I didn't lose it. That someone set the whole situation up, but I can't. I can't give up Samantha Lee. I need Micah. I love him. I need him to know how much I love him.

I reach for the file on the table. "Is this my will? Can I make it legal today?"

"It is. Though why you want to leave everything to that boy you barely know is beyond me. Another one of your rash decisions. No doubt as you mature, you'll change your mind. We can always write a new one."

"I'm not going to change my mind."

He opens the file and pushes the page toward me. "Sign at the bottom."

I glance over the writing. "I Ebba den Eeden do bequeath Greenhaven farm and all my worldly goods to Micah Maystree."

I take the pen he's holding out, dip it in the inkwell, and carefully write my name.

"We need two witnesses," he says. "Not Micah as he's named in the will."

Letti's door is open, so I knock and step inside. She's lying on the bed, pale as a sheet. "Are you okay?"

"Yes." She sits up slowly. "I've just been sick."

"Poor Letti," I feel her forehead. "You're not running a fever. Maybe it will pass. Can you come through and sign my will. I'll get Fez."

She gets up slowly and Fez helps her walk through to the sitting room. Slowly, carefully she prints out her name. Fez is better at writing, and signs with a flourish Fezile Sinxo.

"Well that's that then," Mr. Frye says, drying the ink with his blotter and shoving the page back into his file. "I'll be getting back so I can lodge this at the Council offices. And Ebba, no more shenanigans, do you hear me? Calm down and think before you act or I'll whisk you off to the city. Permanently."

"Yes, Mr. Frye." I dig my toe into the crack in the stoep, wishing I didn't have to face the rest of the day.

He rides off and Fez turns to me, open-mouthed. "You just left everything to Micah? Everything? But we're your Sabenzis."

"What about Alexia?" Letti asks as we go back inside. "She adores you. And she's flesh and blood."

"And Leonid," Fez adds, shaking his head. "Are you mad?"

"I've thought it through carefully. If I die—which I won't, so it's really not such a big deal—there won't be any den Eedens left. My parents both gave their lives for the Resistance. Greenhaven should go to the thing that is dearest to their hearts, and to mine. It's totally unjust that the boat people can't own anything in Table Island city. This way, it's given back to the boat people, to the Resistance."

Letti shrugs, shaking her head. "You are unrealistically optimistic about people, Ebba."

"What do you mean?" That's a bit rich, coming from Letti, the most openhearted and gullible person I ever met, after Shorty.

"I'm not saying anything," she mutters. "I'm going to lie down."

The girls have arrived, and I go out to start the day's work, but they're angry and won't look me in the face. As soon as I turn to go back inside, the muttering starts, and the guards yell to them to be silent.

Aunty Figgy shakes her head when she comes out to hang the washing and finds me picking herbs. "That was a very silly thing to do. You're too trusting, Ebba. Too trusting. Greenhaven is sacred land. You can't leave it to any Tom, Dick, or Harry."

I shrug my shoulders. "It doesn't matter much, does it? After all, the world is going to explode if I don't find the other three amulets in the next few weeks, and I can't see that happening. So there won't be any farm to inherit. Just dust floating around in a great bowl of nothing."

"Hmmmph. Don't underestimate the power of your ancestors."

"So you found your necklace?" Micah asks, when he kisses me good morning. "Where was it?"

"Behind the door, under my clothes. I didn't leave it

there, I swear it. Someone took it from the windowsill and later they hid it on the hook. You have to believe me, Micah. I didn't just mislay it. It was definitely gone. Could it have been..." I want to say it, but I don't dare accuse Samantha Lee. I'll need proof or he'll think I'm acting like a jealous bitch, trying to turn him against her.

He takes my hands and looks into my eyes. "I believe you. Camryn moved it. That's why she ran when they accused her."

"But she died, Micah." The tears spring into my eyes. "She died because of me."

"She died because she was guilty," he says. "She didn't have to run. They hadn't found anything on her. Why would she run if she wasn't guilty?"

I don't believe him. I know it was Samantha Lee.

I drop my voice as one of the guards walks past. "How long will Samantha Lee still be here? I'm worried—they've brought in even more guards. Can't she go home soon?"

His hand runs up and down my forearm. "Just a few more days."

"But what's she doing? How come I never see her?"

"Babe." He pulls me into an embrace. "I can't tell you. But it's nearly done. And then she'll be gone, and you won't see her again." He rubs his nose against mine. "Promise. She won't ever come back here. I understand that it's difficult for you. I know she makes you insecure, and she's not the easiest of people to get on with. I've spoken to her about her attitude to you, and told her if she's rude again, she's got to leave. You're number one, I promise, and you've been incredibly generous letting her stay here, putting yourself at risk when there are so many guards around. You're acting as a buffer between the army and the Resistance, and it's a vital role that only you can do. I'm so proud of you. Thank you for everything you're sacrificing."

My anger melts. "Just make her hurry up, okay. It makes me nervous having her around."

———◄———————►———

It's late Sunday morning, and I've walked right up to the end of the new lands, past the dam and down through the forest, inspecting the work the girls have put in this week. It's the one day they don't come to work, and it feels like the farm can breathe again and relax. Alexia meets me in the kitchen garden. "Can I talk to you?" she asks.

"Sure." We weave our way between the onions and leeks and find an upturned wheelbarrow to sit on. "What's going on?"

"It's a bit difficult." She looks up at me, her curls blowing in the wind. She brushes a lock behind her ear. "Don't be cross. Promise?"

My stomach starts to knot. "What is it? Just tell me."

She bites her lip. "It's about Micah."

I try not to let her see me sigh. Why does she dislike him so much? It's becoming an obsession with her.

Her eyes have gone dark, and she is looking at me with ...it takes me a second to work out her expression. It's pity.

"What? Just TELL me."

"I was feeding the chickens earlier. One of the hens— the speckly brown one that likes to hide away—she was missing, so I went to look for her. She likes to hide in the potting shed behind the barn. I went to look for her there, and...and..."

She checks my face for my reaction. "And Micah was in there with Samantha Lee. They were kissing."

"Rubbish." I stand up and glare at her. "I don't believe you. I know Samantha Lee is on the farm, and Micah has promised that it's purely for work purposes. I believe him because I trust him."

She goes white. "I'm not making it up, I promise you. Why would I lie to you?"

I say the first thing that comes into my head. The only reason I can think why she would want me to be angry with Micah.

"This is about the will, isn't it? You're angry because you and Leonid aren't going to inherit Greenhaven, so now you're trying to turn me against him."

"I don't care about the will," she says quietly. "I only care about you. And he's messing you around. He's not who you think he is."

"You know, Alexia," I say coldly. "I've had enough of you maligning Micah every chance you get. I think you're jealous of him. You probably want him for yourself."

"Is that what you think? Seriously? That I'd be interested in that manipulative piece of rubbish? If you believe that, you're stupider than I thought."

It feels like a slap in the face. "You know, maybe you working here isn't such a good idea. Leonid is going to the harbor tomorrow morning. Maybe you should go back with him."

I'm waiting for her to make some cutting remark, or to beg me to allow her to stay, but she just nods. "I think I will."

I've calmed down by the evening, and I look for her to say sorry. It must have been a misunderstanding. Maybe she saw them together in the dark shed, and presumed they were making out. But she's already packed her stuff, and she won't change her mind. "I can't stay here anymore," is all she'll say. And the next morning at dawn when I hear the wagon clattering down the driveway, I get out of bed and cross to the window. She's really going. She's just as stubborn as Leonid. Nothing is going to change her mind.

Someone else is up too. Samantha Lee and Micah walk around the side of the house, heading for the kitchen. I sneak down the passage and listen outside the door. He's starting the fire in the range as he does every morning. There's the clang of the lid going back on the kettle, and the squeak of the breadbox opening. He's making her breakfast. They're going to be a while.

Something has been plaguing me. What did Camryn mean when she mentioned the old wine cellar? I saw Micah stiffen when she said it, I'm sure I did.

I trust Micah, but Samantha Lee's got her claws into him. I have to know what she's doing here all day. I creep out of the front door and set off through the vineyards to the cellar with Isi at my heels. It's a big building with an arched roof and high wooden doors that open onto the rows of derelict vines.

The doors creak as I push them open. I've never been here and I look around curiously. It smells musty and fermented, like old grapes and mold. Vast metal tanks stand on platforms along one wall. Pipes lead into each tank from the ceiling. Rows of wine barrels lie on their sides, piled higher than my head.

There's a second room opening off it. I go in, and see it's just wine barrels, thousands and thousands of them.

I know what I'm looking for—what my brain suspects though my heart says I'm being suspicious and untrusting. I'm looking for a sign that Micah and Samantha Lee are—I can hardly think it. What if they're more than just comrades in the struggle? What if Alexia is right? I don't want to think about it, but the suspicion is eating away at me like an insect chewing a leaf. I don't want to know, because I can't imagine what I'll do if it's true.

"Come on, girl," I say. My voice sounds very small in the

huge room. "There's nothing here, just barrels."

Isi's ears prick forward and her nose twitches. She trots off into a gloomy corner. I can see her white tail wagging in the half light, then she disappears. She's back a few moments later chewing something.

"Drop it, girl," I say, grabbing her collar. She looks up at me with a look that says, "No way."

"Come on girl, drop." Her eyes go dark but she opens her jaws and a crust of bread drops out.

Bread? I pick it up and turn it over in my hand. It's a few days old. It's Aunty Figgy's bread from the Greenhaven kitchen, I'm sure. Why is it here if Micah is feeding her in the kitchen? He said she was sleeping in the hayloft next to the barn.

"Isi, go find it," I tell her, pointing at the corner.

She wags her tail and trots off and I follow her. There's a tiny gap between the last barrel and the wall, and I squeeze in after her. Isi runs down a narrow passage and into a small room carved out of the barrel pile. From the outside, you'd never know it was here. It's lined with crates, and there's a foam mattress and blankets in one corner. I squat on my haunches and inspect the bed. Who is sleeping here? Isi is sniffing around, wagging her tail. There's an old biscuit tin next to the mattress, with an oil lamp resting on it. I prise open the lid. It's got a hairbrush inside, and a hairclip with red roses on it and a change of underwear. Samantha Lee. It's her hairclip. I've seen her wear it. It would look stupid on anyone else, but on her it just looks cool. Why is she sleeping here?

I lift the cloth off one of the crates. It's packed with bits of metal, all the same. I take one out and weigh it in my hand. What is it? I've never seen anything like this before.

The next crate has metal too, but a different shape. The third one has wooden handles. Handles for rifles. These are gun components?

I hold the lamp up against the side of the crate. I know these crates. They're the ones Leonid takes to market with Greenhaven produce. Is he bringing them back at the end of the day with dismantled weapons? Now I remember seeing him working on the wagon, the day the girls arrived. He must have been making a hiding place for the crates.

Leonid's bringing weapons in from the market. They're in pieces, and somebody is going to assemble them. Samantha Lee. That's what she's doing here.

I check every crate. More of the same. On a hunch, I prise the lid off one of the wine barrels behind the mattress. It's packed with rifles. There must be twenty at least, fully assembled. Ready to shoot.

Deadly weapons, on my farm. If the general finds out about these, I'll be executed for treason.

How could Micah not tell me? How could....Maybe he doesn't know? Maybe he—

But he does know. I'm sure of it.

And so did Camryn.

And Micah lied when he said he's seen her in the stables. He had to—she was about to tell the guards and they would have been here in a flash searching every inch of the building. So he lied, and she was shot.

I lean against a barrel, feeling sick. Micah! This isn't the Micah I know. Or the Micah I *thought* I knew. Would he really let somebody die to protect the Resistance? I don't like facing it, but...

Then suddenly the door creaks. Someone's coming. I look around desperately for somewhere to hide. But there's nowhere. I have to wait here, hoping I won't be discovered. They're coming closer. Oh Goddess, don't let it be one of the guards. What am I going to say? I crouch in the corner, heart thudding, one hand on Isi's collar, hoping she keeps quiet.

My imagination goes wild. What if another girl has found out about the weapons and has reported me? They're all so angry about Camryn, about being cold and overworked and by the brutality of the guards, any one of them could have sold me out to the guards. I huddle there, waiting, waiting for the barrels to be pushed aside, for the rifle to be pointed at me, to be shot dead as Camryn was.

I'm trying to sit still but I'm shaking.

The footsteps come closer.

I hardly dare to look up. Isi is watching, ears pricked. Then her ruff stands up and she edges closer to me. It's not a guard. It's worse than that. It's Micah.

I stand up to face him and I'm shaking so much I have to steady myself against a barrel. The light is behind him, and I can't make out his expression. I open and shut my mouth. What am I going to say to him?

Dr. Iris is here suddenly, scolding me as usual. "Are you a little mouse?" she snaps. "This is one of your employees. You are a den Eeden. Behave like it."

"Who do these guns belong to?" I ask, stepping forward. My voice is chalky, my mouth dry. "It's Samantha Lee, isn't it? That's what she's doing here—assembling guns."

He's not reacting like I expected. He doesn't look guilty or angry that I'm standing up to him. He isn't saying anything. "You think it's okay to have illegal activity on my property without telling me? Because I don't."

"Ebba," he says quietly. "I couldn't tell you about it. It could put you in danger." His eyes are gentle, not angry. "I was protecting you."

"What were you thinking, bringing guns into the city— you've been using the wagon on market day, haven't you?" I grab his arm. "Tell me. Tell me." My voice rises.

"Keep it together, Ebba," he says quietly as we hear marching outside.

The guards are bringing in the girls for work. Did they hear me yelling? I bite my lip.

He waits till their marching footsteps have disappeared before he says, "Babe, let me explain everything."

"Okay. Talk." I sit on the barrel and look him in the eye. "What is going on?"

"We've been using the wagon, yes."

I suck in a breath. "You've put Leonid in danger?"

"Leonid has been in no danger. If they stopped and searched the wagons, which they never do, and they manage to find the secret compartment, which they won't, all they would find would be a few bits of metal."

"How long has this been going on?"

"Years. Since your aunt's time. But we've been bringing in more recently."

I shake my head, disbelieving. "My great aunt knew about it?"

"Of course. She was the person who suggested the old wine cellar."

"But it's my farm. You should have told me. You were treating me like a stupid child, too dumb to know what was going on."

"Babe." He leans forward, looking into my eyes again. "I kept it secret to protect you. You don't need to know this sort of thing. If anything goes wrong, you can blame it on us."

"I don't want to blame it on you. I want to be part of your decisions. I want to be in on what's happening on my own farm. I want to know. I need to know."

He nods slowly. "I see that."

"And I'm not happy about having all these guns on Greenhaven. Find somewhere else to store them. It's bad enough having the army here tramping about every day. I hate fighting and wars and weapons. Get someone to fetch them and take them to Boat City."

It feels good to be asserting myself like this. He's always telling me to get some backbone and face up to the things that scare me, so now I'm doing it. I check to see if he's angry. But he's smiling. He leans over and kisses me on the cheek.

"I love you when you're fierce," he murmurs.

"So you'll take the guns away from here?"

Then Isi goes to the passage, growling. Someone else is coming. It has to be the guards. They must have heard me shouting. Oh Goddess, what am I going to do? I can't say I didn't know about them if they catch me in the hiding place with them.

But then I hear her calling. "Micah, are you in here?" And next thing Samantha Lee is standing in the doorway, looking down her perfect straight nose at me.

"Sam," Micah says, "I'm just explaining to Ebba about the guns. She wants us to remove them from Greenhaven."

I try to be brisk and bristly, but it's harder with her. She's so sophisticated and perfect. And I'm so big and clumsy and young. "I'm not...I'm not happy that you're endangering everyone on the farm....There are so many guards here every day..." My voice wobbles and fades, and I kick my heel against the barrel, feeling like a sulky kid.

"I see." She folds her arms, tapping one index finger against her bicep. "The way I see it, your interfering with the Syndicate pissed off the general, so he took the transport away from the Boat Bayers. So now hundreds of families are hungry, and will likely die this winter because of what you did."

I swallow. She's like a snake with those long flickering eyes that miss nothing.

Isi growls quietly, the ridge on her back standing straight up.

Micah slides next to me and puts his arm around my shoulder. "Babe," he says gently, "do you see how you can fix this? You're so powerful, and you can use that power for the good. To help end this unjust system, so that the city is open again to everyone, so that the resources are shared out, so that no one goes hungry while other people live in luxury. It's what your mother wanted, isn't it?"

"Yes. She wanted that." But would she have agreed to weapons on the farm? "So you're going to attack the Citizens?" I ask. "You're stockpiling weapons for a revolution?"

"We're stockpiling them so we can protect ourselves when the time comes. We need resources, weapons, a way of defending ourselves. Things are only going to get worse. The general is a psychopath. He's going to kill everyone who gets in his way. Don't think he's going to release the remaining workers in the bunker."

I stare at him. "You mean he'll keep them inside indefinitely?"

Samantha Lee smirks. "That's a very sweet idea, but no. Once they're no longer any use to them, it will be genocide."

The blood is draining out of my face and I lean against the barrel, not sure if my legs can hold me. "Genocide."

Micah tightens his grip on my shoulder. "We don't want it to get to that. But we need to be ready if it does." He nods to Samantha Lee. "Sam, please give us some privacy."

She tosses her ringlets over her shoulder and her eyes flicker. "Fine."

She leaves, and he lifts my chin with his index finger. "You are a heroine, you know that? You don't know it yet, but you are. You're brave and strong and beautiful. You're like Joan of Arc, one of those olden day warriors." He cradles my head in his hands and kisses me, slow and deep and pulsing, and I begin to feel a tiny bit like the things he has called me. I am stronger, better, fiercer, braver, through the power of his kiss.

"Okay," I say when at long last we pull apart. "Keep the guns here. Just don't let anyone else know about them, see? And I'm not happy about Leonid bringing them in in the wagon. It's too dangerous. Can you find some other way?"

He nods. His eyes are shining. "Not a problem. I'll get them dropped off on the beach. I promise." He kisses me again. "Thank you, babe. Thank you."

He loves me. He told Samantha Lee to give us privacy. He sent her out of the cellar. I've scored a victory. But why don't I feel happier about it? And why has Isi taken to growling whenever Micah comes close to me? Is she smelling Samantha Lee's scent on him?

Chapter Eighteen

The Colony workers are unhappy. They cluster together, talking in low voices, and I can see by their body
language that it's directed at me. Nobody makes eye
contact with me.

I ask Aunty Figgy to increase their rations. "Make them
your Malva pudding," I say. "For a treat."

She shakes her head, but she does as I say, and that
evening, after their meal of goat stew and dumplings,
Frieda brings out the steaming trays of hot sticky Malva
pudding with cream.

They don't like it. They eat it, but they stare at me
balefully. I wish they could just see how hard I'm fighting
to save them, but they don't want to see past the farm,
the servants, my wealth. Past Camryn, and the necklace
which everyone has noticed, although nobody dares say
anything about it.

The guards are more present, more vigilant. They're
sensing trouble too.

"Keep an eye on the girls," Fez mutters to me as he
helps take the dirty plates into the kitchen for washing. "I
don't like the mood that's developing."

I try my best to appease them. I call a meeting on the
lawn outside the barn. I tell them about our plans for the
farm. How I'm hoping to get the remaining workers out
of the Colony. How if we all work together we can make
sure that we all survive and have enough to eat. They look
bored and sulky.

Frieda has lost her friendly smile. I take her aside when she's finished washing up.

"Listen," I say, grabbing a cloth and starting to dry the dishes. "I'm trying my best here. I'm trying to keep everyone happy, and I care about the Colony workers, I really do. I wouldn't have got you out of the Colony if I didn't. Can't you see that?"

She stares at me coldly. Then she turns back to the sink, and starts scrubbing a plate far harder than it needs.

"I don't know what more I can do. I can't change the army, or demand better barracks or that you're allowed to leave the island and look for your families."

"Really?" she says, one eyebrow raised. "You can't, or you won't? Look at all this. You're super wealthy. You're the most powerful person in Table Island City—that's what I heard anyway. People say you're choosing to go along with the general because it suits you to get free labor."

"Free labor!" I shout. "Have you any idea what this is costing me? I'm having to feed fifty extra people three meals a day, and it will be months before harvest and I earn any of it back, and meanwhile the general is taxing me to death. It's costing me, having you here. I swear it, it's costing me an arm and a leg. You can check the books if you like."

She raises her eyebrow again and looks away. I know what she's thinking—that I'm making excuses and I'm as mean and corrupt as the High Priest was. Suddenly I've had enough.

"Listen," I say, "if you don't like it here, why don't you go back into the bunker? If you don't like everything I'm doing for you, well, get off my farm. Go on, get off it, and take your friends with you. I don't need you here. I only agreed to it so I could get you released from the bunker. But you're not grateful for anything I've done for you, so go to hell. I don't want to see you anymore."

A guard comes walking past the window then, swishing his sjambok against his leg. He stops, his arm raised. "It's okay," I tell him. "We're finished here."

"Time to go back to the barracks," he snaps, pointing the sjambok at her. Her face is sour as she throws the washing cloth on the sink and pulls off her apron. I stand in the doorway, hands on my hips, watching her crossing the yard behind the guard.

But...what have I done? How could I speak to her like that? Frieda is one of my friends. I've known her all my life. I know how confused she must be by this new life with new rules and nothing how it used to be. They must hate being marched onto the farm by armed guards and forced to work, especially when they see that I'm now their boss. Me, who used to be the most junior member of the Colony, and here I am, ordering them around, having meetings with the general, paying for their food. No wonder she's angry.

Samantha Lee wouldn't have blown her top like this. She'd have stayed cool and calm throughout, chin in the air, narrowing her long cat eyes as she thought through everything she said before she opened her mouth.

I really hate Samantha Lee, I think as I grab the cloth and start washing the plates. I bet she's poisoning his head—telling him I'm weird-looking and my feet are huge and my hair is bright red and I'm useless at being a boss. I bet she's telling him that. I can just hear her tinkly laugh where she throws her head back and shows her beautiful long neck.

But then Dr. Iris comes tapping into the kitchen, looking brisk, and starts ordering me around. "Stop brooding. You're working yourself up into a state about nothing. Complete waste of energy. Benefits no one. Now get down to the stables and check that everything has been closed up for the night and that the smithy fire has been put out. You can never be too careful."

And she marches out, after wagging her finger at me. I sigh. She's right. One more thing to worry about. Ever since the Colony workers arrived, I've had even more work than usual, checking up that everyone has done their job properly. I wasn't cut out to be a boss. Not like Samantha Lee. Not like Micah.

Micah is a star. He is out in the fields every day working with the girls, talking to them while they work, calming them down. I don't feel safe around them when I'm alone, but when I'm with him, I see how much they trust him and treat him with a respect they certainly don't show me. And just as he promised, Samantha Lee keeps her distance. Every evening Micah sits with me. We drink our rooibos tea and talk over the day's events, planning what needs to be done the next day. I begin to relax again. This is how it's going to be from now on. Micah and I running the farm together, working as a team. It feels good.

A few days later, Micah comes to find me in the late morning.

"I'm going to be away for a while," he says, sitting on the step next to me.

"Wait," I say, grabbing his arm. "Where are you going? How long will you be gone?"

He moves away slightly, brushing at some imaginary dirt on his tunic. "Business," he says. "If I don't tell you the details, you'll be safer."

"And Samantha Lee? Is she going with you?"

He flicks his hair out of eyes. "I thought that is what you wanted. She'll be off the farm."

"Don't go. Please. Fez is training with the Syndicate today, and Leonid and Jasmine have gone to market. What if something goes wrong?"

"Don't be silly," he says firmly. "You'll be fine."

He kisses me goodbye and I watch him cross the paddock to the forest path. Samantha Lee is waiting there in the shadows with a bag, and they disappear between the trees.

For a moment, I wish he wasn't a Citizen. Then he wouldn't be able to leave so easily. I could force him to stay here with me.

"Stop being so selfish," I tell myself. "He's going to help the people from Boat Bay."

But I don't feel like being unselfish. I want him here, with me. I want him to dump Samantha Lee in Boat Bay and come straight back to me. To be sweet and supportive like Shorty is with Letti. They don't have secrets from each other.

I've just got back to work in the greenhouse when a guard comes to call me. "Miss, the wind pump is broken," he says.

"What's wrong with it?"

He shrugs. "No idea. It's not turning."

Shorty is the only one around and he's so clumsy, he'll be even worse than me. I don't dare ask any of the girls. There's nothing for it. I have to climb up the tower and see why the sails aren't turning. Hopefully, it's something simple like needing oil. I fetch the oil can from the workshop, wedge up the spout with a bit of rag, put it in a shoulder bag, and set off through the sweet potato fields to the dam. I gulp as I look up the height of it. It's eighteen meters, maybe twenty. Do I really want to go up those flimsy metal struts?

I must. The windmill pumps water along the deep furrows that hem each field. The cauliflower seedlings are at a delicate stage. If they don't get water today, they'll die, and we'll have to start all over again, planting seeds and waiting for them to germinate. I'll lose three, maybe four weeks, and I can't afford that. If we don't start earning more money soon, the farm will be in trouble.

I tuck the shoulder bag behind my back and start climbing.

My shoulder starts aching after just a few meters. I push onwards, but not even halfway up, my muscles are on fire. It's useless. It's not like I'm going to be able to fix the pump when I reach the top. I know nothing about engineering or machinery. I may as well get down now before I fall.

But a voice above me calls, "Come on, it's fun up here."

A redheaded girl my own age is hanging off the platform at the top. Her hair is shocking red, waving like a lion's mane in the breeze. Her face is freckled, and she's dressed in pants that end below her knee, like a boy in a painting, a white shirt and waistcoat. Her feet are bare, and she's laughing as she swings from one arm. "Come on, Ebba," she calls. "What's a bit of pain? Come and see what's up here."

She's an ancestor. She has to be, dressed in that old-fashioned clothing. My heart speeds up. She's going to show me an amulet at the top of the wind pump, I know it. This was destined to be. She probably jammed the sails deliberately to get me up there. But when I reach a small platform that straddles the posts halfway up, she's gone. I sit down to rest for a moment, rubbing my biceps. I look across the forest to the sea. No sign of his little sailing boat. I chew my lip, wondering what he's going to do in Boat Bay, and if there's the slightest chance he's lying when he says there's nothing between him and Samantha Lee. She's so beautiful and powerful. What kind of guy wouldn't fall in love with her? I've got to prove that I'm as good as she is.

I stand up, tuck the bag behind my back, and start

climbing again. Maybe I'll be able to get a view of the beach if I'm higher up. He's probably launching the boat now. Hand over foot I climb, rung by rung. The struts are thinner here, eaten away by rust. It wobbles as the wind blows against it, but I keep going. The red-haired girl told me to climb, so it must be safe. I see her now, waving from the very top.

"I'm Sofie," she calls. "Come on, Ebba, come and see the view from up here." And then she's gone again.

It's the end of lunchtime, and the workers are marching back to work. Twenty are coming to finish hoeing the sweet potatoes in the field below me, and another fifteen will be planting cauliflower seedlings in the new lands. Isabella and her two co-workers are heading off to the poultry shed. The new cages are ready, and I look over to the workshops to see if Leano and Thobeka, the carpenters, are coming to install them. A movement catches my eye on the edge of the field below. Something is moving in the irrigation furrow. I crane my neck but I can't see what it is. I'm hoping it's not one of the calves—I'll never be able to get it out without help. It's moved out of sight now, hidden behind a clump of bushes we haven't cleared yet.

It's probably one of the goats. They're always escaping. I'll look for it later and take it back to the paddock.

I haul myself up the last few meters of ladder, and perch on the platform behind the sails, while I get my breath back. It's beautiful up here. I can see the sweep of the mountains all the way from Silvermine to Devil's Peak. The forest my great aunt planted is a thick blanket of foliage reaching halfway up the mountainside. You could hide anything in there and no one would ever find it. Has Micah left already? Has he taken the rifles like he promised?

The wind gusts and the platform wobbles. It's almost rusted through in places—we'll have to repair it. More money to find, somewhere, somehow.

The workers are returning through the fields, their hoes over their shoulders. Ten girls and two guards to each field. Some of the guards are off sick today—apparently there's been flu in their barracks.

A movement in the far ditch makes me stop, focus in. A shape emerges in the shadows. It's a person, crouched low and they're carrying a rifle.

Chapter Nineteen

Is it Micah? Samantha Lee? I can't tell from up here. What the hell are they up to? Will the guards see them? They'll be shot dead instantly. My eyes sweep the landscape, taking a quick inventory. Aunty Figgy is outside the house, filling a jug with water at the pump. A guard is standing lazily by, leaning against the wall watching the stonemasons work on a pothole in the driveway. Shorty crosses the yard and goes into the office. The barn is quiet, the horses are grazing in the paddock. I sweep the orchards...all calm. I don't know what Micah is doing, but he should get away with it if he's lucky.

But there! Down by the wine cellar! One of the girls has just come out of the door. She's checking left and right. She's carrying...I wait for her to turn and the shape of the barrels is distinct against the white wall. It's an armful of rifles.

Where are the guards? Why aren't they seeing her? The sweet potato field begins right next to the vineyard and it runs all the way up to the dam and wind pump where I'm perched. There they are—they're facing the opposite way entirely. One tall and skinny, the other stocky. They only have eyes for the girls who have started work. It's Roxie they're watching—she's laughing, wiggling her hips seductively as she scrapes the hoe over the ground.

Now she's gesturing toward the bushes around the dam. Another girl joins her—it looks like Tia, the pretty dark girl. The guards look around briefly, then turn back

to the girls. The tall guard is kissing Roxie now. Tia takes
the stocky guard's hand and leads him toward the dam,
just below where I'm sitting, where the bushes are thick.

Everyone else is hoeing diligently, ignoring the guards.
What the hell is going on? It's not Micah or Samantha Lee
in the ditch. It's one of the girls—I recognize the tunic
and trousers she's wearing under one of my great aunt's
jumpers.

Should I shout to the guards? But then they'll discover
the rifles and I'll be shot for stockpiling weapons.

Tia and the guard are lying behind the bushes now.
I'm sitting so still that nobody thinks to look up and see
me on the platform of the wind pump. In fact, everyone is
diligently keeping their backs turned, hard at work. You'd
think they'd planned it.

The girl with the rifle is closer now, still hidden in the
ditch below ground level. Tia and the guard are busy—
a bomb could go off and that guard wouldn't notice. Roxie
is kissing her guard. He's running his hands over her body,
pressing her to him, pretending to work, but he's not focused at all on the other girls. And they're slowly edging
further and further away from him toward the edge of the
field. Toward the ditch that runs near the old wine cellar.

My blood goes cold. It's not Micah. That's Leano in the
ditch. And it's Thobeka with the armful of guns. They're
supposed to be in the workshop building the chicken
coops. I open my mouth to shout, but I stop. If they see
me up here, and I interrupt their plan, they'll shoot me
dead. I'm a sitting target.

Silently, the girls nearest the ditch drop their hoes.
Thobeka runs along the row, passing them rifles. They
grab them, turn around, someone yells, Roxie runs and
they shoot the guard dead. I grip the edges of the platform
and lean over trying to see Tia's guard. He jumps up as the
shots are fired, but Tia has his rifle, and she shoots him in

the chest. He drops like a stone, his feet dangling in the edge of the dam. I crouch down, trying to hide. Twenty angry girls with rifles—it's going to be a bloodbath. And I'm probably next.

From my perch, I see how everyone reacts to the gun fire. In the new lands, the guards gather the workers together in a huddle. Their rifles are out, ready to fire anyone who moves without warning.

The guards in the courtyard are rounding up all the workers from the kitchen, shed and poultry cages. Aunty Figgy looks out of the kitchen door and goes back inside, closing the door. Isi comes shooting out of the forest and through the fields toward me. She's tracking me down.

"No, Isi," I want to shout. "Go home. Go home." But I can't or they'll see me here. I have to watch as she runs headfirst into danger.

The girls are lined up on the edge of the field, twenty-two girls with rifles, but they don't seem sure what to do. They're standing there, while Thobeka and Leano argue. They're shouting at each other and waving their arms. The mood is getting uglier. They're pointing toward the house, the new lands, the road.

Then Isi comes hurtling into the field. She sees the workers—pauses to assess their mood, and the ridge on her back rises. Her ears go back and she coils every muscle. She's going to attack them.

Come back, come back. I'm trying to call her in my head, but she faces them head on, body low on the ground, snarling. And then she jumps, going straight for them.

"No," I scream. "Isi, come here."

"There's Ebba," someone shrieks, training her rifle on me.

"She's spying on us," Thobeka yells. "Kill her."

Bullets rain on the wind pump. I curl around myself, head down. "Please, Theia. Make them stop. Let Isi be all right." The bullets are pinging off the metal, ricocheting, hitting the platform from below. I can't look.

Then the pump wobbles. I grab the strut next to me and it comes off in my hand, almost catapulting me off the platform. I regain my balance as another round of shots rings out, and this time they go clean through the metal frame. "Theia, help," I scream, as the tower gives way.

The ground flies upwards and flame-haired Sophie is falling with me. "Woohoo!" she screams.

I'm ready to hit hard Earth, but instead back first, full speed, I hit the water in the dam. The air is knocked out of my lungs. I'm grasping, grabbing, sinking, forcing my way up, spluttering as I swallow water and sink again. Sophie is next to me, swimming serenely, her hair flaming around her like coral. "Come on," she says. "Swim. This is such fun."

She reaches up to her necklace and dangles an amethyst-colored amulet at me. "Come on," she laughs. "You want it. Come and get it!" And she swims just in front of me, holding the amulet and laughing.

I'm try to fight my way to the surface but my lungs are bursting. I try and copy her movements, kicking my legs, but it's no use. I'm sinking. I can barely see Sophie in the churned up mud and thick pond weed. Her voice is fading...

And then someone grabs me and hauls me to the surface.

"I've got you. Ebba, I've got you," a voice murmurs in my ear. I open my eyes, looking up into Micah's worried face.

He carries me out of the water, puts me on the grass and rubs my back. "You okay?" he asks as I spew up brown water, spluttering, coughing, vomiting. "I got here just in time. You'd been under for ages."

"The girls," I gasp. "The guns...Is Isi okay?"

"Don't worry. Samantha Lee has got them into line."

"Three or four saw the gap and ran for it. But don't worry. We've got all the rest on our side now. We'll be able to work together. They're supporting the Resistance one hundred percent."

When at last I'm strong enough, I get up on shaky legs.

"Isi...where's Isi?"

He pulls me to him and kisses me. "You're safe, that's the most important thing. You're safe, my Ebba."

Why isn't he telling me? "Isi. Where is she?"

He strokes my wet hair off my face. "Sorry. I know what she meant to you."

My heart cracks like a rock. "She's dead?"

And then I see her. She's there on the edge of the field, her white fur stained with blood.

Her eyes are open, but she's gone.

She's gone.

I pick her up, cradling her in my arms, and take her back to the house. I'm too bereft to say anything to the girls watching me, or the guards standing extra alert at every corner, rifles cocked and ready to shoot. I huddle over her, wetting her fur with my tears, and carry her into the kitchen.

I lay her in her basket next to the stove. Aunty Figgy holds out her arms to me and I fall into them, sobbing. When at last I've cried out every last tear I go over to the basket and lie next to it, stroking Isi's lifeless body. How will I live without her? She's the one who loves me whatever I do. She's the one who sleeps on my bed and keeps me safe. And she died attacking the girls who wanted to shoot me.

Aunty Figgy brings towels and tries to get me to dry myself, but I'm too heartsore. I want to die too.

I close my eyes and lie there stroking her face. But then I feel a warm lick on my hand. My eyes are blurred with tears, but through them, I see her blinking.

"She's alive, she's alive," I shriek, hugging her. "She's alive."

"Ebba," Letti says gently. "She's not alive. Look, if you let her go, you'll see."

"But she's getting up. Look, she's walking. She's walking." I grab Letti's hands and dance with her around the kitchen. "She's alive, she's alive." Isi follows us, barking and wagging her tail.

Letti pulls away. "Ebba," she says gently. "She's still in her basket."

And it's true. She is in her basket. Her body is lying there unmoving, stained with blood, but she's also with me, her fur clean, her eyes bright, sitting at my feet, her tail thumping the table leg.

Then I know the truth. She's my ancestor dog. She's my girl forever. I haven't lost her.

Shorty comes into the kitchen then, his face creased with worry. "Letti, stay inside," he says. "The guards are rounding everyone up—I don't like the mood out there." He turns to me, and his eyes are bright with tears. "I'm so sorry about your dog, Miss Ebba. She was a lovely, gentle animal. I'll bury her for you—I'll dig her grave in the forest next to the Holy Well."

"That's okay, Shorty," I say. "I'm not sad. She's alive again. You might not be able to see her, but I can."

He and Letti exchange glances. "She nearly drowned," he explains to Aunty Figgy. "I think she's confused. If it had not been for Micah, she would still be floating in the dam."

Aunty Figgy goes into frantic mode then, insisting I change out of my wet clothes and dry my hair. "Go and help her, Letti. I'll bring you a chest tincture," she calls, opening up the doors of the medicine cabinet. "I can hear you wheezing already. The Goddess alone knows what impurities you'll have in your lungs."

"Where is Micah?" I ask Shorty, rubbing my arms. I'm suddenly freezing cold. "Why hasn't he come in?"

"He's left, miss. He's had to go to Boat Bay."

My heart drops. "You're not serious. He's gone now and left me with this mess? The general is going to be furious when he hears. He'll be here, tearing the place apart." He'll find the cache of weapons in the wine cellar. He'll arrest me—I'll probably be tried for treason. And he's just gone?

"He said to tell you that the girls stole the two rifles they used to shoot at you from the guards. They've been returned to the guards now, and everything is safe."

I take a moment to decode it. "And all the girls have been found?"

"All except three, miss. They've run away. But the army will be watching the harbor and border post, so they'll find them. That's what Micah told me to tell you."

"Come along, Ebba," Aunty Figgy pushes me out of the kitchen. "Get changed this instant. You'll get pneumonia."

Shorty is about to leave when he stops and pulls something out of his pocket. "Micah told me to give this to you. You dropped it when you came out of the water."

Suddenly Sophie is in the room, laughing, her hair wet around her freckled face. "We had such fun," she cries. "We should do it again. I'll teach you how to swim. It's easy."

Aunty Figgy's eyes widen and she grabs the small muddy object from his hand. She kisses it again and again. "An amulet," she exclaims. "Ebba, it's an amulet."

She undoes the clasp and clips it into place on my necklace. "Thank the Goddess. We have two amulets at last."

"How long until the solstice?" Letti asks. "How long till the second Calamity?"

"Two weeks." Aunty Figgy shakes her head. "Just two

weeks. Now come on, Ebba. We need to keep you healthy so you can find the last two amulets."

Chapter Twenty

There's more drama that afternoon. Letti is picking vegetables in the kitchen garden when she faints. Aunty Figgy sees her from the window and yells to me to bring a cup of water. Shorty is there in an instant, flapping around her, panicking.

"What's wrong with her?" he gasps as Aunty Figgy lifts her head and tries to get her to sip some water.

"I'm not sure. Help me get her inside."

We half carry her into her room and she sinks onto the bed, deadly pale. Shorty paces the room, running his hands through his hair. "Give her some medicine, Aunty Figgy. Help her. There's something terribly wrong—she was sick again this morning. Do you think she's eaten something bad? Letti, my darling." He rushes back to the bed as she sits up at last. "Letti, don't get up. Stay there. I'll bring you anything you want."

"Just some olives," she murmurs. "I really feel like olives."

"Olives?" I ask. "Are you sure? Why olives?"

Aunty Figgy shoos us out of the room and closes the door. Shorty rushes to the pantry and digs in the back shelves for the crock of olives Aunty Figgy has stored up from the crop earlier in the year. He hurries back just as Aunty Figgy opens the door. She's beaming.

"Come along, Ebba," she says. "Help me finish picking the vegetables."

I follow her reluctantly. "What's up with Letti? It's the

second time she's fainted."

"Low blood pressure. I'm going to make her liquorice root tea."

"That's all? And the vomiting?"

"Nothing to worry about," she smiles. "She's expecting a baby."

I try to imagine a baby Shorty and burst out laughing. "That's the best news. I'm going to be an aunt. Sort of. And you can be a granny." Isi wags her tail and barks, her mouth open like she's laughing too.

Aunty Figgy goes about making the tea, humming under her breath and I grab the secateurs and go off to the kitchen garden. A few minutes later I'm filling the basket with onions when the farm wagon comes hurtling down the driveway. The horses are wet with perspiration, almost dropping in their harnesses.

Jasmine jumps down from the driver seat, her eyes wild. "They've taken Leonid," she shrieks. "They searched us at the border post and they took him."

I grab her shoulders and try and steady her, to steady my pounding heart. "Slow down. Who took him?" But I know the answer. The general has hit back. He's getting me where he knows it will hurt most.

"The soldiers."

"We'll get him back," I say, trying to sound confident though I don't feel it. "I'm on the Council. I'll go and talk to the general."

"Will you?" Her voice wobbles. "Will you do that for me?"

I hug her. "Don't worry, Jaz. I'll bring him home."

She feels like a child in my arms. Tears are shining at the back of her eyes as she says, "I'm so scared, Ebba, I'm so scared."

This is feisty Jasmine who always knows what to do. But now she needs me. I'm the only one who can help her, and in spite of my fear of the general, I feel a little bit heroic. "I'll go right now," I assure her. "Shorty," I call, "can you fetch the carriage?'

He's bringing a bucket of water. "Fez has it," he stutters, sloshing half the water out as he dumps the bucket in front of the horses. "He won't be back till nightfall."

"Can I take the wagon?"

"The horses are tired, miss. I don't think they can go all that way."

"You could ride," Jasmine says, pointing to Ponto the big black stallion grazing in the meadow. My courage evaporates and I look at him, biting my cuticle, knowing that there's no way I can control him.

"I can't...he'll kill me."

"You have to do something," Jasmine wails, but I can't think what.

Shorty straightens his shoulders and takes charge. "I'll ride Ponto. You can sit behind me."

I gulp. "Leonid is the only person who rides him."

"Don't worry, miss. I've been riding since I was born. Back on the farm we rode all the time. You'll be safe with me, I promise. I never fall off..."

"Just hurry," Jasmine interrupts his flow. "Please, Shorty. Hurry up. I'll fetch the saddle. Just hurry."

A few minutes later he swings into the saddle and brings Ponto up to the house. This is a bad idea. Should I send Shorty to Mr. Frye rather? He can go and talk to the general. But his house is too far away, and he doesn't like Leonid. He might refuse to help.

"Come along, miss," Shorty says firmly. Ponto tosses his mane and looks at me with the whites of his eyes showing. I take a step back. But Shorty is adamant. "Jasmine, give miss a leg up."

I've only ridden once or twice, when Hal tried to teach me. I hated it. And Ponto is huge. And I won't have stirrups.

"Um..." I take a step back.

Jasmine turns to me with pleading eyes...but my body is frozen and I can't bring myself to put my foot into her linked hands.

Then Dr. Iris and Sophie are there. "Come along," Dr. Iris commands. "Time is of the essence."

"It'll be fun," Sophie says with a grin. "Something to tell your friends about."

"Yeah, right," I snap. "Like climbing the wind pump was fun?"

"Are you all right, miss?" Shorty asks, reaching down and patting my shoulder. "Perhaps you need more time to rest after the accident?"

"She's fine," Jasmine snaps, hopping up and down. "Please, just go."

So I let her help me onto the saddle, behind Shorty. It's so high up here, and as Ponto starts moving, I feel like I'll fall off any moment. I grab Shorty around the waist and cling to him.

"Look after Letti for me," he calls, as Ponto breaks into a trot.

Jasmine runs alongside us, calling, "Just bring him home. Please just bring him home."

And we canter off down the driveway, me clutching Shorty's waist and begging the Goddess to stop me falling off.

It's nearly evening when we reach the Shrine offices. Shorty has talked the whole way, about Letti and how exciting it is that he's going to be a father, about the horses he rode when he was a child on the farm, babbling about everything that crosses his mind even briefly, and I let him babble on, finding the rumble of his voice soothing. It's only when he says, "You're very quiet back there, miss. Are you all right? It's very odd of Micah to just leave you so soon after you nearly drowned. If it was Letti, I wouldn't let her out of my sight, not even for a moment. I hope you're feeling all right, that was quite a shock to your system, nearly drowning..." that I snap, "I'm fine."

I want to cry. He's right. How could Micah just go without even seeing if I was all right? He and Samantha Lee caused the trouble by hiding guns on my farm, and now they just run off, leaving me to deal with the consequences. It's not fair, and for the first time, I'm really angry with him. Angry in a way that I know is justified and not my imagination or jealousy or anything else.

But we've arrived at the gate to the shrine. Shorty dismounts and helps me down. My legs are shaking from the effort of clinging to the horse, and they ache so much, I can hardly walk. I hobble over to the guard box.

The guard looks at me with lazy eyes.

"I need to see the general," I try to sound authoritative, but I'm not sure I do.

"General de Groot is not here."

"But it's urgent. It's about Council business."

He's looking at me like I'm a piece of dirt. My confidence shrivels even more.

"General de Groot is not here," he repeats, his voice flat and disinterested.

I pause, look up the marble stairs toward the door behind the colonnade; two soldiers guard the doors. They glare down at me.

I go back to Shorty, waiting patiently on Ponto. "No good."

His face falls. "Do you think Leonid is here in the dungeons?"

The vague idea of breaking in and saving him flits across my mind but I know it's useless. I'll never get away with it twice. And anyway, I'm too vulnerable. The general will come for him again. For all of us.

This is his revenge because I took the transport away from the Army and gave it to the Syndicate. There is only one thing to do—I need to go back to tell Mr. Mavimbela that the deal is off.

It takes an hour to reach Pamza's house in Claremont Village. My mind keeps imagining worse and worse scenarios. I see Leonid beaten and shut in a dungeon like Hal was. I see him thrown off the side of the mountain like Shameema and Jaco. I imagine him lying dead somewhere, with a single bullet hole through his chest, like my mother. It's my fault. I should never have signed with the Syndicate. But now I'm going to undo the damage.

The meeting starts well. Pamza's mom answers the door and invites me in. She's all friendly and kind, and I start to feel encouraged. I am one of them. They'll understand my predicament. They'll be supportive.

But when I'm sitting in Mr. Mavimbela's study and he's looking at me from under his eyebrows as I explain the problem, I see I've been wrong.

"You want to cancel our agreement?" he says, shaking his head in disbelief. "You want to break the contract we've agreed on?"

"Yes...please."

He leans forward. "You don't seem to understand, my girl. A contract is legally binding. You can't just cancel it willy-nilly."

"But the general..."

"I understand the general is upset that you have removed the Army as transporters. But that's what business is like. You make measured, thought out decisions and you follow them through, and there are consequences, and you ride the consequences through. You work out what will be most advantageous and least onerous to you before you sign anything, and you follow through."

"But..."

"I can't simply explain away your change of heart to my colleagues. They won't accept that. You've made your bed, my girl, and now you must lie in it."

He pushes his chair back and gets up, and the meeting is over. "Let me show you out," he says, shaking my hand. "You have a long way to ride and it's almost dark."

Pamza is standing by the front door. She gives me a half-hearted wave. "Hi," she says.

She's played me. I see that now. Micah was right. Her father used her anger to manipulate me into signing. I'm such an idiot.

Shorty can see by my face that it hasn't gone well. For once he doesn't chatter endlessly. We ride home along the rapidly darkening road, and I'm dreading facing Jasmine. I've failed her again and there's nothing more I can do until morning. If only Micah was here, or even that stupid Samantha Lee. They'd think up a plan. But my mind is empty. And my heart too.

Chapter Twenty-One

It's still dark when Jasmine hammers on my window. "Quick, wake up," she shouts.

I run to open the front door, my heart racing. "What? What?"

"Chad is here. They're going to...kill Leonid." Her voice cracks. "They're putting up a gallows—the whole of Boat Bay is overrun with soldiers. You have to stop them!"

"Tell Shorty to go and fetch Mr. Frye!" I run into my room and pull on my clothes.

Everyone is awake by the time Shorty sets off. Not five minutes and he's back. "The army is at the gate. No one can go in or out."

"I am going there to talk to them," I try to sound brave though I'm quaking.

Aunty Figgy grabs my arm. "No, Ebba! Don't go."

I see the fear in her eyes and know she's thinking about my mother killed by the Army outside the same gates.

"I have to. It will be okay. I won't step out of the gate." I pat the necklace to make sure the two amulets are safe. But Isi is blocking me, leaning against me as I approach the front door. She growls and barks a sharp, warning bark. I could push past her, but maybe she can see the future?

Dr. Iris comes out of the sitting room then, shaking her head, burning cigarette in her hand. "Don't be foolish, my girl."

"We can't do anything," I want to say, but then I catch sight of Chad waiting on the stoep.

"Your boat! How many can it carry?"

"Four people."

"I'll go back with you," I say. "I have to speak to the general."

"Me too." Jasmine's spark is back.

"I can go," Fez says, but Shorty interrupts him.

"I've been rowing since I was a child. I'll handle the other pair of oars. If Letti's all right without me?" Shorty turns to check with her and she gives him a hug.

"Of course. Fez and I will hold the fort. You go where you can be the most help."

We shrug on raincoats and jackets and set off for the beach. Shorty and Chad pull the boat into the water. Chad unfurls the sail, and he and Shorty take the oars. Before long we're skimming over the waves. Our wet clothes stick to our bodies, and the wind is icy. Jasmine's knuckles are white as she grips the sides of the boat. She's dead quiet, her jaw clenched.

"Let us get there in time," I pray. "Please, Theia, get us there before it is too late."

The wind is behind us, pushing the boat around the curve of the Muizenberg mountains and into the Silvermine Sound. The sweat runs down the men's faces as they row in the shadow of the mountain.

"Tide is with us," Chad grunts. "Luck. And the wind's behind us."

It's the Goddess, helping us, I think. Isi is sitting in the prow of the boat, her tongue hanging out and the wind blowing her ears back. I reach out and stroke her, but she's fragile like air and my hand goes through her.

The sun has risen by the time Chad ties the boat to the jetty. We run to the island. Everyone from Boat Bay is there and the mood is chilling.

People are angry. The guards are alert, watching, guns at the ready. On a platform at the end of the island where the fjord meets the sea, the gallows stands. Two soldiers are hammering the frame together, and my throat constricts as I see the third soldier tying a noose in a rope. It's been elevated so nobody can miss it. They want everyone to see Leonid swing by the neck so they'll know what happens to people who anger the general.

Jasmine grips my hand. "Do something, Ebba." Her fingers are shaking.

"I'll do my best, I promise." I squeeze her hand trying to give her the confidence I don't feel. Where is Micah? I search the crowd, looking for his straight black hair. I can't see him. I see the general, though. He's standing with Major Zungu and Captain Atherton to one side of the gallows. They're flanked by armed soldiers.

"Come with me," I say to Jasmine. Together we cross the island, pushing through the angry people who glare at me as we pass. Soldiers turn their guns on us as we approach and I flinch.

But Dr. Iris is next to me, cigarette in hand. "Back straight, chin up," she snaps.

I never thought I'd be glad to see her but I am. I'll be all right with her next to me, and laughing brave Sophie— she's here too, as tall as I am, her hair like flame, and Isi too. Four of us standing together. I let go of Jasmine's hand, pull my shoulders back, put my hands on my hips and announce, "I wish to speak to General de Groot."

Two soldiers step in front of me, rifles blocking me from going any nearer.

"Go on," Dr. Iris instructs. "Speak up, girl."

"I wish to speak to General de Groot." I take a step forward, looking the soldier in the eye. "Do not stand in my way. Let me through this instant."

The soldier flickers his eyes toward the general who has been watching us. The general gives a curt nod and the guard gestures with his rifle to me.

"Come, Jaz." She follows me as I march over to where the general stands. "This is an outrage," I state, looking him straight in the face. His eyes are cold as glass. I feel myself shrivel but Sophie digs me in the ribs so I straighten my neck and shout so everyone can hear me, "I insist on knowing why you have arrested a member of my staff. And what is the meaning of this?" I point to the gallows on the general's right.

"Your staff member has been transporting illegal weapons in your wagon."

"Weapons?"

"Do not toy with me, Miss den Eeden. You know perfectly well what I am talking about. Your employee is fomenting revolution. He is guilty of treason, and there's nothing more to say."

He turns his back on me and inspects the gallows, shaking the uprights to see if they are sturdy enough.

"Ebba!" Alexia's voice breaks through the angry murmur of the crowd. She and her mother are behind the guards, waving frantically. Natasja's eyes are red and swollen. I run to them. Alexia meets me halfway. "What did he say?"

Jasmine never cries but she's close to tears now. "He says Leonid is guilty and has to die."

I put my arm around her shoulder and pull her to me. I have no words. I've tried everything. "Where is Micah?" I ask Alexia over Jasmine's head.

"He's around." Her eyes flicker to mine, then away. "With Samantha Lee."

Shorty pats my arm. "I'll climb the hill and look for him. I'm sure I'll see him from up there. Don't you worry, miss. I'm sure everything will be all right."

He runs for the boardwalk. But right then, the crowd's murmurs become louder. An army wagon pulls up at the first boardwalk and four soldiers jump down, dragging someone with them.

It's Leonid. He's been beaten—there are red sjambok welts across his arms and legs. He's limping, dragging one foot, and one of his eyes is swollen shut. Jasmine half sobs when she sees him, and I crane my neck, searching the crowd. Where is Micah? Does he know what's happening? How can he be missing at a crisis like this?

Shorty is halfway up the hillside perched on a rain tank, searching the crowd. He's seen something—his eyes are focused on one spot at the far end of the island. Then he looks back to me, catches my eye, and points. I wave to show I've seen him.

Alexia pulls my arm down. "Don't." She gestures with her head toward a burly soldier with a jaw like a boulder who is watching me, rifle cocked.

My legs want to give way. Dear Goddess, are they ready to shoot anyone, even me, a member of the Council? Is the general that desperate? But I have to find Micah. I have to take a chance that the soldiers are just trying to scare me. I spot an upturned row boat and clamber on top of it. Leonid is almost at the gallows. He's climbing the first step. I search every corner of the island but I can't see Micah.

I'll have to think of a plan. I try to remember what I know about the island. It's made of barrels lashed together. It solid enough to hold five-hundred people at least. It's been here since before the Calamity. It's covered with a thick layer of soil. But that's all I have. My mind is a blank. I can't think of any way to save him, not when there's a row of guards standing around the gallows, rifles raised.

Then finally I spot him—at the wrong end of the island, as far away from the gallows as it is possible to get. Can't he see what's going on? He's just talking to people as though there's nothing wrong. I look back. Leonid has reached the top of the platform. The general stands next to him. He points to the wooden box and Leonid, chin in the air, his trademark scowl on his face, steps onto it, and stands there, glowering.

The crowd falls silent. An ugly, angry silence that hangs over the island like a cloud of angry bees. The tension buzzes as the general pulls the noose over Leonid's head and tightens it around his neck. Natasja sobs into Alexia's shoulder. Jasmine stands alone, her arms crossed, jaw tight, her small body brave and indomitable.

And then as the general is about to kick the box from under Leonid's feet so he'll swing by the neck, a scuffle breaks out at the opposite end of the island. Micah is yelling, someone fires a gun, the crowd roars, "Get him, get him." They rush toward the gallows. The soldiers surge to meet them, pushing them back, firing into the air. They retreat, the soldiers forcing them back, back, back until the three officials are alone, unguarded in front of Leonid. The gallows rocks. The general and Major Zungu grab each other to stop themselves falling. Major Atherton seizes the side of the gallows.

It's another earthquake. The whole island is going to collapse. We'll drown. "Run," I shriek, jumping off the boat. I grab Jasmine. "Run..."

"Wait." She's standing dead still. "It's only them moving." She points to the section of island under the gallows. "They've loosened it..."

I grab the necklace. "Goddess, Goddess..." I don't even have words, just a desperate clawing in my gut as the box slides out from under Leonid's feet and he's swinging, the rope tightening around his neck. Jasmine breaks into a run.

"They'll kill you," I shriek, grabbing her.

She pulls free. "I don't care."

And suddenly the gallows overturns, tossing the general into the air. Zungu bellows as he and Atherton follow, and they land in the water with a huge splash. Their section of island has turned turtle, the rows of barrels exposed, the newly cut ropes that tethered it dangle free.

The crowd burst into cheers. Jasmine rushes to the edge. "Leonid," she yells. "Leonid!"

There's no sign of him.

At least ten soldiers jump into the sea and rescue the general and Zungu. They're spluttering and choking, swallowing water, and I hope with all my heart they'll both drown.

Jasmine and Alexia are frantically searching the water for a sign of Leonid, any sign, but the soldiers are back in force, rifles trained, ready to shoot anyone who goes near the water.

"My boy, my boy," Natasja keens next to me, her voice rising in a wail. "My boy..."

"Come," I say putting my arm around her shoulder. "You don't want to see this. Let me take you home. We can wait there."

She resists, but I lead her away. It's going to be ugly when they bring up Leonid's body.

We push through the crowd. Their anger is growing as they realize that Leonid is dead, and the soldiers are on knife's edge, ready to shoot anyone who makes a sudden movement.

We reach the second boardwalk, the nearest one to her house, and I'm about to take her across it when I see someone underneath the wooden planks. It's Micah.

He holds his finger to his lips and I pause, then whisper to Natasja, "Look."

Samantha Lee is under the boardwalk, cutting the rope off Leonid's neck. He's alive.

"Shhhh," I hiss, before Natasja can react. "Don't say anything. Just go home. I'll go back to the front to distract the soldiers."

As I push my way back to the front, the crowd senses my urgency because they let me pass. I stand right at the front, watching as the general scrambles out of the water, dripping wet and sullen. I want to laugh as he's followed by Major Zungu, his uniform clinging to his large stomach, and Major Atherton glowering at the smirking crowd. As he passes me, the general lifts his head and stares straight into my face. It's a look of pure hatred and a shiver runs down my spine. What have we done? Leonid is alive, but at what price?

They get back into the carriage. It rolls slowly away and they're gone. The soldiers leave too, marching four abreast up the road toward the harbor.

Now the party begins. Leonid is brought out, toasted and celebrated. They bring out big jugs of moonshine, the smoke from the braai fires is rising, and the band strikes up. The general was defeated. Leonid is safe.

But I have a sick feeling. I want to get home.

Samantha Lee and Micah are the center of the celebration. It was Samantha Lee's idea to dive under the island and cut the ropes. Everyone drinks toast after toast to them and she stands there beaming, her chin in the air, looking pleased with herself. They start to dance. Micah sees me watching and waves at me to come and join in, but then the dance sweeps him out of view and I turn away. I can't celebrate. I know the general. The repercussions will be swift and they'll be brutal. Who will he choose to destroy next?

Shorty comes to find me. He sits next to me on the boat.

"You don't look happy, miss. Don't you want to join in the festivities?"

"I'm worried. The general was humiliated today. He's not going to take that lightly."

"You think he'll hit back?"

"He's probably already started."

Shorty pales. "Greenhaven! We left it unguarded. I'll look for Chad." He heads off toward the braai fires. "You find Leonid and Jasmine."

But Jasmine isn't ready to go back to Greenhaven. "They're taking Leonid to the Mainland," she says. "I'm going with him."

She's leaving? It dawns on me that Leonid will never be able to come back to the farm again. What am I going to do? I can't run the farm without him. He knows exactly how to keep things running properly.

"It won't be for long. We'll rally the Resistance—we can work as well from the Mainland. We're getting ready for the revolution. And when it happens, Table Island will be open to everyone again."

"Look at it this way," Shorty says. "You can tell the general that you fired her. It will make it safer for you. Safer for everyone on Greenhaven. We must go now, miss."

Down at the jetty, Leonid is getting into a dhow. They're right. It's safer for them to be far away from the island.

"Go," I say. "Go. Give Leonid my love. But come back soon."

There's a lump in my throat as she reaches up and kisses my cheek. "Be back soon," she murmurs.

She dashes off down the hill to the jetty.

"Wait," I tell Chad. "I won't be a moment. I'll meet you at the harbor."

I run down to the dancing circle where Micah is swirling around, arm in arm with Samantha Lee. I push my way between the crowd and pull him by the sleeve. He stops, wiping the sweat from his forehead. "You coming to dance?" he pants.

"I need to get home. I...I need you to come home too.

Please." I don't want to plead. I want him to see how much I need him right now. To put me first, just once.

"Come on, Micah," Samantha Lee calls above the music. "Dance with me."

"Stay, babe," he says, waving to her. "Stay and enjoy yourself. You never let yourself go and have a good time."

I glance across at Samantha Lee twirling at the center of the ring. Her blouse is low cut, and wet with perspiration, clinging to her body. Her head is back and she's laughing. She's way out of my league. Every man on the island is aware of her, wants her. I haven't got a chance.

I can't stay and watch her flirting with my boyfriend.

"Please, Micah."

He pauses as though he's reconsidering. But then Samantha Lee comes past and grabs his hand. "Come on!" She laughs and drags him off. She doesn't even see me there. She can have any man in Boat Bay. But she's got to have mine.

And all I have to hold onto is my trust that Micah will be true to me, and that they really are nothing but partners in the Resistance.

Chapter Twenty-Two

It's taken an hour of hard rowing but we're almost home. We're rounding the Muizenberg mountains and I look eagerly for Greenhaven and the little bay where Micah leaves his boat. Isi stands in the prow, sniffing the air. She puts her head back and howls.

"What is it, Isi?" I say. "What's wrong?"

Shorty glances at me with worried eyes. "Are you all right, miss? You know Isi isn't here, right?" Then he stops rowing and stares at the shoreline. A ribbon of smoke is rising over the farm. "Where is that fire?"

The boatman is battling the sails in the strong wind. I grab the other pair of oars and start rowing. The tide is going out, and the wind is against us. It seems that for every meter we go forward, it pushes us back two. I'm trying to calm my panic but the thoughts pound my head like waves.

Is it my house on fire?

It can't be an accident. The general's sent the army, or maybe it's the girls who escaped with the rifles. Oh Goddess, everything I love is in that house. Everything that belonged to my family.

"Row harder, miss," Shorty gasps, his face almost purple with effort. "Letti...Letti's not well."

The ribbon has become a thick funnel by the time the boatman pulls the boat into the shallows. We jump out and dash for the culvert.

The soft sand sucks in our feet, slowing us down until

I want to scream. We reach the grille and Shorty wrestles it out of position. "Go, miss. Hurry."

I crawl through and we race for the house.

The air is thick with smoke. Shorty is right behind me. "It's the barn, miss," he yells. "The barn's on fire. Where are the horses? Did anyone let them out this morning?"

Fezile and Aunty Figgy have got there before us. The terrified horses, whinnying and rolling their eyes, gallop out of the barn and past us down the driveway. Fez comes after them, bent double with coughing. He collapses on the grass, holding his chest.

Aunty Figgy is at the water pump, filling buckets.

"Where's Letti?" Shorty shouts.

"She's lying down. She fainted earlier." Aunty Figgy hands him a bucket. "She's fast asleep. Pass this to Ebba."

We're getting nowhere. As fast as Fez and Shorty pass me the buckets, I throw them on the flames, but they're still growing, leaping higher. Then a huge gust of wind blows a pile of smouldering thatch off the roof, and Fez yells, "The house. The roof is alight."

I drop the bucket of water and run to the front of the house. The roof is already shooting up flames.

"Letti?" Shorty yells. "Letti." He sprints through the front door, straight for the bedroom they share.

Aunty Figgy pushes past me. "The book," she gasps. "Have to get the Holy Book. And my statue."

She's coughing and spluttering, and I push her back. "I'll go," I yell.

I dash through the front door. The house is filling with smoke and I grab a scarf from the hallstand and wrap around my nose and mouth. I push open the library door. There's an ominous crackling coming from above, and flames are reaching through the wooden ceiling boards. It's too smoky to see the books, so I feel along the shelves. The Book of the Goddess is shorter and fatter than any other book in the library.

I can't find it. It always stays here, on the third shelf near the door. The smoke burns my eyes and the flames lick right through the ceiling to the top shelf of books. I can't breathe. Where is it?

"Get out, Ebba." A tall figure pushes me toward the door.

There's a crash, and a flaming beam falls across the table. Another dangles above, burning orange.

"Get out!" It's Lucas, shoving me into the passage.

The front door is blocked with flames. I can't get out that way. I'll have to run through the dining room and along the passage to the kitchen. Through the roar of the flames, I can hear Shorty screaming for Letti. Why wasn't she in their bedroom? The air is black. I can't find my way to the passage. I feel along the wall until I find the opening. Then I'm in the kitchen at last. Someone is screaming. The statue. I need the statue. She's on the windowsill. But which way is the window? Choking, I drop to the floor. "Goddess," I gasp. "Help me."

It's Letti screaming. I try to orientate myself. She's close by, it has to be the pantry. Crawling across the room I feel for the door, but this door swings open too easily. I've opened the bottom of the dresser. I'm next to the stove. It's the wrong wall. I've turned the wrong way. Swing to the right, I tell myself. The smoke is getting heavier, searing my throat. There's a crackle overhead as flames surge through the ceiling boards. Should I go left or right? Which way have I just turned?

A strange woman grabs my shoulder. "Get out," she hisses, shoving me forward. Barking frantically, Isi seizes my sleeve and drags me across the room. The smoke clears for an instant—I'm under the window.

I stand up, grab the statue, look for the door. "There's no time. Smash the glass," the woman cries. "Throw the statue."

I hurl it through the window. The glass shatters, the flames flare, leaping higher. Scrambling onto the sill, I elbow out the remaining glass and jump. I almost knock Shorty over as I land.

"Letti," he screams. "Have you seen Letti?"

"She's in the pantry."

He's clambering onto the sill.

"Shorty, no."

But he's inside. I can't watch. They're both going to burn. He won't find the way through the smoke to the pantry. She's still calling. And then she stops.

But then there's a shadowy shape at the window and Letti falls through. She lands like a bunch of rags onto the grass. I grab her legs and drag her away from the flames, from the smoke. "Come on, Shorty," I yell. "Get out of there."

I sit Letti up, patting her back. She splutters, coughs, and half opens her eyes. "Shorty... where's..."

He should be climbing out the window. Instead there's an explosion of flame. The roof has caved in.

———————

We gather under the Ficus tree, away from the smoke, while Greenhaven burns. I hold Letti in my lap, wishing I could take some of her pain into myself.

I can't even think of Greenhaven, of everything I have lost. None of it compares to hers. How can she survive such a terrible loss?

I hold her, rock her gently, leaning against the tree where just a few months ago they were married. I'm too numbed to think about what we're going to do.

I touch the necklace, running my thumb over the amulets. Why didn't it protect us?

Theia, where are you? I pray. *We've lost the house and the barn. The coach house is burning. Any minute the Jonkershuis will go up. Where are you?*

For a second Sophie is with us, and I catch a flash of the blue amulet under her white shirt. Dr. Iris is there too, and the strange woman who helped me out of the kitchen. "We're here," they seem to be saying.

Without warning there's a roll of thunder and the rain begins to pour. Within seconds, it's so heavy it's hidden the house. I pull Letti into the forest and we huddle under a bush. "Shorty," she sobs. "Shorty."

When the rain finally stops, I push my wet hair out of my eyes and try to dry Letti's face with my sleeve. We stagger out of the forest. Aunty Figgy gathers Letti into her arms.

"I wanted some olives," Letti wails. "I just wanted some olives. I don't know what happened."

"Shhh," Aunty Figgy murmurs. "You must have fainted again."

Fez takes my hand and we walk slowly back to the house. Greenhaven is a sodden, ashy mess. Cinders glow in the blackened rubble. Only the walls are standing. The barn and coach house are gone too, and everything in them.

By the kitchen door I find the statue of the Goddess. It's lying in two halves, and as I pick them up something falls out of the top half. I sink down onto the steps, shaking, holding it in my palm. It's an amulet, a silver circle holding a flame carved from red stone.

———

We bury Shorty at nightfall. There's nothing to wrap him in, no coffin, no shroud, just an old tarpauline Fez finds in the storeroom. Fez and Lucas dig a grave near the house, just a few steps from where we found him crushed by a beam. I turn away as they carry his charred remains to the grave and drop him inside. I can't watch.

Letti has cried herself out. She has no more tears. "I want to be with him," she says, her voice is raspy as she watches them fill the grave. "I want to die."

I do too. I've lost Greenhaven. The one thing entrusted to my care, and I've lost it.

Chapter Twenty-Three

I'm furious with Micah. How could he stay partying on the island instead of making sure I got home safely? If he'd been here, maybe Shorty could have been saved. And Letti's heart wouldn't be broken. By the time we go to sleep in the old Slave Lodge, I'm raging.

Letti and Aunty Figgy share a bed in Aunty Figgy's room. I'm in Jasmine's old room next door, and I keep waking through the night to hear her sobbing and Aunty Figgy soothing her. On the other side is Fez, and I'm sure he's awake too, distraught for his sister, for me, for himself that the books in the library are burned and he never got a chance to read them all.

I lie in bed, staring at the moon behind the oak trees, and I think about how much I hate Micah, Samantha Lee, the general, Zungu and Atherton and everyone in the army, Mr. Mavimbela and all the rest of the Citizens. Most of all, I rage against the girls whom I saved from the Colony and who repaid me by trying to kill me. Maybe they started the fire.

I think of Lucas sleeping out there in the forest, under the light of the moon, in the shadow of the trees. It feels like he's the only one who can understand what I've lost, because he's lost everything too.

By morning, I've remembered something else to worry about. My taxes are due at the end of the month and I have no way to pay them. The fields are full—the cabbages, cauliflowers, potatoes need harvesting, but I have no one to do the work.

I can't lie here fretting. I may as well get up and start picking.

I get outside and look for the familiar outline of the house and barn against the skyline. There's nothing—just a blank space and a smell of smoke. And it hits me—without the barn, there are no baskets to store the vegetables, no wagon, no place to sort them, no way to get them to market, no money coming in. My farm is bankrupt.

I reach the Holy Well as the sun's coming up. The water glows, the stone wall shines with a pinkish gleam, reflecting the dawn light, and I sit down, leaning against the edge of the wall and finally let myself cry.

A woman emerges from the trees, carrying a blanket. She's younger than Dr. Iris, older than Clementine. She's the age my mother would be now if she had not gone out to talk to the army that day. For a minute, my heart leaps. She's my mother, come back to be with me. But her dress is full, skimming the ground. Her hair, the color of autumn leaves, is woven into a braid that she's wound around her head. She's wearing the necklace. The necklace with all four amulets. She's the woman from the fire. My last ancestor.

Sitting next to me, she drapes the blanket around my shoulders. "I'm Emilie," she murmurs.

I drop my head into her lap, she pulls the blanket around me, and I drift off to sleep while she strokes my smoke-riddled hair, murmurs quiet words in a language I don't know.

———◆———

Someone is watching me. I open my eyes and sit up. What is the smell of smoke? Then I remember, and I want to pull out my hair and tear my clothes to shreds. What am I going to do?

"You looked so tired," Micah says. "I didn't want to wake you."

I glare at him, turning my head so his kiss lands on my cheek. "Oh. It's you. Have you seen my house? Have you seen Letti? Shorty..."

"I've seen them." He puts his arm around me, pulling me against his strong body.

I stiffen. He's not going to persuade me that everything is all right.

"It's terrible about Shorty. He was a really solid guy. But don't despair. You've still got so much—the Jonkershuis, the wine cellar, the laborers' cottages, the land...all this." He waves at the forest. "Don't give up hope. We can start again. We can rebuild Greenhaven. What matters is that you and I are safe, and together."

"But where were you? Why didn't you come home?"

He looks me in the eye, but there's something about his expression I can't read. "I couldn't leave," he says. His voice is sincere, but his face is stiff. "I knew the army would be back. I had to stay until the people were safe. I couldn't have done much here anyway."

What is he not telling me?

"But what about me?" My voice starts controlled and ends in a wail. "You always put me last. You're always there with the Resistance, you and Samantha Lee, and you always pick them first, and I'm losing you to her, I know it. I've lost everything, my house, my clothes, my furniture, and now I'm losing you, too."

"I promise I won't leave again," he murmurs again and again as he holds me. "I promise I'll stay until you're settled again. I'll help you get what you need. You can survive this, believe me. You're stronger than you think."

The winter sun has disappeared behind cloud, and I shiver. The wind is picking up, cutting through my robe and the thin blanket. "What am I going to do?" I rub my arms. "I can't even change my clothes."

"I told you, I'll find you whatever you need."

I shake my head in disbelief. "Where? Where will you find beds and chairs and saucepans and shelter for the horses and clothes and bedding and...?"

"Ebba!" He gets up and pulls me to my feet. "You're getting hysterical. Trust me. The forest has plenty of abandoned houses. People left behind what they couldn't take across to the Mainland. We'll be able to find you everything you need. You can sleep in the laborers' cottages. You can shelter the horses in the wine cellar. It's not the end. Now you go and find Aunty Figgy and I'll fetch you the things you need."

Chapter Twenty-Four

For another week, we limp along. Micah forages in the abandoned houses and finds us enough to get by. We have plenty of vegetables to eat and water to drink. The carriage horses come back on their own, and Micah finds Ponto grazing in the orchard and brings him back.

Mr. Frye comes to assess the damage. "So much destruction," he says, blowing his nose in his handkerchief. "So much history gone. That beautiful old house."

As he's leaving he says, "The general's called a Council meeting a week from now."

"I'm not going," I snap. "He's crazy if he thinks I'm going to sit there watching him gloating about what he's done to me."

"Ebba, Ebba, you have no proof it was the general who started the fire. It could have been anything—lightning, or a spark from the forge."

"Oh please. The timing is far too good to be an accident. I'm not going, and you can tell him from me."

He shakes his head. "Don't be impulsive. It's going to be an important meeting. He will discuss what to do with the remaining young people in the Colony. And the ones who were working here. You need to be there to stick up for them."

I turn away. I'm not defending those ungrateful cows. He swings into the saddle and clicks his tongue to tell the horse to move.

"I'll send my carriage for you, in case you change your

mind."

On market day, Mr. Mavimbela sends a wagon to take the vegetables to market. Fez and I spend our waking hours in the fields picking them and stashing them into crates Micah brings up from the wine cellar.

I just have to think about one hour at a time. One day. If I think ahead, I despair so I focus on what we need to get by just for now.

I don't want to think about the future. How we will plant for next season. How we're going to irrigate without the wind pump. How I will make enough to pay the taxes the general is demanding.

But maybe we won't have to. It's only three days until the solstice. Aunty Figgy is at the Holy Well every day searching for the last amulet. As the days pass, her face gets grimmer and the moon gets fuller. She mutters prayers as she goes about her work, begging the Goddess to send the last amulet.

It's lost forever. I'm sure of it.

It's nightfall. The air is still, and slate gray clouds are piling over the mountain, closing up the patches of light. A single star twinkles and then the clouds blow across it and the sky is black, the mountain barely visible. Micah finds me sitting on the swing at the end of the meadow.

"Shift up," he says.

He squeezes in next to me, and puts his arm around me. I lean my head on his shoulder. He's been working from first light until nightfall doing the jobs that Leonid used to do, bringing home piles of things we might need, scratching through the ashes of the house to see what he can salvage. He hasn't left the farm and he's been tender with me, and his presence is like a balm on my sore heart.

We swing quietly for a while, our fingers laced together, my head on his shoulder.

"So, the sacred task—you haven't completed it?" His voice is gentle.

"No. I've found three amulets, but the one my mother gave me is gone. Major Zungu might have it. Or it may have been washed down the river in the earthquake. It's probably buried under a mountain of sand on the beach."

"Hmmm." He sits quietly for a while.

"What are you thinking?"

"I got a message today from Boat Bay. The Colony has run out of growing medium. There's no more planting happening. No more food to grow. They're surviving by eating the stored food."

"So the general must let them out. He can send them to the Mainland."

His fingers tighten in mine. "He won't do that. He's seen how dangerous it is."

"Is he going to force me to supply their food?" It's just the kind of revenge I'd expect from him.

But his answer makes the hair on the back of my neck rise. "He's going to kill them."

"No! He's not that evil." But as I say it, I know that this is just what he'll do. "You've got to get in there. We must rescue them."

"How?" He lifts his hands, palms up. "Every soldier on the island will be guarding the entrance."

"The ventilation shafts. We could climb in through the shafts and rescue them."

"And get our heads blown off."

I know he's right. Anyone climbing the side of the mountain will be an instant target for the guards. "Maybe you're wrong," I say hopefully. "It might be a mistake."

"It's not a mistake. Chad told me. The maintenance team has been called in to seal shut the ventilation shafts. They've started already. Then they'll pull out the soldiers, lock down the entrance, and..."

"And they'll suffocate. It will become a huge coffin."

I sit down again, twisting my fingers together. There's got to be another way. There has to be, but I can't think of anything.

"So if you don't find the amulet, the Sacred Book says we'll all die anyway in two days' time?" he asks.

I'm surprised. He's always acted like the amulets are fairy stories. "That's what it says."

"So each amulet is linked to one of your ancestors?" he asks. "They each did something remarkable?"

"That's what Aunty Figgy says. Not everyone becomes an ancestor. Just those who did something bigger than themselves. Who were braver than everybody else."

"Ebba..." he begins, kicking his feet so we start to swing. I'm waiting but he stops mid-sentence. Then a minute later he says, "I love you so much. Do you know that?"

"I love you too," I whisper, tears filling my eyes. "I'm sorry I'm such a mess."

"You're not a mess. You're the bravest girl I know."

"Really? Braver than Samantha Lee?"

"Much braver. You're extraordinary."

A glow of pleasure warms me—the first one in weeks. He kicks his knees out and we begin to swing higher.

"I was just wondering," he says as we sway to and fro under the big Ficus tree. "I'm speaking right out of turn here, and you can stop me if I'm wrong. I can't help thinking...and listen, I don't know much about the Goddess and religion and ancestors, but..."

"What, Micah?" I peer into his face, trying to work out why he's being so tentative. "What are you trying to say?"

"Well, there is a way to stop the general from killing everyone in the Colony, but it will have to be done by someone with incredible courage."

"What is it?"

"Somebody needs to assassinate him. You need to

assassinate him."

I jump off the swing. "Kill him? Me?" I grab the rope and stop the swing. He slides off, stands up, facing me eye to eye. I am a descendent of Theia, the Goddess of Life and growth. I can't kill, I wouldn't know where to start. But... what if it's so that other people can live? Is it still wrong?

"Maybe this is your sacred task," he says, laying both hands on my shoulders. "Perhaps you're destined to be the one who saves two thousand lives by killing the general."

I gulp. "I...I have to think."

"It's just a thought," he says gently. "It's a different interpretation of the sacred task, but maybe Aunty Figgy isn't right? She's old, and confused, and so focused on her idea of what the sacred task is that she can't see the bigger picture."

I turn away from him, pace the meadow, thoughts stabbing at me. It's two days to the solstice and there's no hope of finding the amulet. If Aunty Figgy's right, we're all going to die so the general's plan doesn't matter. If Micah's right, nothing's going to happen to the planet. And I could save the two thousand people I grew up with. I could prevent a genocide.

"Think about what I've said," he says. "This is your chance to show everyone in Boat Bay, in the whole world, that you're a hero. You'll be the greatest hero the Resistance has ever known."

———◆———

There's only one day left. Aunty Figgy paces the court-yard clutching the Book of the Goddess, praying relent-lessly. As soon as we've eaten breakfast, she makes us all go down to the forest to search for the lost amulet. I haven't seen Micah this morning. She doesn't give me a chance to check on him. "Go, go, go," she scolds. "We've got less than a day to find it. And the less you have to do with that boy the better."

"Do you really believe the old book?" Fez whispers as we hurry down the forest path after her. "I mean, there's no scientific evidence that tomorrow is the end of the world."

"I haven't a clue. She says yes, Micah says no, but I'm not sure I want to take the chance. Anyway, I want to find the amulet, so with four of us searching there's a much better chance."

I need time to think. I wish I could tell Fez about Micah's plan, but he's sworn me to secrecy. All morning we search the well, the river banks. Fez even goes through the culvert and scratches through the sand in the estuary, but we find nothing. Isi comes with me, sniffs around for a bit, and then disappears into the forest.

At lunchtime, Aunty Figgy lets us take a break. We go back to the laborers' cottages and eat the vegetable stew she's cooked in a potjie over the open fire. The potjie that Micah found, and the chipped plates and spoons and mugs he brought back from foraging in dead people's houses. Aunty Figgy isn't grateful to him though. She's suddenly taken a violent hatred to him. She dishes up four plates of food, although he's sitting right there with us.

"Aunty Figgy!" I exclaim. "You're being so rude." I take Micah's plate and serve him an extra large portion to make up for her nastiness. She hmmmmphs and turns her back on him. On us.

When we've finished eating, she gets up and gathers the plates, ignoring his, which he's holding out to her. "You lot go and start searching again," she orders. "I'll finish cleaning up. Look under the rocks—maybe it's trapped in the sand at the bottom of the well."

Fez sighs. He's already spent over an hour in the freezing water. We set off, but Micah pulls me aside. "Come to the wine cellar. I want to show you something."

"Aunty Figgy is really losing it," he says, as he leads me through the narrow passage between the wine barrels into the little room where Samantha Lee stored the guns. He's sleeping here, on her blankets. "I think she's got dementia. The shock of the house burning down has pushed her over the edge."

He opens the tin where Samantha Lee keeps her things and takes out the hairclip. "Look here." He passes it to me.

I push his hand away. "I don't want that. It's her stuff."

"Open the hairclip," he says.

I flick open the clasp. It springs apart revealing a knife, small but sharp.

"You can wear this in your hair," he's saying. "Nobody will suspect a thing when you go into the meeting. I got a message from Chad this morning. They've almost finished closing the ventilation shafts. Then they'll have air for a day, two days at the most. He's heard your Council meeting is tomorrow."

Tomorrow. The solstice. The end of the world, one way or another.

"They'll kill me, won't they? The guards. When I've stabbed him, they'll kill me."

"We'll do our best to get you out alive," he says smoothly. "You'll be the biggest hero the world has ever seen. I'm telling you, babe, you'll make Samantha Lee look like an amateur."

I bite my lip. I don't know who to believe. Who to trust.

"Do it for me, Ebba," he begs, gazing into my eyes. "You know I've loved you since we were children. We'll protect you, I promise. And you'll be a hero, and we'll save the two thousand, and we'll get married and rebuild Greenhaven. We'll have a perfect life together with our children running in the meadow." He searches my face. "I won't let you down. I'll tell Samantha Lee to get lost. I'll send her to the Mainland. I won't ever see her again."

"Tell her today. Make her go today."

"I'll send a messenger pigeon right now. You'll never see her again."

I want to vomit. What am I doing? Mr. Frye's carriage is waiting, the coachman holding open the door. It's time to go.

Aunty Figgy's face is gray. "Ebba, don't go to the meeting," she pleads. "Stay here. We'll find the amulet, if we just keep searching, we'll find it. The Goddess won't let us down."

I hesitate. Maybe she's right. But Micah pins the clip into the top of my pony tail. "Remember what we practiced," he whispers.

"I knew it," Aunty Figgy shrieks, grabbing my robe. "He's up to something. He's...He's...you can't trust him, he's evil, he's evil."

"Poor old lady," Micah murmurs as I pull her hands loose. "She's totally lost her mind. Don't you worry. We'll look after her."

Maybe I shouldn't go. What are the chances of our plan working anyway? But the coachman coughs and says, "Excuse me, miss, Mr. Frye said you mustn't be late for the meeting."

Micah gives me a little push toward the open door. "Go. Be a heroine."

So I climb aboard. The coachman slams the door and jumps into his seat. He flicks the reins and we're off.

I look back. Micah has gone, but Aunty Figgy is standing alone in the driveway staring after me. Isi's running alongside the carriage barking. And someone is coming out of the orchard waving.

"Stop!" I shout, banging on the glass.

The coachman stops and Lucas climbs up next to him.

What is he doing? I watch his long back swaying as the carriage jolts along the dirt road, and wonder why he wants to come along. And why did he wait until we were out of sight of the house to join us?

"Wait until the meeting is about to start. Remove the hair clip and hide it in your sleeve. When the general enters the chamber, stand with everyone else. Wait until he is directly behind you, then swing around. Aim for the heart."

I say the words over and over as we canter along the road to the Shrine offices. Micah and I have practiced the maneuver until I can do it in my sleep.

It will be easy to kill him if I can just focus. But I can't. I'm going to die, I can feel it. I've walked over a precipice and I'm falling, like Laleuca pushed over the cliff by her sister.

When we reach the bottom of Wynberg Hill, the carriage slows down, and I think about jumping out and running away. But where could I go where the army or the Resistance won't find me? The carriage labors up the hill and as we climb I look up at the mountain, towering over us. Ahead lies Devil's Peak, then Table Mountain, and inside Table Mountain the remains of the two thousand are going about their daily chores, weaving and spinning, trying to grow food. Ma Goodson will be organizing the laundry. Is she starting to feel a little breathless yet? How long does it take to suffocate?

I close my eyes trying to calm myself. When I open them again, my ancestors are with me. Sofie, Clementine, Dr. Iris and Emilie. How can Clementine be here when I don't have her amulet? She's misty and almost transparent, but she's there, squeezed between Emilie and Sofie.

Emilie is looking at me with kindness. She knows what I'm feeling. Clementine's little boy slides off her knee, and stands with his little hand resting weightlessly on my leg. My throat constricts. I'll never have children now. Micah and I won't have the future I wanted, living together, growing old at Greenhaven, raising a family in a house filled with laughter and love.

I wipe away a tear with my sleeve. Dr. Iris wags her finger at me. "He who puts his hand to the plough and turns back, etcetera etcetera." I haven't got a clue what she's talking about. "Stay focused," she says.

I sink my head and sigh. I want to go home but I can't. I'll lose Micah. I'll have two thousand deaths on my conscience.

I'm doomed. I may as well just accept it. If Aunty Figgy's right, we're all going to die today anyway. I may as well just do my part.

We reach another hill and Lucas jumps down to lighten the load for the horses. He strides up the hill on his long heron legs. The sight of his thin frame toiling up the incline gives me heart. It will soon be over. One way or the other, it will soon be over.

Chapter Twenty-Five

Mr. Frye waits at the entrance to the Offices next to the empty stone plinth. He kisses me on both cheeks. "Ebba, you don't look well." He brushes my hair off my forehead.

I mustn't cry. I clench my lips together and shake my head. "I'm fine. Just a headache."

"What are you doing here, Lucas?" he snaps. "Go and wait in the carriage."

Lucas's hangdog look is back. His shoulders are hunched, his face haunted. His eyes flicker toward mine.

"He's coming with me," I say. "I...I couldn't face the Council meeting alone."

"All right then," Mr. Frye says. "I'll inform the Council that you have brought your secretary."

I wait at the door for the soldiers to finish searching him. My heart is thudding. What if they find the clip? Sweat is building up on my forehead and Major Zungu is looking at me suspiciously.

"You look hot and bothered, Miss den Eeden," he says coldly. "Something worrying you?"

"No. I'm running a slight fever."

He nods to the soldiers and they begin their customary search, patting my sides, my arms and legs. One searches through my hair, pushing aside the curls in my pony tail but they don't think to search the clip.

Inside the Council chamber, we take our places behind our chairs, ready to greet the general as usual. Lucas has pushed his way next to me. A door bangs in the distance and I hear footsteps. Sweat is running down my legs. I wipe my sleeve across my face. It's time. I flick my hand back as though I'm scratching my head and squeeze the clip. It opens, I pull it out, and hide it in my sleeve. My hand drops to my side. Instantly Lucas shifts over shoulder to shoulder with me. His arm is against mine, and as the general enters the room, his hand closes around mine. I can't pull away. If I push him away, the guards will notice.

The general is three steps away, two steps. One step and he'll be in the perfect position, just as we planned. I tighten my grip, but Lucas's fingers are around the hairclip and I can't get them free.

Then...then...I hear voices in the passage. "Miss den Eeden" and "Hair" and "Assassination." I freeze. That's Micah's voice.

My world disintegrates.

I barely notice Lucas drawing the hairclip out from my hand, or pushing something else into it. Major Zungu and Captain Atherton are on me. They shove me against the wall. My head cracks against the marble.

They rip open my robe, looking for the weapon. Atherton pulls my hair loose and tugs it, shakes it. They force open my hand and Atherton swears when he sees nothing but a small silver oval.

"The amulet," Lucas screams. "Join the amulets." Zungu hits him in the stomach.

"What have you done? What have you done?" Mr. Frye yells.

The general is being hustled out of the chamber. It's too late. He's got away.

"Join the amulets," Lucas yells. He lunges forward and plunges the knife into the general's chest.

I feel for the necklace for the empty clasp. My shaking fingers open the fitting and slide the amulet into position next to its three companions. Instantly there's a throb-bing, vibrating running through the soles of my feet, up my legs, into the pit of my stomach. Lights flash in my head, green, gold, peacock blue.

I shake my head. What the hell is happening?

General de Groot has collapsed.

Zungu and Atherton are firing shot after shot. The sound reverberates in my skull. Mr. Frye screams as he tries to get out of the door. The soldiers push him back into the room. Lucas. Where is Lucas?

I begin to rise. The general is dying. They're giving him CPR, but I can see his spirit, small and twisted, writhing out of his body like a scorpion.

As the soldiers move aside I see Lucas at last, on the floor, peppered with bullets. He's still moving...

The shouting fades. I'm in the air, looking down on the city, on Greenhaven. There's Micah, addressing a crowd of soldiers in the courtyard; Aunty Figgy weeping in the orchard; Samantha Lee landing on the beach at Greenhaven with a flotilla of boats behind her.

I drift up, up, up, through the clouds, into the blue nothing. A sense of calm fills me. The amulets are re-united. The portal has opened. The Goddess is coming back to Earth. She will make everything new.

My task is complete.

ABOUT THE AUTHOR

Helen Brain was born in Australia in 1960 and raised in Durban, South Africa. After school, she studied music at the University of Cape Town.

Before settling to a life writing and teaching writing online, she was a freelance journalist and editor, a screenprinter and crafter, and taught English, music and Ancient Greek.

Helen Brain lives in Muizenberg, a suburb of Cape Town, South Africa. She lives with her husband Ted and dogs. She has three sons and a grandson.

9 781946 395498